The Eye of Shiva

By

Alex Lukeman

Copyright 2014 by Alex Lukeman

http://www.alexlukeman.com
https://www.facebook.com/alexlukeman?

5

*"I am created Shiva, the Destroyer, Death,
the shatterer of worlds."*

- from the Bhagavad-Gita

6

CHAPTER 1

Rain from the South China Sea beat a monotonous rhythm on the rain forest canopy overhead. Nick Carter pulled his MP5 close to his chest and wished it would quit. The water fell in sudden streams through the leaves and down the back of his neck.

The rain forest stank of rot and mud and heat. Ahead of him, soldiers from the Philippines Special Forces Regiment moved in silence through a world lit with endless, green twilight. More followed behind. The trail under Nick's feet was churned into muddy ooze, slippery, laced with treacherous roots and crawling vines waiting to trip him.

Roots and vines were the least of his problems. Trip on a root and he'd get a sprained ankle. Step on a mine or trigger an IED, that step would be his last.

The objective was an abandoned rubber plantation on Mindanao being used by Abu Sayyaf, a brutal jihadist group that had left a trail of headless corpses and bombed out markets across the breadth of the island. All the other Islamic separatist movements on the island had agreed to recent peace accords with the government. Abu Sayyaf's response to Manila was to intensify their terror campaign.

The terrorists were flush with money and were using it to buy the latest in modern weapons. There were rumors they had made an alliance with the Taliban. If the stories were true, it would be an international terrorist alliance from hell. Those rumors and the unknown source of money were the reasons Nick was slogging through the Philippine rain forest.

Officially, he wasn't there. If things went wrong, there would be no posthumous medals or heroic speeches about valor when they buried whatever was left of him.

The leader of the Filipinos was a short, muscular man named Rafael Gabuyo. Captain Gabuyo had gone through Army Ranger training at Fort Benning and knew what he was doing, which gave Nick one less thing to worry about. Earlier, Gabuyo had sent his sergeant ahead to scout the objective. Nick saw the man return. The captain signaled a halt and beckoned Nick forward. The three men stood together on the trail, water dripping off the brims of their camouflage covers. Nick's green jungle fatigues were dark with sweat and rain.

At six feet and two hundred pounds, Nick dwarfed the smaller Filipinos. The heat and humidity of the jungle wrapped around him like a damp fist. A change in the sound of the water hitting the leaves signaled that the rain was letting up.

Thank God for small favors, he thought

"We are very close," Gabuyo said.

His voice was soft, muffled by the humid air. He pulled a folded black and white satellite photo from under his shirt and opened it out. It showed what was left of the plantation. A large house that had been living quarters for the overseer and his family still stood on the edge of the jungle. The rain forest was taking back the land, but the house and a broad, cleared space in front of it were still visible. Evenly spaced rows of neglected rubber trees marched away in the thick undergrowth. Vehicles were parked near the building. A winding, narrow

track led away from the house and back to the
nearest highway, miles away.

Gabuyo traced his finger along the photo and
rested it at the corner of the cleared area.

"This trail we are on comes out here," he said,
"a few hundred yards from where we are standing."

"Sentries?" Nick asked.

"Sergeant Ramirez says only one." He pointed
out the spot on the map where the trail entered the
clearing.

"I saw two more men walking around outside
the building," the scout said. "They have AKs. I
don't know how many are inside. There are two
Land Rovers parked by the side of the house. Also a
Toyota pickup with a heavy machine gun mounted
in the bed. That's parked in front."

"Every terrorist's favorite ride," Nick said.
"How do you want to do it, Captain?"

Gabuyo looked at his watch. "It gets dark soon.
We can't approach from the front, it's too open. The
jungle has grown close to the building in back.
We'll take out the sentry on the trail and work
around to the back along the perimeter, then toss a
few grenades through the windows. After that it
should be easy."

Nick thought about it. Sweet and simple,
nothing complicated. Simple was good. It should
work. But he knew that when the attack started,
simple plans could become complicated.

Gabuyo said, "Pass the word to the others. We
move out in five minutes."

"Yes, sir." The sergeant moved off.

Gabuyo looked at Nick. "When we go in, I
want you in support only. This is a Philippine
operation. You are here as an observer. Your
presence is secondary."

Nick had expected nothing different. It was all right with him if others took the brunt of an assault for a change.

"Understood, Captain."

Gabuyo nodded once. "Good," he said. "Let's move out."

They moved down the trail and Nick felt the adrenaline kick in. His body vibrated with sudden energy. He was just an observer but the terrorists didn't know that. There was nothing like it, that adrenaline hit before a firefight, addictive as any drug. His mouth was dry and he breathed deep as he walked, calming himself. Too much of a good thing would get him killed.

The signal came back to halt and he crouched down and waited. The sounds of rain had slacked off to a faint patter of drops on the leaves. A bird called in the distance, then another. A silver mist began rising from the jungle floor.

They moved forward again, past the body of the sentry lying by the side of the trail, his eyes wide open and sightless. His throat was cut deep and wide, his chest covered in blood.

A minute later, Nick saw the clearing. The old plantation house was a long rectangle made of logs with a wide, covered porch in front. The roof had fallen in at one end. The foundation was going and the building had started to lean. Smoke rose from a chimney in the middle of the roof. He saw the parked Land Rovers and the armed Toyota. There was no one on the porch.

So far so good, he thought, *they're all inside.*

Gabuyo's men moved like silent wraiths through the trees. The captain moved to the back of the building and armed a grenade.

Then it went wrong.

A burst of automatic rifle fire came from the house and caught the Filipino in the chest. Gabuyo was knocked backward. The grenade flew out of his hand and detonated. Two of his men were caught in the explosion and went down.

More shots came from the building. Bullets ripped through the leaves over Nick's head with a sound like tearing paper. The Filipinos began returning fire. The sounds of the jungle were drowned out by the barking of automatic weapons.

Later, it was hard to remember exactly what happened.

He darted from cover and ran to the front corner of the house and leapt onto the porch. A man came out of the house with an AK. Nick shot him and ran to the doorway. He pulled the pin on a grenade and tossed it through the open door and got out of the way.

The grenade sent smoke and debris flying through the door. Nick leaned around the doorway and shot the first person he saw. Bullets struck the wooden doorframe by his head, showering him with splinters. A bearded man dressed in a loose white shirt and baggy pants shot at him with a pistol. Nick fired a three round burst that bloodied the white shirt and drove the shooter backward and down. His pistol skidded across the floor. Nick ran across the room to an arched opening and glanced around it into the next room. Bodies lay on the floor. Two men were firing at the Filipinos through an open window. One of them turned and let off a burst that peppered Nick with pieces of wood and plaster.

He ducked back and tossed a grenade into the room. The explosion shook the building and brought down part of the ceiling.

He risked another glance. It looked like
someone had set off a bomb in a butcher shop. The
white washed walls were covered with blood and
shreds of flesh.

At close quarters, a grenade was a terrible
weapon.

It was the last room in the house. Nick lowered
his rifle. The sound of firing from outside stopped.

"Clear," he called. He looked around.

A meal had been cooking over the fireplace in
the main room. The pot had spilled over onto the
flames and the smell of burning food made Nick
realize he was hungry.

Gabuyo's sergeant came into the building with
two of his men and looked at the bodies strewn
across the rooms. He turned to Nick.

"That took some cojones," he said. "I think you
must be a little bit nuts, but thanks."

"You're welcome. Sorry about your Captain."

"Yeah. We're out of here in twenty minutes.
Better start looking for whatever it is you're looking
for. We're going to torch the place when we leave."

"Roger that," Nick said.

Nick began searching the bodies lying around
him and found nothing of value. He went into the
main room. A large table lay on its side. A cigar
box on the overturned table had spilled its contents
across the floor. Something glittered in the smoky
light from the fire and Nick bent down to see.

Gold.

A dozen gold coins lay scattered on the floor.
Nick asked himself when he'd last seen a gold coin
outside of a coin shop. The answer was easy.

Never.

He picked one up. It was round, a little
irregular in shape and it looked old. Arabic writing

covered both sides. He picked up the rest of the coins and put them in a collection bag. He began searching the bodies of the dead terrorists, looking for cell phones, letters, anything useful. He found a throwaway phone and put it in his pocket. He found a few papers and put them into a collection bag. He came to the body of the man with the pistol and the white shirt and began searching it.

The dead man wore a skullcap and sported a full, unkempt beard that reached halfway down his chest. He was big and he didn't look Filipino, more like a Pakistani or an Afghan.

It could be the rumors of Taliban involvement with Abu Sayyaf are true, Nick thought.

A small cloth sack hung around the bearded man's neck on a braided thong. Nick pulled it off and opened it. Inside was another one of the coins. Nick put the coin back in the sack and put the sack in his pocket with the phone. Most of what he found would go to the Filipinos but he wanted Harker to see one of the coins for herself.

The dead man had a sophisticated satellite phone. Nick pocketed the phone to take back to Virginia. He took out a camera and began photographing the faces of the dead terrorists. If any of them were in the computer databases back home, they'd be identified. It was always good to know which of your enemies were no longer a problem.

He was here because the bad guys were spending a lot of money on fancy weapons and everyone wanted to know where the funds were coming from. Now he had some of the money but he was no closer to knowing the source. Nick wasn't sure what one of those coins was worth but he knew it had to be a lot.

The Sergeant came to the door. Nick heard the sound of helicopters approaching.

"Time to go," the Filipino said.

Nick took a last look around. "I'm done here," he said.

By the time the choppers lifted off, the old plantation house was engulfed in flames. Nick watched the glow of the fire recede into the darkness below. The rush was gone and fatigue had set in. He ached, a deep, wide ache that reached into his bones. It was getting harder to recover from these missions, harder to motivate himself.

Getting old for this, he thought. *It's a young man's game.*

Sometimes he just wanted to go somewhere where no one knew who he was or cared. For what was probably the thousandth time he told himself that what he did made a difference. He still believed it.

He had to believe it.

CHAPTER 2

"One year, perhaps more. Perhaps less."

Doctor Singh set aside the folder with the scan results and looked at Ashok Rao, not without sympathy. The background sounds of New Delhi drifted through an open window.

Curious, Singh thought. *The man shows no reaction.*

"You are absolutely certain," Rao said. "There's no possibility of a mistake."

"I'm afraid not. The tumor is inoperable. The headaches will begin to occur with more frequency. Eventually there will be blackouts."

"Will there be pain?"

"Yes, and nausea. Disorientation. Like a migraine. I'll prescribe medication for you. The symptoms will become more evident in a few months. Over time it will become more and more difficult for you to function. Are you married?"

"No."

"I suggest you make arrangements while you're able to do so."

"Arrangements?"

"For terminal care." Singh had the grace to look uncomfortable.

Rao listened to Singh pronounce his death sentence and resisted an urge to reach out and choke him. Outwardly, there was no sign of his rage. He'd learned long ago to conceal his true feelings. Concealment meant safety.

Rao was the Secretary of the Office of Special Operations for the Research and Analysis Wing, India's CIA. He directed a network of spies, informers and military units that carried out targeted assassinations, false flag operations and counterterrorism. In India, Rao was a powerful man. All of that power could not stop the cancer growing in his brain.

Rao barely listened to Singh's instructions for follow-up appointments and tests. He knew he wouldn't be seeing the good doctor again.

If word of Rao's illness reached the agency, he'd be shuffled aside and forced to resign. That couldn't be allowed to happen. Without agency resources he would never get his revenge. The tests and records were under a false name and Doctor Singh was the only one who knew what Rao looked like. Something would have to be done about Doctor Singh.

A few minutes later Rao stood on the sidewalk outside Singh's building. He wanted to scream at the people hurrying by. *Look at me! I'm alive!* No one did. If any of them had bothered, they would have seen another aging civil servant in a rumpled suit. Rao was 61 years old. For his age, he'd thought he was in excellent condition. Then the headaches had started a few months ago. And now, this.

He flagged down a cab, a shiny black and yellow Ambassador.

"The temple of Shiva near the market on Peshwa Road. Do you know it?"

"I know it," the cabbie said.

Twenty minutes later, Rao took off his shoes and placed them by the temple entrance before he entered. The temple on Peshwa Road wasn't one of the largest temples in New Delhi, but it sheltered a statue of Shiva unique among the many thousands found throughout the city. Inside it was dim and quiet, calm contrast to the glare and noise outside.

The floor under foot was cool stone, worn smooth over hundreds of years by devotees come to worship. Overhead, the ceiling rose in a perfect stepped pyramid toward the heavens. The air was heavy with incense, the sweet fragrance of a thousand flowers.

The heart of the temple was an ancient statue of Shiva in his wrathful form, the god who unleashed divine fire and karmic retribution from his third eye. The figure stood on the crushed bodies of slain demons. Four arms wielded terrible weapons. A belt of skulls encircled Shiva's waist and poisonous snakes of silver coiled around his neck.

Carved into Shiva's forehead was an empty socket for the third eye. Centuries before, the space had been filled with an enormous ruby. The jewel had been stolen in the sixteenth century by the Muslim ruler, then looted from the emperor's treasury during the sack of Delhi in 1739. No one had ever seen it again.

Rao often came to the temple to contemplate the god's image and remind himself of Muslim treachery. For Rao, the Eye was a symbol of the heart of India, violated by Muslims who had ripped the nation apart to create the abomination of Pakistan. A prophecy predicted the downfall of India's enemies if the Eye was returned. Over the last few years Rao had become obsessed with finding the missing jewel.

Rao knelt before the statue. He was about to begin his meditation when he felt someone watching him. He turned and saw an elderly, well-dressed Indian man standing motionless nearby.

The man's gnarled hands rested on the gold handle of a walking cane made of polished rosewood. His shirt was a soft, perfect cream color.

Gold cufflinks glittered at his wrists. He wore an expensive gray suit and handmade shoes. His skin was a medium brown. He was thin, with high cheekbones and dark eyes, his face grooved with the passage of years. Rao had never seen the man before. He would have noticed him if he were a regular devotee.

"Many seek Lord Shiva." The man's voice was quiet and powerful. "Few dream of restoring the eye to its rightful place."

"How did you know that?" Rao was shocked. He had told no one of his obsession.

"I know a lot of things about you, Secretary Rao."

Rao's heart began hammering inside his chest. He stood and glanced at the entrance, long yards away. Few people knew who he was. Rao looked for the telltale bulge of a gun under the tailored jacket but there was nothing to be seen. The man's hands rested on his cane. Besides, he was old for an assassin. He seemed to pose no threat.

"You know who I am but you have the advantage," Rao said. "Who are you? What do you want?"

"My name is Krivi. What I want is the same thing you do. I represent an organization that wishes to help you."

Rao laughed. There was no mirth in it. "What organization? You don't know what I want." He thought of Doctor Singh. "Besides, there isn't much that can help me now."

"Oh, but there is," the suited man said. "We know about your medical condition. It's true we can't cure it, but we can prevent the worst effects for quite some time and keep the pain away. Our medical expertise is beyond most capabilities. It will give you time to achieve that which you most desire."

Rao couldn't believe this man knew about his illness. No one knew. He'd just found out himself less than an hour before.

"What is it you think I desire?"

"The destruction of Pakistan. Revenge for the death of your family."

Rao was speechless. It was true. Rao's wife and son had died years before, during an attack by Muslim terrorists seeking to drive India from Kashmir. The operation had been planned and carried out with the blessing of ISI, Pakistan's Inter-Services Intelligence Agency. Rao loathed Pakistan. He loathed all things Muslim, especially the jihadists.

He found his voice. "An organization that wants to help me? Why me? What organization?"

"We are a group of patriots unhappy with our government's policies toward Islamabad. Like you, Ashok. We're going to do something about it. Our intention is to provoke war with Pakistan. Our goal is to reunify India and reclaim the land stolen from us during the partition."

Rao looked around. There was no one nearby to overhear.

"That is treason. I could have you arrested."

Krivi laughed. "Treason is a relative word. We both know you're not going to have me arrested. You asked who we were." He gestured at the statue. "We call ourselves the Eye of Shiva. We are the instrument of India's retribution."

Rao looked at the fine suit, the polished cane, the expensive shoes, the outward signs of wealth. In India, as in most places, wealth equaled power. Krivi was a serious man.

"You haven't told me what you want in return."

"You are in a unique position to help us," Krivi said. "You have an extensive network of agents. You know the secrets of the government, what they are doing, what they are planning. You can find and track almost anyone. These are all useful assets. In return, we can add six months to your life, perhaps longer. Before your time is finished, you will have the revenge you seek. You will be a hero of the New India."

Krivi was offering what every Hindu nationalist in India dreamed of. *Too good to be true,* Rao thought.

"How do I know you are serious? Why should I believe you?" Rao said.

"Why indeed? I don't blame you for being skeptical. I assume you are unhappy with the fact that Doctor Singh can identify you?"

Rao said nothing.

"I see that I am correct," Krivi said. "As a gesture of good faith, we will take care of this small difficulty for you."

He handed Rao a white card of heavy linen stock. The only thing on the card was a telephone number, embossed in elegant black letters.

"Call this number when you are ready. Use your encrypted phone."

Rao looked down at the card, thinking. When he looked up again, Krivi was already at the entrance of the temple.

"Wait," Rao said.

By the time Rao reached the street, Krivi was getting into the back of a silver Mercedes limousine with tinted windows. The car pulled away. The license plate was unreadable.

The next day, Rao read about a fire in Doctor Singh's building. The structure had been gutted and six people were dead, Doctor Singh among them. Krivi had kept his word. Whoever he was, his organization was ruthless and efficient. Rao appreciated ruthlessness and efficiency.

Rao called the number on the card.

"Meet me in Bhuta Jayanti Park," Krivi said. "You know the pavilion near the temple?"

"Yes," Rao said.

"Be there tomorrow. Two o'clock in the afternoon."

Rao put his phone away.

On the other side of New Delhi, on the top floor of one of the new temples of commerce rising throughout the city, Krivi set his phone down on a polished conference table and turned to the man sitting across from him.

Johannes Gutenberg was dressed in an Italian suit made of material not available to the average customer. The jacket fit with perfection across his narrow chest, creating an impression of a larger, more powerful man. Gutenberg owned one of the oldest and largest banks in Europe. He was no relation to the man who had invented the printing press, though he appreciated the use of Gutenberg's invention to produce clean, crisp euros and dollars by the billions.

"Rao has agreed to meet," Krivi said.

"Good. He believed your story about a group of patriots?"

"It's what he wanted to hear. He assumes we are Indian nationalists like him. He'd change his mind if he saw your European face."

Gutenberg laughed. "You're a closet racist, Krivi."

Krivi shrugged. "Most everyone is."

Gutenberg said, "People always make assumptions based on what they want to hear. Do you think he'll find a way?"

"We may have to make a few suggestions, but yes, I think he will. He's motivated."

Gutenberg nodded. "He may balk at launching the missiles when the time comes."

"It's possible, but we've spent a lot of time on understanding his psychology. He'll do it. We'll let him stir things up first. Once things are in motion, it will be easier."

"If he does his job well, the government will do it on their own."

"That's so," Krivi said, "but I don't like leaving things to chance. Rao is our first choice."

"Everyone knows Indian missiles are inaccurate," Gutenberg said. "When some of them land in China, it will be blamed on faulty technology."

"The missiles will go where they're needed," Krivi said. "The lesson will be painful. It will take Beijing years to recover."

"We warned them," Gutenberg said. His voice was dismissive, touched with contempt. "They think they can go their own way, meddle with the financial system. They don't understand who we are. It's past time they learned who was in charge."

"In a way, you can't blame them. We've concealed our existence for a long time," Krivi said. "It's unfortunate their leaders didn't listen."

Gutenberg looked at his watch, a gold Patek-Phillipe. "I need to get back to Geneva."

"You'll brief the others?"

"Of course."

Gutenberg stood. Krivi rose with him.

"It's good to see you, Johannes."

"And you. You must come home soon."

"I'll come before the war starts. Tell Marta I miss her chef's cooking."

The two men shook hands. After Gutenberg had left, Krivi thought about Marta's desserts and the fine, rich chocolate of Switzerland.

He was fond of chocolate.

CHAPTER 3

Selena Connor didn't think of herself as stubborn. More like determined. There was a difference between stubborn and determined, wasn't there? The gym in the underground level of Project headquarters was cool with air conditioning but Selena's body glistened with sweat.

Ever since the wound in Mexico that almost killed her she'd been trying to regain the level of skill she'd had before the surgery. The bullet had nicked a vertebra and come close to putting her into a wheelchair for the rest of her life. It was months before she could risk a light workout. Her back still ached at the end of a day, no matter what she did.

She had her strength back, that part was all right. What bugged her was that she still couldn't get the height and speed she wanted for the lethal kicks she practiced in her martial art.

She aimed a kick at the target on the hanging dummy, where an attacker's throat might be. Her foot landed six inches below. She swore under her breath and kicked again with the same result. The heavy bag shuddered and swayed from the impact. An opponent would have been knocked across the room but that wasn't what mattered to her. What mattered, damn it, was placing her foot where she wanted it, on the target.

Selena wiped her arm across her brow, brushing aside a wisp of hair.

On the other side of the gym, Nick was working out on one of the Nautilus machines. The scars along the side of his chest rippled as he brought the bars of the machine together. He grunted with the effort. He let the machine return to neutral and wiped sweat away from his forehead with a towel.

"How about a break?" he said. He'd been back from the Philippines for two days but he still hadn't told her what she wanted to hear.

Selena aimed another angry kick at the bag. After two years of a rocky relationship Nick had finally proposed. Now it seemed to her that he was dragging his feet. He couldn't make up his mind about a date for the wedding. He couldn't make up his mind about buying her a ring. It was beginning to piss her off. She aimed a vicious kick at the dummy and came up short of her mark by about two inches. Better, she thought, but not good enough.

Nick went to a bench by the wall, picked up two bottles of water and came over to her. At thirty-nine and pushing forty, the workouts were getting harder. He wasn't about to admit that to Selena.

He took a swig of water. "Why don't you give the bag a rest and try your moves against someone who can kick back?" he said.

She gave him a dangerous smile. Selena had the kind of face that made people look again when she went by. Her eyes were sometimes deep blue, sometimes violet, an unusual color that might have been painted by van Gogh or Picasso. The color was complemented by her reddish blond hair. One of her cheekbones was a little higher than the other. She had a mole, a natural beauty mark, just above the right side of her upper lip. Selena was an attractive woman.

"You never learn, do you," she said. "You know I'll kick you all over the mat."

"You can try," Nick said.

"How's your hand?" she said.

The last two fingers on his left hand had been broken a few months before by one of Fidel Castro's sadistic policemen. They'd healed, but they were stiff and painful. He didn't have the flexibility he'd had before. Sometimes the fingers itched.

"It'll be all right," he said. "Don't worry about it."

Selena sighed and shook her head. "I promise I won't say I told you so when we're done," she said. "After you." She gestured at the large, square floor mat they used for their workouts together.

They faced each other on opposite sides of the mat, bowed, and began. Nick had height and weight on her, but with Selena that was no advantage. She was far beyond him in skill when it came to hard-core martial arts. She'd been studying with a Korean master for more than twenty years.

They sparred for the next half hour. After Nick had landed flat on his back for the eighth or ninth time and taken a dozen hits to his ribs and hips and legs, he surrendered. If she'd landed those blows at full strength, he'd be going to a hospital or the morgue. But this was practice. Nick had seen what she could do when it counted.

"Uncle," he said from the floor.

"I told you so."

"You promised you weren't going to say that," he said.

"So? I lied." She held out a hand and helped him up.

Nick looked at the clock on the wall. "We're supposed to meet Harker in 10 minutes."

"Then we'd better get cleaned up."

They undressed and went into the showers together. Nick watched her walk ahead of him and thought about the night he'd proposed to her. It had seemed right at the time, a natural in the romantic, tropical evening, with moonlight and the scent of flowers coming through the open window of their bedroom.

He still hadn't gotten her a ring. On the one hand, he wanted to surprise her. On the other, he thought it might not be a bad idea if they picked it out together. They hadn't set a date for the wedding, either. He wasn't sure why he kept putting it off but he figured the ring came first. After that they could move on to the next step.

He held her close under the running water and kissed her.

"You're not worried someone may come in?" she said.

"It's just a kiss."

"And then another, and then you know what happens."

Damn, it was hard to stay mad at him. She glanced down and smiled. "See what I mean?"

He kissed her again and went over to another shower head and turned on the cold water.

CHAPTER 4

Elizabeth Harker was a small woman. More than one self-important politician or general had learned the hard way not to underestimate her because of her diminutive size. Most people guessed her age at around fifty, but it was hard to tell. The stress of the job had left premature streaks of white in her black hair.

Harker wore one of her favorite combinations, a tailored black Prada suit and a crisp, white blouse with a Mao style collar. A butterfly-shaped emerald pin edged with small diamonds rested over her left breast. The pin and a pair of emerald earrings brought out the green color of her eyes.

Harker ran the Project, a small intelligence unit that acted in the shadows. Elizabeth's unit was the hidden point of the president's sword. Invisible compared to the giants at Fort Meade and Langley, the Project operated under the radar and outside the conventional rules. The free hand given to her by the president made her unpopular in the fiercely competitive world of Washington's intelligence community. Nick and his team did things the others couldn't or wouldn't, but freedom of action came at a price. Everything Harker and the unit did was deniable. If things went wrong, her head would be laid on the chopping block. There were plenty of people who wanted to see it there.

From the outside, Project headquarters looked like an upscale ranch house. The house had been built after the Cold War by a civilian millionaire over a decommissioned Nike missile site. The computers, armory, gym, emergency living quarters and operations center were underground. There was even a swimming pool. Harker's office was on the ground floor. It was a large, pleasant room, with a wall of bulletproof windows graced by French doors. The doors opened onto a flagstone patio and looked out over a green lawn and beds of flowers. A large, flat screen monitor was mounted on the wall across from Elizabeth's desk. A row of clocks showing world time zones was mounted over the screen. A comfortable leather couch and two chairs were grouped in front of the desk.

An enormous orange tomcat named Burps slept on his back on the couch, paws in the air. He snored and drooled. Nick had brought him from California to Virginia.

Nick and Selena came in and sat down. Nick's hair was still wet from the shower. He rubbed his left ear, where a Chinese bullet had torn off most of the earlobe. He had gray eyes flecked with gold and a face women thought of as rugged. No one looking at him would mistake him for someone who worked 9 to 5 in an office.

Selena had changed into jeans and a loose, dark blue top. Her Sig pistol was tipped forward in a quick draw holster at her waist. On her, the gun was a fashion statement.

"I've got the breakdown on the Philippine operation," Harker said. She gestured at a file folder on the top of her desk.

"Who was the guy with the beard?" Nick asked. "He wasn't Abu Sayyaf."

"His name was Abu Khan," Elizabeth said, "and you're right about him not being Abu Sayyaf. He was second in command of a terrorist group called ISOK."

"Eye sock?"

"Short for Islamic State of Kashmir. They're based in Pakistan."

"Kashmir is a long way from Mindanao. What was he doing hanging out with a bunch of Philippine terrorists?"

"That's what we're trying to find out. If it's an alliance between ISOK and Abu Sayyaf, it means trouble. Whatever they're up to, it can't be good. "

"I've heard about ISOK," Selena said. "They set off bombs in Srinagar a few years ago. Didn't they kill a bunch of people at the train station?"

"That's them," Elizabeth said. "It almost started another war between India and Pakistan. The Srinagar attack was pulled off with the help of Pakistan's intelligence agency. It got settled with a little arm-twisting diplomacy, but a lot of people weren't happy about it. There are factions in both India and Pakistan that don't want peace and it wouldn't take a lot to trigger another war. They hate each other too much."

"And they both have nukes," Nick said.

Elizabeth nodded. "That they do. The nukes, and the missiles to deliver them."

"Gee," Nick said. "Why can't we all just get along?"

Selena rolled her eyes.

Elizabeth reached into her desk drawer for the coin Nick had taken from the dead man's neck. She handed it to Selena. "What do you make of this?"

Selena was one of the world's leading experts in ancient languages, especially those from the Far East. Before she'd joined the Project she'd lectured on the university circuit and worked as a consultant with NSA. She spoke more than a dozen foreign languages. Her skills were a major asset for Elizabeth.

Selena studied the coin, turning it over in her hand. She was silent, her focus intense. After what seemed like a long time, she said, "Fascinating."

Elizabeth picked up her Mont Blanc pen and began tapping it impatiently on her desktop.

"What, exactly, is so fascinating? Would you care to enlighten us?"

"Sorry," Selena said. "I've never seen one like this before. It's from India. The writing is a form of Arabic current in the time of the Mughal emperors. It's the Shahada/Kalima, the affirmation of Allah as the only God and Mohammed as His last messenger. That could explain why a Muslim might wear it."

"How does an Indian terrorist end up with an ancient gold coin for a good luck charm?" Nick asked. "And who were the Mughal emperors?"

"I don't know how he got the coin, but the Mughals ruled India for over three hundred years," Selena said. "It was one of them who built the Taj Mahal."

"What happened to them?"

She shrugged. "What usually happens. A succession of weak rulers, lost battles and decline. It finally ended when the British co-opted the last ruler in 1857."

She looked at the coin again. "This is an odd thing to find in a terrorist camp."

"There were a dozen more," Nick said. "The Filipinos have them."

"A dozen more? One would be unusual. That many seems beyond belief. A coin like this has to be worth thousands of dollars."

Ronnie Peete came into the room. He was wearing a Hawaiian shirt with scenes of Kilauea erupting in vivid reds and yellows.

"Sorry I'm late," he said.

Ronnie was Navajo, born and raised on the reservation. He'd lied about his age, joined the Corps when he was seventeen and retired twenty years later with a Gunnery Sergeant's stripes. He had broad shoulders and narrow hips and stood about two inches below Nick's six feet. His eyes were a sleepy dark brown. He and Nick had been in the same Marine Recon unit.

"Glad you could join us," Elizabeth said.

Ronnie didn't seem embarrassed about being late. He sat down on the couch. "What did I miss?"

"Selena was telling us about the Mughals," Nick said.

"Mughals? Sounds like the title of a movie. You know, like *Meet the Mughals*."

Nick sighed. "They ruled India a long time ago. Selena thinks that gold coin I brought back from the raid in the Philippines comes from the Mughal Empire."

"Those coins could explain the sudden flow of money for weapons," Elizabeth said.

"Where would they get the coins?" Selena asked. "They're very rare."

"I'm hoping Abu Khan's phone will tell us more. The memory chip is encrypted. Stephanie's been working on it."

Stephanie Willits was Elizabeth's deputy and the Project's computer guru. Elizabeth had recruited her from the NSA. Steph had never met a computer or a chip she couldn't hack into. Sometimes it just took a little longer.

"When is she going to be done?"

"Let's ask her," Elizabeth said. She punched a button on her intercom. "Steph, could you come in here, please?"

In a moment Stephanie came through the door.

Selena thought Stephanie looked radiant these days. She was in love with Lucas Monroe, a long time agent with the CIA. He was on track to become Director of National Clandestine Services, one of the four major directorates at Langley.

Steph had the kind of average face you wouldn't pay much attention to if you passed her on the street. Her hair was full-bodied, a gleaming dark brown. Her eyes were the same color as her hair. She liked dangly earrings. Today they were large, gold hoops.

"Nick was asking if you'd gotten anything from Khan's phone," Elizabeth said.

"That's a heck of a phone," Steph said. "As good as what we use. It was a real challenge to get through the encryption. There were three calls in the log. Two went to a throwaway cell somewhere in the Quiapo District in Manila. That's right in the center of the city where most of the Muslim population lives. It doesn't help. "

"And the third call?"

"It came from a number assigned to the American Embassy in Manila."

"Who would call a terrorist from one of our embassies?" Ronnie said.

Elizabeth said, "Whoever it was, I don't think they were talking about getting a visa."

"They must have a plant working inside," Nick said. "Someone local. Part of Abu Sayyaf."

"We don't know that," Elizabeth said.

"What else could it be?"

"It would help if we knew what was said. Can you pull the calls out of the data banks, Steph? NSA tracks everything overseas. They have it somewhere."

"I've been looking but I haven't found them yet. Do you know how many calls there are in that database?"

"Why would Abu Sayyaf get involved with ISOK?" Selena asked. "The Philippines have nothing to do with Kashmir."

Harker's pen beat a rapid tattoo on the desktop. She looked at it and set it down.

"ISOK is led by a jihadist named Abdul Afridi. He's Indian, but he doesn't do anything without permission from Pakistan's intelligence service. Whatever he's doing with Abu Sayyaf, ISI is behind it. It means trouble for sure."

"What are you going to do?" Nick asked.

"All we have is a phone call and speculation," Harker said. "I'll pass the info to Langley and let them follow up. Steph, after you check out those calls in the NSA data banks, see what you can find out about this coin."

She handed it to Stephanie. "Anybody have anything else?"

"When is Lamont coming back?" Steph asked.

Lamont Cameron was the fourth part of Nick's team. A few months before he'd gone down with an infection, the result of a wound he'd taken in Jordan. It had almost killed him. Lately he'd seemed depressed. Nick was worried about him.

"I'm not sure," Elizabeth said. "I'm letting him have as much time as he needs to heal. I shouldn't have sent him on that last mission, it was too soon."

"It wasn't your fault, Elizabeth," Selena said. "He's the one who wanted to get out of the hospital."

"I know," Harker said. "But even so..."

"He'll be okay," Ronnie said. "Lamont is one tough cookie."

CHAPTER 5

Ashok Rao was in his office at RAW headquarters, reading a report from the Philippines and trying not to think about his limited future. He felt a sudden, sharp pain, as though a spike had punched into his skull. He got up from his desk and steadied himself. He walked to the private washroom he rated as Secretary of Special Operations, took the bottle of pills Krivi had given him from the medicine cabinet and shook four tablets into his palm. He filled a glass with bottled water and gulped them down. He turned on the tap and splashed cold water on his face. He patted the skin dry with a towel and combed back his receding hair.

The image looking back from the mirror showed a balding man with a moon shaped face. Deep pockets of shadow sat like bruises under liquid brown eyes. His skin was a medium brown color with a yellowish cast to it. He was clean-shaven. Rao was sixty-one years old, but today he felt ten years older.

His office was on the top floor of the agency's new headquarters building on Lodhi Road. He had a fine wooden desk and bookcase, a couch and upholstered chairs of good quality. The walls were painted yellow, with off-white, enameled trim. The floor was covered with thick, blue carpet. A row of windows looked out over the busy road below and across the rooftops of New Delhi.

One wall bore a mandatory picture of the current Prime Minister, a man for whom Rao felt only contempt. Below it was a picture of Lakhan

Gupta, the current Secretary of RAW and Rao's
boss. On another wall was a picture of the founder
of the first Hindu nationalist party. Next to it hung a
painting of an eighth century Hindu philosopher
called the Great Revivalist. A gold frame with a
picture of Rao's murdered wife and son sat on his
desk, next to a computer monitor.

He picked up the picture and gently touched the
glass over his wife's face.

The marriage had been arranged by their
parents, as was customary. Before the wedding, Rao
had little contact with his bride-to-be. That, too, was
customary. Marriage was a contract, a necessary
part of the social agreement. Love was secondary,
of little importance. What mattered was the alliance
between the families. At best, he'd hoped Lakshmi
would bear him sons and not argue with him too
much.

It hadn't taken long for Rao to see that Lord
Krishna had blessed him. Lakshmi had made him
feel like a poet, like a prince. Within months, he
was hopelessly in love with her. The feeling was
mutual.

When their son Arjuna was born, it seemed as
though the gods had filled Rao's life with joy. If
there was any one thing that interfered with his
happiness, it was his work. It was dangerous and
unpleasant, taking him away from Lakshmi for
weeks and months at a time. But it offered
advancement and the kind of security that came
from being an instrument of state power.

One day Lakshmi and Arjuna had been waiting
for a train on a packed station platform in Srinagar
when a terrorist from Abdul Afridi's group opened
fire on the crowd. Twenty-seven had died, his wife
and son among them. Whatever part of Rao was

drawn to poetry and love died with them that day. The attack had been planned by Pakistan's intelligence agency. Rao filled the empty space in his heart with hatred for ISOK, for Pakistan, and especially for Abdul Afridi.

Rao set the picture down and leaned back in his chair.

Since the meeting with Krivi, Rao had thought of little else except revenge. At night his dreams filled with half remembered images of black skies filled with fire. Now, it seemed, vengeance was within reach. He wasn't sure how Krivi would make it possible, but it didn't matter. Rao knew what needed to be done. He had to create a provocation, an incident to start India on the road to war. Krivi and his organization would fan the flames. But how was it to be accomplished?

The search for an answer kept Rao awake at night. Meanwhile there was work to be done, the daily oversight of his network of spies. He had to maintain an illusion of loyalty.

He picked up the report he'd been reading. It detailed a Filipino raid on an Abu Sayyaf camp and the death of Abu Khan. The report of Khan's death cheered Rao, but it raised questions. What was Khan doing in the Philippines? Had ISOK formed an alliance with Abu Sayyaf? If so, why? A second report speculated about a phone call from the American Embassy in Manila to Abu Khan. In the world of counter terrorism, a call like that was a red flag.

Rao's agent in Manila was Prakash Khanna. Khanna thought Abu Sayyaf was planning a major attack on the Americans, with the American Embassy the likely target. The phone call was a piece of intelligence he pointed to in support of his theory.

Rao didn't like Americans. He thought them arrogant and rude, little better than the British oppressors that had ruled India in the past. Washington claimed to be India's friend but played a double game by aiding Pakistan. America needed to understand that Pakistan was their enemy.

Rao decided against warning Washington. If Abu Sayyaf attacked the Americans there might be a way to turn their anger against Pakistan, by making Washington think Islamabad was behind it.

There can be no peace and rebirth without destruction, Rao thought. The concept of death and destruction as the seed of renewal and peace was deeply rooted in Indian culture. So was the concept of sacrifice. Sometimes sacrifices were necessary for the greater good and the glory of God.

Sacrifice.

Krivi's pills were taking effect. Rao's headache was gone. He felt good. The seed of a plan began to grow in his mind. He picked up his phone.

CHAPTER 6

The Indian Embassy to the Philippines was located in Dasmarinas Village in the Makati district, a peaceful, tree shaded island of calm in the restless chaos of the city. The saffron, white and green flag of India hung limp in the humid air over the entrance to the embassy.

Prakash Khanna's official title was Second Counselor Attaché, attached to the trade ministry. He'd been an agent with the Research and Analysis Wing for twelve years.

Khanna's last name was derived from a Sanskrit word for sword. It marked him as a guardian who would defend the values of Mother India. True to his name, he belonged to the *Kshatriya* caste, warriors in the tradition of the great Prince Arjuna. The caste system was still legal, still a universal part of Indian social and cultural life. Caste was hereditary and unchangeable. Many of the best RAW agents were Kshatriya.

Khanna thought of himself as a warrior, though his slight frame and thinning hair didn't match the virile image people saw in the Bollywood spectacles. Times had changed. In the modern era, a computer was of more use than a sword and analytic skills could be more deadly than the bow and arrow of the ancient epics.

Khanna's encrypted phone signaled a call from Ashok Rao. Rao was Khanna's superior but the two men were friends and shared many things in common. Like Rao, Khanna was a fundamentalist who saw all Muslims as the enemy.

Rao got right to the point. "I read your reports. Give me your thoughts."

"The meeting with Abu Khan is significant," Khanna said. "As far as I know, it's the first time there's been any involvement with the so-called Islamic State of Kashmir over here."

"Your report said gold was found during the raid."

"The Filipinos are concerned. Everyone's wondering where it came from. A dozen gold coins were recovered. Converted to cash, they'd buy some serious weapons."

"Abu Sayyaf could be getting money from ISOK. It would explain why Khan met with them."

Khanna thought about it. "Pakistan gives ISOK money but why would they use it here? Their focus is on Kashmir."

"I have good intelligence on the money trail from Pakistan to ISOK and nothing they get from Islamabad explains the gold. We tracked a shipment of weapons to their source. I sent in one of my best men to talk with the dealer. ISOK paid him in gold. The money didn't come from Pakistan."

"What happened to the dealer?" Khanna asked.

"He won't be selling more weapons to them or anyone else."

"Where are they getting the funds, if not from Islamabad?"

"I don't know, yet." Rao paused. "Your report puts a lot of emphasis on the call to Abu Sayyaf from the American Embassy."

"I'm convinced they plan to attack the Americans," Khanna said. "There are rumors on the street. They're seldom wrong."

"And you believe it's the embassy?"

"Yes. It's the logical choice."

"Why would Abu Sayyaf pick such a high profile target? It would be like poking a hornet's nest," Rao said.

"Washington wants to reestablish a military presence in the islands. Manila is demanding help with a new offensive against Abu Sayyaf in exchange. That could be reason enough."

"Let me pose a question to you," Rao said. "Suppose ISOK attacked our Embassy? What would the Americans do?"

"They wouldn't do anything," Khanna said. "They don't care about us. There would be expressions of outrage and official condolences, nothing more."

"And if they attacked the American Embassy?"

"That would be a different story. But ISOK doesn't have any reason to target Americans here."

"What if there was proof ISOK organized an attack against the Americans with Pakistan's backing, using Abu Sayyaf as surrogates?"

Khanna paused for a moment. He was beginning to see where Rao was going. "It would make ISOK a priority terrorist group for direct action. The Americans would be very angry at Pakistan."

"I have an idea," Rao said.

"What idea?"

"I'm sending a message that will explain. It should be on your computer a few minutes after we're done talking. I'll use the cipher."

The cipher was only used for the most sensitive communications. Anyone who managed to intercept a transmission would mistake it for a more commonly used code. It would appear to be a normal message sensitive enough to encode. The real message lay within the outer one. The cipher's beauty lay in its transparent simplicity.

"Read it and you'll understand," Rao said. He ended the call.

Curious, Khanna put his encrypted phone away and went to his computer and waited for the transmission. He printed it out, deleted it and started to decode it. As the message within a message emerged, Khanna shook his head in admiration. Rao was a cold son of a bitch. If his plan worked, it would mean serious trouble for ISOK and for Islamabad. It meant the sacrifice of a few of his countrymen but sometimes sacrifices were necessary.

Khanna finished the message and smiled.

CHAPTER 7

Selena's surprise showed in her voice. "I
thought we were going to have lunch."

She stood with Nick in front of a jewelry store
on 20th Street in Washington. It was just past noon.
Smog had settled over the city in a noxious haze.
The air smelled of exhaust fumes from the endless
traffic.

"We are," Nick said, "but I thought we might
stop in here first."

They stood in front of a jewelry store window.
Selena started to speak, then stopped.

"Lots of shiny things in the window," Nick
said. "See anything you like?"

"I see lots of things I like," she said. "I know
the store. People from the White House shop here,
whenever they need a bauble or two."

"Let's go inside."

The store was a testament to chic modernity.
Circular stools on elegant chrome stands were
strategically placed for customers to sit on while
they examined the goods. The goods were mostly
diamonds, though Nick saw a lot of gold and a
variety of gemstones in brilliant colors. Round,
open front cabinets at eye level displayed special
pieces under discreet lighting. An elderly woman
and a younger man sat at one of the counters,
looking at a man's wristwatch with a diamond
studded band. Nick and Selena were the only other
customers in the store.

A thirtyish man in a tailored suit approached
them. "May I help you?" he said. His tie was
perfectly knotted dark blue silk. It rested over a

light blue shirt that would have cost Nick a week's pay.

"We're looking for an engagement ring," Nick said. He looked at Selena and suppressed a laugh.

"What?" she said.

"The look on your face. You thought I'd never get around to it, didn't you?"

"The idea had occurred to me," she said.

The clerk watched them, a small smile on his face. It wasn't a new situation for him.

"This way, sir." He led them to a row of display cases filled with diamonds and gold and silver and platinum rings that gleamed under the lighting.

"Let's get that one," Nick said. He pointed at an elaborate ring with a central diamond and a pattern of leaves worked in tiny stones all around a platinum band.

"Are you sure you want to do this now?" Selena said. There was an edge to her voice.

"Why not? You want a ring, don't you?"

"Yes, but..."

"But?"

"But this feels rushed. It's not just another ring. I have to think about it, look in catalogs, visit stores, things like that."

Nick felt a headache start. "This is a store. There must be a hundred rings to look at here."

"That's not the point."

"What is the point? I thought you'd be pleased if we got something today."

The smile on the clerk's face was starting to look strained.

"The point is that I want to take more time to think about it," Selena said.

"Think about what? The ring or whether you want to get married?"

"Both," she said. She turned and walked out of the store.

Nick stood for a moment. He looked at the clerk and the man took a step backward.

"Don't say a word," Nick said.

He stormed out of the shop in time to see Selena get into a cab and pull away from the curb. He began walking toward Dupont Circle and then cut over to 19th Street, where there was an Irish bar he knew about. An Irish whiskey would be about right for his mood, maybe two or three of them. What the hell was it with Selena, anyway?

The bar was a three-story establishment built to resemble an Irish pub. The ground floor featured wooden floors, pub food, a fireplace and comfortable couches and chairs. The bar was polished wood, with wooden stools for the patrons. The back bar had a brick wall, two flat screen television sets and an impressive array of beers, whiskeys and liquors. The mellow glow of wood and comfortable lighting made it a place for serious drinking, if that's what you wanted. The pub looked more or less authentic, in an American kind of way. Missing were the Irish and two or three hundred years of music, tobacco smoke and spilled whiskey.

Nick took a seat at the bar and ordered a double Jameson neat, with a soda back. It was early in the day. He had the bar to himself except for a corporate-looking guy in a dark blue three-piece suit at the other end, drinking a martini. Nick sipped the whiskey and felt the mellow heat of Ireland descend into his stomach. The pub wasn't authentic but the whiskey was.

He'd thought Selena would be happy, surprised. She'd been surprised, all right, but she sure as hell didn't seem happy about it. What did he do wrong?

He finished his drink and signaled for another. The whiskey made a soft bed for his anger. Maybe he hadn't done anything wrong, he thought. Maybe it was just that age-old disconnect between men and women, the impossibility of either sex understanding the other. Why should he expect it to be any different between him and Selena? He was damned if he was going to let it spoil his day completely. But still, it pissed him off.

It hadn't been that way with Megan, back when he was almost done with his first tour in the Marines and ready to make the move into civilian life with her. It might have gotten that way after a while but he'd never had a chance to find out. She'd died in a plane crash as he watched, unable to do anything to save her. A piece of him had died that day as well, until it came alive again after he met Selena.

The whiskey helped. He debated having a third and decided against it. He paid for the drinks and left a five dollar bill and walked out into the fall afternoon.

I guess the ring is on hold, he thought. *Maybe it's a good thing.*

CHAPTER 8

It was the evening of the same day. Nick sat with Ronnie and Lamont at a table in The Point, a bar popular with current and former members of America's Special Forces. For a while the three of them had been barred from the premises, after a wild brawl provoked by a patron who'd taken exception to a song they were singing. Since then, all had been forgiven. The joint had a jukebox loaded with rock 'n roll. *Sweet Home, Alabama* played in the background.

Ronnie had a glass of club soda with a lime in front of him. Lamont and Nick were drinking beer. Lamont had lost weight in the hospital. The corded muscles that lined his wiry frame seemed more prominent than usual. His coffee colored skin was pale from being indoors. The scar he'd picked up in Iraq stood out like a thin, pink snake running across his forehead and the bridge of his nose. But the blue eyes he'd inherited from his Ethiopian forebears had lost none of their intensity.

It was early and the place wasn't crowded. It made conversation easy.

"How you feeling, Lamont?" Ronnie asked.

"Better with this beer."

The last few years had been rough on Lamont. He'd been badly wounded in Jordan. He'd almost died in Cuba. Now he was ready to come back and Nick was glad to have him. But he could tell Lamont had something to say.

"Better spit it out, Shadow," Nick said.

Lamont's mother had named him for Lamont Cranston, *The Shadow* of radio fame. His Navy

SEAL teammates had dropped the nickname on him. It was a natural.

"What do you mean?"

"Come on," Ronnie said. "You've been sitting there like you're hatching an egg, all quiet."

Lamont grinned at him. "Hey, I'm a quiet guy, you know that."

"Not when you've got a beer in front of you," Nick said. "Not usually."

Lamont fooled with his beer bottle, making rings of condensation on the table top.

"I've been thinking," he said.

"That's dangerous for someone like you," Ronnie said. "You ought to be careful about that."

"At least I can think, which is more than I can say for some people I know."

Nick signaled the waitress for another round. "So, what have you been thinking about?"

"I had a lot of time in the hospital to do nothing but think."

"And?"

"And I think it's about time for me to hang it up."

Nick and Ronnie looked at each other.

"Hang it up?" Nick said. "What would you do?"

"There's a dive shop for sale down in Florida. I called the real estate agent. It'd be perfect, just what I'd always dreamed of. I'd have to upgrade some of the gear but the price is right. I've got enough money saved up to take care of the down payment and I can borrow the rest."

The waitress came and set a new round of drinks on the table.

"You sound like your mind is pretty well made up," Nick said.

"Yeah, I think it is."

"There you go with that thinking stuff again," Ronnie said. He was joking but Nick could see he wasn't happy about what Lamont had said.

I should've seen this coming, Nick thought. Lamont had taken a lot of hits in the past two years. It would be enough to make anyone think about getting out. Hell, he had his own thoughts about getting out, and he hadn't been hurt as bad as Lamont. Sooner or later, everyone got out. The only difference was whether you went out on two feet or in a box with a flag over it, if there was enough of you left to put in a box.

"When were you planning on leaving?" Nick asked.

"It'll take time to replace me," Lamont said. "I don't want to leave the team short."

Nick knew that if Lamont had made up his mind to go, nothing he could say would change it.

"You'll stay until we find someone to take your place?" Nick said.

"Yeah. Until the end of the year, anyway. Harker ought to find someone by then. Then I'm gone."

"Ah, shit," Ronnie said. "Who's going to jump in the water if you're not around?"

Because of Lamont's time with the SEALS, anything involving boats and water on missions had fallen to him.

"Didn't they teach you Jarheads to swim in Recon? Course, that's kind of like the YMCA. I guess you're finally going to have to learn how," Lamont said.

"Marines are smart enough to stay out of the water. Fish crap in it." Ronnie sipped his club soda.

Lamont changed the subject. "Nick, how's it going between you and Selena? When's the wedding?"

"You're asking me? How would I know?"

"Oh, oh. Like that, is it?"

"I never know where I stand with her," Nick said. He told them about what had happened earlier at the jewelry store. "I wanted to surprise her. I thought she'd be pleased."

"You surprised her all right," Ronnie said. "You should've just bought the ring and given it to her without taking her into the store."

"What if she didn't like it?'

"What if she didn't? Then you could just go back to the store with her and have her pick a ring she liked."

"But that's why I went in there with her in the first place."

"You know what your problem is?" Lamont said.

Nick was beginning to get annoyed, thinking about what had happened with Selena.

"No, I don't know what my problem is. Why don't you enlighten me?"

"The problem is you're thinking like a guy instead of like Selena. A guy says to himself, self, I think I'll go in this store with my honey and buy a nice diamond ring. It's a jewelry store, right? Got to be a lot of rings in there. Shouldn't take long."

"So? What's wrong with that?"

"Nothing, so far. Where it went wrong was when you picked the first one you saw and said, 'let's get that one.'"

"It was a nice ring."

"That's got nothing to do with it," Lamont said. "That's how a guy shops. We go to a store, we see something that works and we buy it. We don't spend a lot of time thinking about it. Women don't do it that way."

Ronnie was nodding his head in agreement.

"What was I supposed to do?"

"You were supposed to let her look at rings until she decided she wanted to think about it some more."

"But what's there to think about?" Nick asked. "There must've been a hundred rings in that damn store. Any one of them would of worked."

Lamont turned to Ronnie. "See what I mean?"

"Hopeless," Ronnie said. He turned to Nick. "That's not what Selena wants."

"You, too? Okay, Einstein, what does she want?"

"She wants it to be special when she chooses a ring." It was Lamont's turn to nod his head. Ronnie continued. "You made it seem like buying a pair of socks."

Nick looked at his two friends and their serious expressions.

"I think you're wrong. I'm picking up on second thoughts about getting married."

"Hers or yours?" Lamont said.

CHAPTER 9

Jagadev Muhkerjee walked the grounds perimeter of the Indian Embassy in Manila and looked again at his watch. It was a very nice watch, with a little button he could push to light the dial. It was 3:30 in the morning, a half hour from the end of his shift and exactly 2 1/2 minutes since the last time he'd looked.

Jagadev was bored and tired. He wanted nothing more than a quiet smoke and hours of sleep on his bunk in the security barracks. The night sounds of Manila were muffled by the trees and landscaping that made Dasmarani Village seem more like a rural estate than an enclave of important government buildings. Only the glow in the night sky was there to remind him that he was in the heart of one of the great cities of the world.

Jagadev wasn't really a soldier, even though he wore a jaunty beret and uniform and carried an Indian made 5.56 mm INSAS rifle that put out six hundred rounds a minute. Security guards for India's embassies abroad were civilians. It was a job, like any other security job. In difficult areas like Jammu and Kashmir, security fell on the shoulders of specially trained commandos. But Manila wasn't Kashmir. The main requirements were that the applicant be an Indian citizen, have had the proper security or military training and be able to deal as required with the constant stream of people visiting the Embassy.

He looked again at his watch. Another minute had passed. A three-quarter moon cast pale light on the tropical flowers and trees of the embassy grounds. A few stars glimmered in the night sky, flickering in the smoggy haze thrown off by the city.

There was a garden bench tucked away in the far corner of the grounds, under the trees. Jagadev decided not to wait until he went off duty to grab a cigarette. The bench and the overhanging branches of the trees were a perfect spot to take a minute and handle the nicotine edge that kept him looking at his watch. No one would see him there and no one would know that he'd taken a short break from his perimeter duty. He reached the spot, stepped into the shadows and took a cigarette from the pack concealed under his shirt. He lit it and took a long, satisfying drag.

There was a faint sound behind him. A gloved hand covered his mouth as he started to lift the cigarette to his lips and pulled his head backward. There was a terrible, hot pain across his throat. Blood fountained into the night, spraying over the bench where the ambassador liked to sit for his afternoon meditations. Jagadev's last thought was only a confused, unspoken question.

The man who had just slashed Jagadev's throat was dressed all in black. He had been born in the slums of Mumbai, back when the city was still called Bangalore. His name was Ijay. His ski mask concealed the discoloration of large, dark spots on his face. The spots had earned him the nickname *Tendu'a*, after the silent and deadly leopard that was feared throughout India. The elite unit of black op commandos he led was known as the Leopards.

Ijay had three kilos of Semtex high explosive in a backpack. He signaled the others. Four men in black with identical packs emerged from the shrubs and trees and fanned out at a run toward the back of the embassy. No one would miss the guard for several minutes. There was more than enough time to plant the charges and melt back into the trees before anyone saw them.

They worked quickly, placing enough high explosive to take out most of the building. When the Semtex detonated, the wall and the back of the embassy would cease to exist. The ambassador's quarters were on the second floor in the back, directly over one of the charges. Only a miracle would save him.

As he worked, Ijay thought about how all that Semtex was going to make one hell of an explosion. He wondered why an embassy of his own country had been chosen for the target, but it didn't matter. It wasn't his place to question orders. As long as he was creating chaos, Ijay was happy.

The others finished setting charges. Ijay gave the signal to arm the detonators. In a movement they had practiced over and over, all five men knelt and triggered the timers at the same instant. All five rose as one and headed back for the cover of the trees. In seconds they were gone from sight.

Prakash Khanna had watched the entire operation from his hiding place in the shrubbery on the side of the grounds. He waited until the quiet of the early morning was shattered by the explosion. The back of the Indian Embassy rose toward the sky in a geyser of fire and stone. A billowing cloud of smoke and dust rolled out over the green lawn as bits and pieces of the building fell back to earth. The cloud thinned and Khanna saw that more than half of the embassy was gone. The remaining floors and rooms gaped at him like an open mouth with crooked teeth.

The ambassador never could have survived that, Khanna thought. His lip curled in unconscious contempt. The man had been a pawn of the Americans, a weakling, just like the Prime Minister. Unwilling to do what needed to be done, to take the steps necessary to eliminate the Pakistani threat once and for all.

In the distance, Khanna heard the first siren. *Time to go*, he thought. He walked to where the crumpled body of the guard lay by the secluded bench. The stench of voided bowels filled the night. Khanna held his finger under his nose, reached in his pocket and pulled out a crumpled pack of Pakistani cigarettes. He tossed the cigarettes into the bushes near the guard. He'd already filed false intelligence reports to New Delhi about a possible ISOK incident in Manila. Along with the Filipino report about ISOK's involvement with Abu Sayyaf, it should be enough to point the finger at them and at Pakistan.

Before the Partition of 1947, Khanna's family had lived in Lahore, now part of Pakistan. The family had lost everything, choosing to leave rather than live under Muslim rule. His grandfather had died a bitter man. His father had taught him that Muslims were evil and Khanna had seen nothing to make him change his mind. Pakistan was the enemy, a thief that had stolen his ancestral home. If what had happened here tonight pushed India into striking a first blow, Khanna would be cheering every missile.

Fire was climbing the broken wall on the side of the embassy. The sound of sirens was closer. Khanna lit a cigarette and walked away into the night.

CHAPTER 10

Selena finished her morning workout in the exercise room in her condo, went into the bedroom, dumped her sweats and headed for the shower. Usually the workout and shower helped her relax, but it wasn't working today. She shut off the water, grabbed a thick, Turkish towel, and dried off. She rubbed steam off the bathroom mirror with the towel, stood before the mirror and gave herself a critical look.

Still pretty good, she thought, resting her hand on her hip and turning her head slightly. She touched the scar left by the bullet she'd taken in Mexico and felt a faint memory of pain. There were shadows under her eyes. Were those new lines at the corners? She leaned forward and stretched the skin a bit, trying to see. She hadn't slept well, not after leaving Nick standing in the jewelry store. She was still sorting out why she'd acted on impulse like that.

She'd been on edge that morning, annoyed with Nick and the way he was taking her for granted. Assuming she'd just go along with what he wanted. But that wasn't it. It was deeper, some fundamental doubt the engagement was a good idea in the first place. In hindsight, if she tried to be objective, she could see Nick had meant well and was only trying to surprise her. Somehow her objectivity kept slipping away, lost in a mix of conflicting thoughts and emotions about the whole damned relationship.

Why was she thinking about getting married anyway? She was self-sufficient, able to do whatever she wanted on her own. She had her own money. She didn't even need to work unless she wanted to. She could go anywhere she wanted, do almost anything she wanted to do. She could have her pick of intelligent, handsome and educated men from about any walk of life. So what was so damned attractive about a battered, stubborn man whose principal goal in life seemed to be jumping in where angels feared to tread and whose primary skill was shooting at people and blowing things up?

When Nick asked her to marry him, she'd barely hesitated. Maybe it was the context of a Caribbean night, the moonlight, the afterglow of sex, the warm strength she felt radiate from him as he stood next to her. Maybe it had been the knowledge that the next day meant one or both of them had a good chance of getting killed.

Or maybe you're just a closet romantic, she thought. *Moonlight, flowers and guns.*

She smiled to herself. Not too many people would put those three things together and think of romance. Nick would. Things like that were why she loved him.

The thought rippled through her. It was true, she really did love him. She wasn't sure that was enough of a reason to marry him. Too much had happened over the last few years.

She walked from the bathroom to the closet and picked out a bra and panties, then a pale lavender silk blouse that went well with her eyes. She added black slacks and low heeled, comfortable black shoes. She dressed, went into the kitchen and made herself a cup of coffee and sat at the counter.

Love. Once before, she'd thought she was in love. His name was Ted. He was rich, educated, and sophisticated. They'd been on vacation in Greece, spending a week on Mykonos. He'd gotten drunk and they'd gone back to their room overlooking the harbor. An argument had started and he'd hit her, hard enough to send her staggering backward. She hadn't even thought about it. She'd decked him and kicked him where it hurt. It hadn't taken long to pack the few things she'd brought with her. She'd walked out and never looked back.

After that there'd never been anyone serious. Not until Nick.

Selena glanced at the clock on the counter. It was time to get going over to Virginia for the morning briefing. She and Nick could go out for coffee together afterward. They needed to talk.

CHAPTER 11

Elizabeth looked over her team and felt a vague sense of unease. Selena and Nick were sitting together but they might as well have been in different rooms. Something was off between them.

Lamont looked tired. His coffee colored skin was pale. The scar crossing his face seemed more vivid than usual. Elizabeth reminded herself to ask him if he was still taking meds. This wasn't a good time to have things getting in the way of the team's usual high level of performance. At least he was back in the mix. That counted for a lot.

Ronnie sat next to Lamont. He wore one of his many Hawaiian shirts, an endless scene of surfers at Waikiki done in unnatural colors that looked dreamed up by a mad chemist on an acid trip.

Elizabeth began. "There's been an attack on the Indian Embassy in Manila," she said. "They cut the night guard's throat, planted Semtex and did their best to blow up the building. The ambassador and his wife were killed in the explosion."

"Who did it?" Nick asked.

"Nobody is certain, yet. Possibly ISOK."

"That could explain why Abu Khan was on Mindanao."

She looked at Nick. "President Rice is trying to get new base agreements in the Philippines. With the Chinese claiming islands right off their coast and building bases in the China Sea, Manila is getting nervous. It's important that nothing disrupts those negotiations."

"The Filipinos kicked us out and now they need us," Lamont said. "Why am I not surprised?"

"American bases and our nuclear weapons are a sensitive subject over there," Elizabeth said. "There's a demonstration scheduled two days from now to protest any new agreement, with a planned march on the Embassy. Demonstrations like that have turned violent in the past. After the Indian Embassy bombing, Rice is worried the terrorists may use the march to create an incident. He wants me to send the team to Manila."

"What do you want us to do there?" Nick asked.

"Think of it as a preventative mission. See what you can find out. If Abu Sayyaf or ISOK is planning an attack, head it off at the pass."

"You want us to go in blind, sniff around for terrorist activity and then prevent an attack that might or might not happen?"

"Is that a problem?"

Nick sighed. "Anything else?"

"That's about it. Try to stay out of the way of the demonstrators."

"Mob, you mean. How do we get there?"

"Clark Air Force Base is open to us again. You'll go in on military transport. That puts you about forty miles from Manila and avoids the complications of civilian travel. Take weapons but keep it light and easy to conceal. We don't want to upset anyone. Take a comm package for the satellite uplink back here."

"When do we leave?"

"Wheels up at 0200 tomorrow from Andrews. "

"What about Langley?" Ronnie asked. "They've got to have a man in the embassy looking into the same things we are. Do we let them know we're there, or keep our distance?"

"Keep your distance," Elizabeth said. "I don't see any need to involve the agency. I'll decide if we need to bring them in."

"I know the U.S. Ambassador in Manila," Selena said. "Not well, but she attended a series of lectures I gave at Stanford a few years ago and we got to be friends. I could arrange to see her. She might be helpful."

"Good," Elizabeth said. "Definitely, go see her." She turned to Lamont. "How are you feeling, Lamont? Are you ready to go back in the field? You haven't had an easy time of it the last few months."

"I'm fine, Director. I'm going crazy sitting around doing nothing. Yeah, I'm ready."

"All right then," Elizabeth said. "Any other questions?"

No one had any.

"I'd better get going on the gear," Ronnie said. He got up and left the room and headed downstairs to the armory.

"I'll give you a hand," Nick called after him. He stood and went after Ronnie.

So much for a quiet talk over coffee, Selena thought.

CHAPTER 12

Selena decided where they would stay in Manila. Most of the time they were in places where accommodations were lousy or nonexistent. She tried to upgrade whenever they had a choice. She had the money and she was damned if she was going to be uncomfortable just because they were on a mission in some foreign country.

She'd picked one of the large chain hotels with a five star rating, a modern businessman's hotel within easy walking distance of the American Embassy. There was nothing particularly unique about it. It was clean and you could drink the water. It was a slice of commercial America set down a block and a half from Roxas Boulevard and the waterfront on Manila Bay.

She was sharing a luxury suite on the twentieth floor with Nick. It had two bedrooms and separate bathrooms, which would come in handy if things didn't smooth out between them. There'd been no opportunity to talk when they were getting ready for the mission and trying to hold a conversation in the aluminum belly of a C-130 was a lost cause.

Ronnie and Lamont were down the hall. Nick looked out the window at the impressive view of the bay and the eight lanes of Roxas Boulevard and thought the wide, modern highway along the waterfront made a perfect route for marchers and protesters. It would also work well if the government had to bring in the tanks and water cannons.

There were signs the protest was going to be a big one. Thousands of people were coming in from the countryside and the outlying districts of the capital. Temporary campgrounds had sprung up everywhere in the parks along the bay, complete with cooking fires, makeshift shelters, and a nervous police presence. The demonstration was scheduled to begin early the next morning.

There was a feeling of tension in the air, a kind of unpleasant, electric anticipation, like the way things felt before a big storm. There was going to be trouble.

"I have a bad feeling about tomorrow," Nick said.

Selena came over and stood next to him at the window. "So do I."

They looked out at the fabled waters of Manila Bay. A large tanker was heading away from the port toward the distant entrance of the bay, where the island of Corregidor stood silhouetted against the most amazing sunset Nick had ever seen. The broad bowl of the sky was filled with colors of flaming orange, gold and red. Billowing black clouds taller than Everest scudded across the horizon, forcing the light of the setting sun into a kaleidoscope of fiery golden rays that spread across the sky.

They stood in silence looking at the spectacle. Selena felt Nick take her hand. She glanced over. His eyes had a distant look in them as he watched the sunset. As the sun vanished on the horizon, there was a brief, brilliant green flash.

"Did you see that?" he said.

"Yes."

"I've heard about the green flash but I'd never seen it," Nick said. He turned to her and took her other hand. "We need to talk."

"Yes, we do."

"I'm sorry about the other day. I shouldn't have surprised you like that."

"I'm sorry too." She paused. "It's just that...things seem to be moving too fast."

"Too fast?"

"We're talking about getting married," she said, "but we don't know what it would be like to live with each other all the time."

"We already spend most of our time together," Nick said. He kept his voice neutral.

"A lot of that is in the field," Selena said, "like right now. It's not the same."

"No, I suppose it isn't."

"I mean, why aren't we living together? My condo is more than big enough for two people."

"So is my apartment," Nick said. "Well, not in the long run. But I like it there. I like the privacy, doing things my way."

"And I like my place," Selena said.

Nick looked out the window again at the growing tropical twilight. "I meant it when I asked you to marry me," he said.

She heard an unspoken *but* in his voice. She wasn't sure where he was going with this. Was he backing out? Was she pushing him away?

"Have you changed your mind?" she said.

He looked at her. "No, I haven't changed my mind. I was wondering if you had."

If she were honest with herself, she definitely had second thoughts. Why else had she reacted like that in the jewelry store?

"Because of the ring?"

"That was a pretty strong message," he said.

"I told you, it took me by surprise."

"Yeah, I get that, but I think most women would have at least looked at the rings they had in that store. It wasn't like I was trying to force you into making a decision right then. It makes me wonder if I'm pushing too hard."

"So what are you saying?" Her heart was beating hard in her chest.

"I think we need to back off a little. Like you said, we haven't tried living together. It might be a good idea. See if it works."

"What about our engagement?"

"Nothing's changed," Nick said. "That jewelry store will still be there when we get back."

Nothing's changed. That's easy for him to say.

Selena took a deep breath. "I think I'll give Ambassador Cathwaite a call."

CHAPTER 13

Omar Madid was a small man, even for a Filipino. His eyes were deep brown, with large, black pupils. They should have been beautiful eyes, but there was something about them that made people turn away, as if someone you didn't want to meet lived inside him.

Omar had grown up in the poverty-stricken slums of Manila, a lawless collection of shanties, makeshift houses and desperate people. He had never known his father. As a boy, life had revolved around his mother and days spent playing along the banks of the polluted creek that ran through the shanties. Then his mother was trampled to death by a mob running from the police as they made one of their periodic sweeps through the district.

After that, life held no joy for Omar except for one thing; death. Death was always interesting. He began to torture and kill small animals unfortunate enough to cross his path. He killed his first man when he was eleven, a drunken Chinese tourist who'd been looking for a male prostitute but who had found Omar instead. The older criminals used him to carry drugs and guns, sometimes as a lookout for one of their operations. His small size meant he could get into openings no adult could climb through.

When he was seventeen, he was arrested and beaten by the hated police, then taken to Navotas Municipal Jail. The police threw him into a cell crowded with filthy, desperate men. When three of them came for him, Omar killed the first with a blow to his throat. He crippled the second with a knee to the groin and stomped on his chest. He broke the knee of the third with a vicious kick. After that, no one bothered him.

In the jail he was recruited by Abu Sayyaf. That had been eight years ago. He'd become devout in those years, a true Jihadist. It was why he'd been chosen to lead this mission.

Omar sat in the bow of a small boat piloted by one of his comrades as it bounced across the choppy waters of the bay. He kept his binoculars trained on the American Embassy passing to his right. The grounds were protected by a curving sea wall. A high, black barrier rose from the sea wall and extended the length of the embassy grounds. All that could be seen beyond the barrier were palm fronds and the tops of trees rippling in the breeze coming off the water. In the middle of the sea wall was a glassed security tower with a commanding view of the bay.

Through his binoculars Omar saw a Marine guard in the tower looking back at him through his own set of lenses. Omar lowered his binoculars, smiled a toothy grin and waved at the guard. The man was too far away to see that the smile never reached Omar's eyes.

The Americans thought their walls, their fences and their security forces would keep them safe.

They were wrong.

CHAPTER 14

The American Embassy was a three-story, flat roofed, federal style mansion, built early in the twentieth century to house the United States High Commission. It had always been a seat of power. In World War II the building had served as the residence of the commander-in-chief of the Imperial Japanese Army, then as the Embassy of Japan in the puppet Republic set up by Tokyo in 1943. After the war, the building became the center for the Japanese war crimes trials. After independence in 1946, it became the U.S. Embassy.

A ten foot high wall and a black iron fence separated the embassy grounds from Roxas Boulevard. A large guardhouse sat to the right of the main entrance. Double-gated passages for vehicles were placed on either side of a central wall bearing the sign identifying the embassy. The gates operated electronically from the guardhouse and opened and closed one at a time. They formed an iron cage.

Once through the gates, visitors turned onto a continuous drive lined by a row of three foot high iron bollards. A car or truck bomb would never reach the front doors of the building. Internal security at the embassy was covered by a small detachment of Marines commanded by a Staff NCO. Filipino security forces were responsible for external security.

A building to the right of the embassy housed numerous offices and living quarters. The Chancery complex was directly behind the original structure. Several more buildings were under construction on the embassy grounds. The U.S. presence in the Philippines was growing.

A growing crowd of demonstrators had already gathered in front of the gates. Selena showed her ID to the Marine guard and passed into the compound. Inside the embassy, a security desk manned by a Marine Corporal faced the double doors of the entrance. A second Marine manned a metal detector and x-ray machine by the doors, screening everyone who came into the building.

Selena showed the Marine her credentials. Not many people had ever seen that particular badge with the presidential seal. She wore a light weight linen jacket. She lifted it away to show the Marine the pistol at her hip.

"I'm armed," she said. She kept her hands where he could see them.

"You'll have to leave your weapon with me, Ma'am."

"I would prefer not to."

"I'm sorry, Ma'am. It's regulations."

Selena unclipped her holster and handed it to him.

"It's de cocked, loaded and ready to go," she said.

"I see that. I'll take good care of it for you," he said. He took the Sig and locked it in a small safe. "You can go through now."

"Thank you."

Selena looked around. The embassy had been built during America's colonial era, designed to impress visitors as the outpost of a nation on the rise as a world power. A stairway with a wide, mahogany railing led to the upper stories. Selena spotted an elevator to one side. A wide hall that doubled as a gallery ran to the back of the building and a large ballroom used for events.

Two muscular Marines wearing spotless white hats with the globe and anchor, short-sleeved tan shirts and dress blue trousers stood at parade rest by the entrance, observing the crowd forming beyond the gates. They were armed with pistols and radiated alert tension. Selena had seen that look before, when Nick and Ronnie and Lamont expected trouble. She touched the radio transmitter in her ear that kept her connected to the rest of the team outside the embassy. It felt reassuring.

Like other presidents before him, President Rice had rewarded generous donations to his political campaign with ambassadorships. But Rice wasn't a typical politician. When it came to posts he considered critical for the security of the United States, he picked qualified people he knew to be competent. Rice considered the Philippines too important to entrust to a rich amateur with no diplomatic experience.

Ambassador Margaret Cathwaite was a career veteran of the State Department's diplomatic corps. Cathwaite looked out the windows of her office and wondered if the day would bring violence. It was nine o'clock in the morning. The main demonstration had not yet begun and protesters were already parading in front of the gates with signs denouncing the United States, President Rice and the Philippine government.

Today wasn't the first time or the first country where she'd looked out an embassy window at angry people who blamed the United States for all their problems. America was the perfect scapegoat when foreign politicians with an agenda needed a distraction.

She took off her glasses and rubbed the bridge of her nose, stretched in her chair and rotated her head from side to side, trying to free up the stiffness in her neck. She put her glasses back on and looked at a picture of her late husband, displayed in a prominent position on her desk. She wished he was here with her. The pain of his death would never go away, but after three years it had dulled somewhat. A second picture next to the first was of her daughter and two smiling children. Her daughter lived in Seattle and was happily married.

This was Margaret's last post. She was sixty-two years old and had decided to leave the service at the end of the year. She was tired of the constant pressure that went with her job and dealing with the egos and turf wars within the State Department. Margaret Cathwaite looked forward to retirement and spending time with her grandchildren.

A knock interrupted her reverie. Her secretary entered the room.

Helen Martinson was the kind of woman people called *willowy*. She was tall and supple, with straw colored hair pulled back in a tight bun, a pleasant looking woman in her late forties. Margaret thought she was one of the most efficient people she'd ever met.

"Doctor Connor is here to see you," Helen said. "She's your only appointment this morning. I haven't scheduled anyone else because of the demonstration."

"Wonderful. Send her in. No, wait, I'll go out to meet her."

"Did you remember to take your pills?" Helen asked. She'd been with Margaret a long time. Sometimes the ambassador thought she acted more like a mother hen than a secretary.

"Yes, Helen, thank you." She got up out of her chair and went to meet Selena.

"Madam Ambassador," Selena said. She smiled. "Hello, Margaret. Thanks for seeing me."

"Selena, it's been too long. Come on into my office."

Selena followed her in, feeling the absence of weight on her hip caused by her missing holster.

Across the street Nick stood in the shade of a tall flame tree, watching the crowd and the Filipino police outside the embassy. Branches loaded with feathery green leaves and brilliant red flowers spread over his head, breaking up the heat of the sun. He wiped away a light coating of sweat from his forehead. It was already hot and humid. The weather forecast was for a scorcher.

Lamont and Ronnie were with the crowd of demonstrators and speakers at the beginning of the march, some distance away down Roxas Boulevard. The color of their skin made it easier for them to blend into the mob than it was for Nick. No one would mistake him for a Filipino. So far there'd been no sign of unusual activity, unless you counted the gathering of thousands of people opposed to an American presence in the Philippines as unusual.

Nick's earpiece crackled. He heard Lamont's voice.

"The march is moving," Lamont said. "Lots of people and they all seem pissed off."

"Roger that," Nick said. "You and Ronnie stick together. Try not to get separated."

Lamont said, "There's going to be trouble."

"Don't get caught in the crowd. Stay on the edges."

"Roger. Out."

Nick waited in the shade of the tree. Soon he heard a rumble of sound in the distance. As the crowd got closer the rumbling became distinct words.

USA OUT!! USA OUT!! USA OUT!! NO MORE BOMBS!! NO MORE BOMBS!!

Nick watched the march approach and felt his adrenaline kick in. The hair prickled on the back of his neck. There was something primal about mobs like this, an echo of a time before humans became civilized. It was more than a gathering of angry people. It was an entity unto itself, a force that could not be reasoned with. The chanting vibrated underfoot and echoed off the walls of the buildings.

Nick looked for Ronnie and Lamont and saw them on the outer fringe of the marchers, a few rows back from the front. They looked stressed. He held his hand over his ear.

"Ronnie, Lamont, I see you. I'm under that big tree with the red flowers across from the embassy. Break out and get over here." He saw them look his way.

They pushed through the protesters toward Nick. No one paid any attention. The march halted in front of the embassy. A double line of nervous national police in riot gear with helmets, clubs and shields blocked the front of the gates. The protesters ignored them and focused on the leaders. A man took out a crude American flag and set it on fire. A man with a bullhorn began haranguing the crowd, waving his fist in the air and shouting out slogans.

Inside the embassy, Selena and the ambassador watched from Cathwaite's office.

"Does this happen often?" Selena said.

"Not on this scale. Every once in a while somebody sprays slogans over the embassy sign out front. There hasn't been a big demonstration like this for a year or two. This one seems well organized and larger than most."

There was a knock and the door of the office was opened by a Marine wearing Gunnery Sergeant's stripes.

"Ma'am, I'd like to break out weapons and lock down the building. I don't like the looks of what's happening out there."

"Sergeant Crowder," she said. "If you think it's necessary, go ahead."

"Yes, Ma'am." He saluted and turned away. Selena could hear him giving orders to his men.

"I'm afraid you're stuck in here for a while, Selena," Margaret said. "These things can last for hours."

"Your sergeant looks competent," Selena said.

"He's a good man, commander of the security detachment. He watches over the others as if they were his family. As far as I know, they're the only family he's got."

Cathwaite pressed a button on her intercom. "Helen, would you assemble everyone in the ballroom please?"

The speaker crackled. "Right away."

"Let's join the others," Margaret said.

She swept out of the room, very much the Ambassador. *You never know who someone is until things get difficult*, Selena thought. Margaret Cathwaite looked like she was up to the task, whatever it turned out to be.

CHAPTER 15

The Museum of the City of Manila was located to the Northeast of the American Embassy. Ahmed settled himself comfortably in a sitting position on the roof of the museum. He placed the barrel of his Russian SV-98 rifle on the rampart, adjusted the bipod and peered through the telescopic sight. From the top of the four-story building, Ahmed had an unobstructed shot to the sentry tower on the back wall of the embassy. His rifle was chambered for the .338 Lapua Magnum. The range was about 1200 meters, well within the round's 1750 meter accuracy.

Ahmed was the best marksman in Abu Sayyaf and proud to have this fine rifle. The SV-98 was an older design but it was still an effective sniper weapon, especially in the larger caliber. The rifle had a Russian PKS-07 scope with 7x magnification and a compact muzzle brake that acted to suppress the sound of the shot and reduce the powerful recoil. Even with a fiberglass stock, the SV-98 was heavy, weighing in at almost eight kilos.

Ahmed mentally calculated the breeze and the weight of the humid air and adjusted his sights accordingly. Shooting the way he did was an art, born of a natural gift and countless hours spent practicing. He made a slight adjustment to the scope and watched the uniformed sentry in the tower come into sharp, clear focus.

Bang. Ahmed pictured the man's head exploding. The heavy bullet would punch through the glass of the sentry tower as if it were paper.

Out on the bay, the boat with the assault team
had turned toward the sea wall. Ahmed looked at
his watch. Once the sentry was down, the others
would scale the wall on the water side and move
through the embassy complex toward the main
building. There was a construction site near the wall
that was usually busy with workers, but today it was
abandoned. The Chancery was a large building
situated directly behind the embassy. There might
be trouble there but with the protest scheduled, most
of the workers had stayed home. The chances of
reaching the embassy unseen were good. Plenty
would be going on in front to distract everyone.

Ahmed settled behind the scope. He took a
breath and let part of it out, willing himself
motionless, his mind focused on the head of the
Marine in the sentry tower. He felt himself become
one with the gun. His finger rested next to the hair
trigger. The sentry was looking at the boat with
Ahmed's comrades through a pair of binoculars.

Ahmed touched the trigger. The sound of the
shot rolled across the bay, sending dozens of gulls
screeching into the air. The rifle jumped with the
recoil. Ahmed saw the Marine's head turn into a fog
of red mist. The binoculars flew through the air.
The man fell out of sight.

The boat moved in close, seconds after the
shot. Grappling hooks and chain ladders locked
onto the barrier wall. Men swarmed up the ladders
and onto the grounds.

Inside the embassy, Master Gunnery Sergeant
Crowder wasn't having any luck raising the tower
on his radio. Crowder had been a Marine for
twenty-four years. He'd developed a fine sense for
trouble, honed in Iraq, Kuwait, and Afghanistan. No
one lasted long in the kinds of places he'd been if

they didn't develop that sense. Now it was telling him there was more than a communications glitch behind the radio silence.

"Shit," he said. "Parker, Martinez, lock and load. Get your ass to the back of the building."

The two Marines carried M4A1's they'd taken from the arms locker. Crowder heard the metallic clacking of the bolts as his men charged their weapons on the run. One of his men came up carrying a rifle and handed it to him.

"Thought you might like one of these, Gunny."

Crowder nodded his thanks. Better than the Beretta 9mm he carried. "Take Rodriguez and Jackson and get over by the front. Keep an eye on that crowd."

"Roger that."

The last stragglers were coming down from upstairs, headed for the ballroom. On a normal day there might be anywhere from fifty to eighty people inside the building. Today wasn't a normal day and the place was nearly empty. Most of the civilians and nonessential personnel had stayed home, anxious to avoid the demonstration. The Commerce Department attaché was there and his assistant, CIA's man in Manila. In addition to the ambassador, the only other Americans were Helen Martinson, Selena and a young woman who was the attache's secretary. Her name was Jean Wilson. Manila was her first overseas assignment.

Six American civilians, plus Sergeant Crowder and his Marines. A half dozen Filipinos rounded out the list, cleaning personnel and maintenance workers unwilling to be intimidated by the demonstration and lose a day's pay.

Selena was a step behind Margaret as they moved toward the ballroom. She heard sudden shouts from the rear of the building and the unmistakable sound of automatic weapons, followed by an explosion.

Grenade, she thought. Without thinking, her hand went for her gun. It wasn't there. *Great. Locked away.* She reached up to her ear and activated the comm link.

"Nick, do you read me?"

"Loud and clear. What's happening?"

"We're under attack. In the back."

Nick heard the background chatter of small arms fire over his earpiece. Out front, the only sound was the roar of the crowd. Ronnie and Lamont heard everything Selena was saying. Lamont's chronic tiredness seemed to have vanished. They stepped close to Nick and waited for his lead.

Nick cupped his ear. "Can you get to cover?" he said.

Selena was about to answer when men dressed in black shirts, white trousers and wearing black headbands spilled out of the ballroom into the central hall. They carried AK-47s. Sergeant Crowder shot the first man through the doorway before a burst from an AK cut him down.

The three Marines in front opened fire. The foyer echoed with gunfire and the eerie sound of high velocity rounds ripping through the air. Two more terrorists went down. Selena grabbed the ambassador from behind and pulled her down to the floor. The terrorists concentrated a stream of fire on the Marine guards. The open space echoed with shouts and the staccato blasts of the weapons and the ping of empty casings bouncing across the hard wooden floor.

Then it was silent except for the clacking, metallic sound of an empty magazine hitting the floor. The smell of spent rounds and fresh blood filled the air.

Selena looked at the carnage and whispered into her comm link. "Negative cover," she said. "Three terrorists dead. Six left that I can see. The guards are dead."

She stopped whispering as a pair of feet wearing Nike running shoes stopped nearby.

"All right," she heard Nick say. "Stay cool, don't do anything heroic. We'll get you out of there. Don't say anything unless you have to. I can hear everything going on around you."

"Get up." The voice was hard, almost bored. The Nike foot kicked her. "You are not hurt. Both of you, get up now." The speaker kicked her again for emphasis.

Selena got to her feet and leaned down to help Margaret stand.

"You are going to regret this," the ambassador said. "You, and all your cowardly comrades." She looked at the blood soaked body of Sergeant Crowder lying on the floor. Selena watched her get herself under control.

The terrorist leader was a small man with eyes that looked dead. Like the others, he wore a black headband, black trousers and a white shirt.

"I don't think so," he said. His English was good. "Unless you want to join your sergeant over there, you'll do as I say, *Madame Ambassador*." He turned his attention to Selena.

"Who are you?" he said. "You are not one of the people in our photographs."

Nick's voice sounded in her earpiece. "Tell him you're a journalist, visiting for a story. He'll like that."

"I'm a journalist," Selena said. "I work for the Times. I'm doing a feature piece on Manila and the American presence here in the Philippines."

"Ah, a journalist. Surely Allah has smiled upon me. You will tell our story to the world."

"Allah?" Selena said. "You are Muslim?"

Like a snake, the man's hand whipped through the air and slapped Selena across the face. The blow rocked her. Her cheek began to burn. At least he hadn't hit the side with the earpiece.

"You do not say the name of God," the man said. "In your infidel mouth it is an abomination. Look at you. Your hair uncovered, your legs and arms exposed for all to see. You are whores, both of you. But useful whores."

Selena wanted to rub her face where he'd hit her but wasn't about to give him the satisfaction of seeing how much it bothered her. She also wanted to kick him in the balls. *Who is he?* she thought. *Get him to tell you so Nick can find out.* She looked him in the eye and said, "If you want me to write about you, I need to know your name."

"Why not? You may call me Omar." Omar gestured to one of his men. "Take them into the big room with the others," he said.

The man pushed them toward the ballroom. He wasn't gentle about it. Selena heard Nick's voice in her right ear.

"Good work, Selena. I'll get Harker on it." He paused. "I'm right here, I'll get you out of there."

She almost answered and caught herself in time.

The ballroom faced out the back of the embassy onto the Chancery through a wall of tall windows. Many of the windows were broken, blown in by the attack. Glass and bits of stone and wood littered the room. Two Marines lay dead on the polished ballroom floor. The rest of the embassy staff clustered together against one of the walls, under a large painting of Admiral Dewey's flagship at anchor in Manila Bay. The Americans sat together. The Filipino staff formed their own group. Omar herded Selena and the ambassador over to the others.

Cathwaite's secretary got up and hugged the ambassador. "Margaret! Thank God you're all right."

"I'm fine, Helen. Is anyone else hurt except for our poor Marines?"

"Just cuts and scratches from the glass. Nothing serious. Carmichael doesn't look good. I'm worried about him."

Matthew Carmichael was the Commerce Department attaché. He was sitting to the side of the group, holding his hand against his chest and taking labored breaths. Sitting next to him was a blond haired man who appeared subdued. Selena figured him for the CIA spook. Carmichael's secretary sat huddled on the other side of her boss. The Filipinos looked frightened. They stared at the floor, avoiding eye contact with anyone. It wasn't the kind of group she would have picked to go up against a dozen terrorists.

Omar jabbed Helen in the ribs with the barrel of his AK-47. "You, slut, shut up. All of you, sit. Now, or I kill you."

Selena sat down next to Margaret.

For now, she was on her own.

CHAPTER 16

"How many inside the building?" Harker asked. She and Stephanie were in Elizabeth's office in Virginia, talking to Nick over the satellite link.

"Uncertain. Selena said six. There could be more. The terrorists took out the Marine guards. They're led by a man named Omar."

"That helps," Elizabeth said. "It's a common name but they're probably Abu Sayyaf. We'll look in the database." She paused. "Don't do anything stupid, Nick."

"If it's only six we can take them. But we have to get into the building. They're going to have people watching the entrances. Can you get plans of the embassy? Blueprints?"

"I can do that. Give me a minute." Stephanie's voice came over the link. In Virginia, she entered a string of commands on her keyboard. "I'm looking for them now," she said.

The Project computers were Crays. A search for the embassy building plans was child's play for their enormous power. The drawings were up on Stephanie's monitor within a minute.

"I'm looking at the plans," she told Nick. "The whole complex is built on an artificial extension into the bay. They sank six hundred concrete pillars into the bay floor and filled it in."

"How does that help?" Nick said. Stephanie heard impatience in his voice.

"There's an underground drainage system combined with a service tunnel for utilities serviced by a pumping station on the surface. The tunnel is big enough for a man to walk in. The pumps are

gone but the groundskeepers use the old pump
house for a storage facility. If you can get into the
tunnel and up into the building it would put you on
the grounds next to the Chancery."

"You see a way into the tunnel?"

"There's a building over it now and no way to
tell until you get there. The access might be sealed
off. There are three buildings on the next street
over, to the right of the embassy grounds. The one
in the middle is the one you want. I'm sending a
satellite shot now."

Nick looked at his phone. A satellite picture of
the embassy complex appeared. He saw the
buildings Steph was talking about.

"Okay, I've got it."

Nick looked across the boulevard toward the
embassy. The speakers were riling up the crowd.
The riot police fingered their batons. Some of them
held guns that fired rubber bullets. Nick could see
half a dozen teargas guns being held at port arms.
Things were about to get ugly.

"Hold on," Nick said into his phone. "Looks
like more cops are showing up."

A Kia SUV with police markings and four men
dressed in police uniforms pulled up. An officer got
out and signaled his men into the street. They were
armed with AK carbines.

Something bothered Nick about the scene.
Then he realized what it was.

"This isn't right," he said to Ronnie. "The
Filipinos don't carry AKs."

The officer walked to the guardhouse. A
Marine corporal came to the door and opened it.
The officer raised his carbine and shot him. His men
opened fire on the line of police stretched in front of

the embassy gates. The crowd erupted in panic as people scrambled to get out of the way.

"Holy shit," Nick said.

"Nick, what's happening?" Elizabeth's voice crackled in his ear.

"Terrorists, dressed like cops. They shot the Marine guard and they're firing on the riot police and the crowd. They're taking over the guardhouse."

"Nick, we gotta take cover," Lamont said.

There was a parking lot full of cars and a restaurant behind them. They ran behind one of the parked cars and watched what was happening across the street. A window in the front of the restaurant shattered, hit by a bullet. Another stray round whined through the air with a peculiar singing sound.

Nick was still on the link with Harker. "Everything's turning bad," he said. "The crowd's running. People are going down. The cops are getting slaughtered."

In a few minutes it was over. The demonstrators had fled, leaving trails of blood behind. Bodies lay in the street. Backpacks, pieces of clothing, shoes lay scattered on the ground. Banners and signs littered the pavement. The riot police lay where they'd fallen. It was a massacre.

A man walked among the bodies and fired an occasional kill shot. The embassy gates swung open. The terrorists took out black headbands and put them on. They got back in the Kia and drove into the compound. The man who had shot the Marine guards emerged from the gatehouse as the gates swung closed and followed them into the embassy.

Nick said, "They're not covering their faces. That's a bad sign. It means they don't care if they're identified. It could be a suicide mission."

Lamont said, "If they're the ones who blew up the Indian Embassy, they could be planning the same thing here. We need to get in there, get Selena."

"You think I don't know that?" Nick's voice was strained.

"Take it easy Nick, just sayin'."

"Yeah. All right, let's figure out how to get over to that building where the tunnel is."

Nick studied the urban terrain. Beyond the restaurant parking lot was a children's playground, then a building with another parking lot. If they could get through the playground and to the end of that lot without being seen, they'd be right across from where they needed to go.

"We'll move down to the end of the lot behind the cars, then through that playground," he said. "Keep going until we get to the end of the next lot. From there we can make it across the street. We time it right, they won't see us."

"They might not care," Ronnie said. "We're just three civilians trying to get away."

"Or they might want to add a few more to the score," Lamont said.

"Nick." It was Harker. "I'm going to call the president. Don't talk to me unless you need to. But keep the line open."

"Copy that," Nick said. He looked up and down the Boulevard. "Looks like all the bad guys are inside. Let's go."

They got up and sprinted to the end of the parking lot and into the playground. The playground was flat and green, full of mature trees. Big trees, big enough to stop bullets if somebody shot at them. But nobody did. They made it past the playground and into the next parking lot. There was good cover behind the cars. It would be a difficult shot from the embassy.

The lot bordered on a street called United Nations Avenue that formed a T with Roxas Boulevard. Across the boulevard, three long rectangular buildings stretched toward the bay. Their goal was the one in the middle.

They started across the boulevard.

CHAPTER 17

Stephanie and Elizabeth looked at a picture of Omar Steph had found in the international terrorist database.

"He's Abu Sayyaf," she told Harker. "One of their principal lieutenants."

"Look at his eyes," Elizabeth said. "The man's a psychopath. Rice needs to know what he's dealing with."

President Rice was in the Oval Office, where he'd just been informed of the events in Manila. Elizabeth had access to him at any time.

When his phone signaled Harker's ID, he knew what it was about.

"Director. You are calling about Manila."

"Yes, Mister President."

"What can you tell me?"

What Rice needed was a factual briefing with as much as she could tell him in as few words as possible.

"The terrorists are from a Muslim extremist group called Abu Sayyaf. One of my team is a hostage inside the embassy. The rest of them are working on getting into the building as we speak."

"Who's inside?"

"Selena Connor."

Rice knew Selena, had known her since she was a child. Her uncle had been a close friend and supporter. It made the crisis a little more personal.

Harker continued. "The terrorists breached the embassy from the rear. The Marine guards were killed. The ambassador and her staff were taken hostage. A second contingent of terrorists arrived at the front gates, opened fire on the police and the crowd and gained access. There are at least ten hostiles inside the building, possibly more."

"I expect to hear from President Navarro at any moment," Rice said. "We don't get along well and I anticipate problems controlling the situation. He's going to want to go in there and teach the terrorists a lesson."

"Sir, that would be a very bad decision. These could be the people who destroyed the Indian Embassy two days ago and they could be planning to do the same with us. Abu Sayyaf is a fanatical jihadist group. If troops assault the building, the terrorists will kill everyone inside. Dying for Allah is right up their alley."

"You have a way with words, Director. What do you suggest?"

"Sir, it might help to get an American unit on the scene. I realize this will create political problems for you, but we have to keep Navarro from going in there guns blazing. He might be more reasonable if it looks like there could be a confrontation."

"Go on."

"Yes, sir. The terrorists will have demands. They'll want to make a statement of some kind. We have a little time before the end game plays out. You know how good my team is. If you can stall Navarro until they have a chance to get into the building, they may be able to handle it."

Rice considered what Harker had said. President Navarro was a difficult man and Rice did not like him. He thought about assets in the area. The helicopter assault carrier *USS Boxer* was visiting Subic Bay. On board was a full Marine Expeditionary Unit, with 2200 Marines and the helicopters to take them into Manila. He could have the embassy surrounded within an hour if he gave the order. But if he sent in the Marines it would complicate the chances of reaching an agreement with Navarro about re-opening American bases.

Rice needed those bases to offset the growing Chinese military threat in the region. He needed Subic Bay and the facilities it could provide for the U.S. Navy. The sudden appearance of armed American forces in the heart of Manila would blow any possibility of successful negotiations out of the water. It would probably end the agreement to use Clark as well. Filipino pride and anger would see to that.

There were times when Rice truly wished he had never run for office. He was between a rock and a hard place. Whatever he did was liable to turn out badly. On the one hand, he faced the diplomatic nightmare that would result from putting boots on the ground and criticism from his political enemies for undermining America's future security interests in the region. On the other, American lives had been lost and more were at risk. Rice had decided long ago that he would never let political expediency outweigh what he believed to be the right thing to do.

The embassy was an important symbol of American prestige and power. Failure to respond with everything at his disposal would send the wrong message to terrorist groups everywhere. The attack could not be allowed to pass without immediate American response, whatever the consequences might be. Rice knew the value of decisive action. He decided to give Harker a free hand.

"Director, I don't have troops on the ground but the USS Boxer is visiting at Subic Bay. She has a Marine Expeditionary Unit on board. I could send in a detachment."

"Sir, that would be an excellent choice."

"Wait one, Director." Rice pressed a button on his desk. The door to the Oval Office opened and an aide stepped into the room.

"Get me the captain of the USS Boxer," Rice said. "Call a meeting of the National Security Council and get the National Security Advisor in here. But get me the Boxer first."

"Yes, Mister President," the aide said. He left the office and closed the door behind him

"Very well, Director. I'll send in the choppers and set up a perimeter. Navarro can bitch all he wants. But Elizabeth..."

Rice seldom addressed her by her first name. "Yes, Mister President?"

"You don't have a lot of time. I can only hold Navarro off for so long."

"Then let's hope that it's enough, sir."

Rice broke the connection. He touched a button on his desk. The aide came back in the room.

"Get State in here right away."

"Yes, Mister President. Sir, Captain Addison is waiting on line two."

Rice activated the speaker. "Captain Addison, this is the president."

"Mister President." Addison had a deep voice that boomed out of the speakerphone.

"Captain, we have a situation. I have a mission for you."

Rice ran down the attack on the Embassy and told Addison what he wanted. Addison listened to the president and thought about the CH-46 Sea Knight helicopters on his flight deck.

"How many men do you want on the ground, Mister President? Each one of my Sea Knights carries seventeen Marines. "

"A dozen choppers ought to do it, Captain. How soon can you get them to the embassy?"

"Loaded and in the air in half an hour, sir. Fifteen minutes after that to the LZ."

"Do it faster if you can, Captain. Cut them loose. Patch me through to the commander of the Marine unit."

"Yes, sir. One moment." Rice heard Addison give an order. There was a brief pause. Rice tapped his fingers impatiently on the surface of his desk. A new voice came on line.

"Sir, this is Lieutenant Colonel William Kroger speaking. What are your orders?"

"Colonel, terrorists have attacked our embassy in Manila. They've taken the ambassador hostage and there are casualties. The Marine security detachment has been killed."

Rice heard a sharp intake of breath on the other side of the world.

"Yes, sir."

"I want you to set up a perimeter around the embassy and secure the area. There may be trouble with the Filipinos and I need you to keep them at bay. Don't take any crap from them. I'm relying on you to keep your men in hand. Things could get heated on the scene. Under no circumstances can the Philippine forces be allowed to assault the embassy. You are authorized to resist any such attempt up to but not including lethal force."

"Yes, sir."

"We have friendlies on-site," Rice said. "They are going to attempt a penetration. They're Americans in civilian dress, so they'll be easy to spot if you have to go in."

"Do you anticipate sending us in, sir?"

"I'm hoping to get control of the situation before things get worse. I will send you in if I need to. In that event, lethal force is authorized."

There will be no giving in to terrorists on my watch, Rice thought.

"Understood, sir."

"Colonel, I want to emphasize that you are in command. You have full authority to act as you think appropriate. This is going to get big, fast. Don't let anyone push you around. I don't care if the Chairman of the Joint Chiefs tells you to stand down, you take orders only from me. Any problems, contact me through the *Boxer*."

"Yes, sir. Thank you, Mister President."

"Go buy our people some time, Colonel."

"I'll do my best, sir."

As Rice broke the connection he hoped Kroger's best would be good enough.

CHAPTER 18

Prakash Khanna was talking with Ashok Rao. The connection between Manila and New Delhi was crystal clear. Both men used phones with encryption that made listening in on the conversation harder than winning the lottery.

"Abu Sayyaf has attacked and occupied the American Embassy," Khanna said. "Many have been killed. Turn on your television."

Rao picked up a remote and turned on a large monitor mounted on the wall of his New Delhi office. The network was running footage taken when the terrorist attack outside the embassy gates had begun. The picture switched to a live telephoto shot of the front of the embassy. The camera zeroed in on the bodies of the riot police. The network ran the attack footage again while an excited announcer in the corner of the screen rehashed the details in a voice of modulated outrage.

Rao turned off the sound. "What is the current situation?"

"Abu Sayyaf has control of the building," Khanna said. "The initial attack came from the bay. Then the others showed up."

"There are hostages?" Rao asked.

"Yes, including the American ambassador. I'm not sure how many. As yet, there have not been any demands. The attack happened only a short time ago."

"What are the Filipinos doing?"

"For the moment, the police are hanging back. They'll probably send in the army. Navarro has made several public statements about being tough on Abu Sayyaf. He can't back down."

"If he storms the embassy, it will create a major international incident," Rao said.

In Manila, Khanna lit a cigarette. "Nonetheless, I think that's what he'll do. Navarro is no friend to the United States. His political base is opposed to an American presence in the islands."

"Perhaps they would prefer a Chinese presence instead," Rao said.

Khanna laughed.

Rao continued. "You were able to get everything in place?"

"Yes. The Americans will discover convincing evidence of ISOK's involvement. They'll think ISOK and Abu Sayyaf have formed an alliance to attack American and Indian targets with high public visibility."

"They *have* formed an alliance," Rao said. "We're doing Washington a favor, helping them fight their war on terror." Rao paused. "What do you think Abu Sayyaf will do?"

"My guess is that they will start executing hostages until their demands are met. Navarro will never give them what they want," Khanna said. "I don't think anyone will come out of there alive. Abu Sayyaf believes in Jihad. They think God will be pleased if they die fighting the Crusader infidels."

"They are fools."

"There is only one possible outcome once the hostages begin dying. I estimate an assault on the embassy within twenty-four hours of the first execution. Once it's all over, the Americans will discover that Pakistan is behind the attack."

"Excellent," Rao said. "I imagine they will be very angry at their Paki allies." He paused for a moment. "How do you feel about the bombing of our embassy?"

In his office on Lodhi Road, Rao couldn't see Khanna shrug.

"Sacrifice is sometimes necessary," Khanna said. "The ambassador here was useless, an appeaser like the Prime Minister. Perhaps it will serve as a wake-up call to those idiots in New Delhi."

It was what Rao wanted to hear. "I doubt that anything will change the way our Prime Minister and his cabinet think."

"If your plan works it won't matter what he thinks," Khanna said. "He'll be forced to take a hard line with Islamabad and Washington will have to get involved. My only concern is that the Americans have a habit of creating problems once the door has been opened for them."

"Mother India is not Afghanistan or Iraq," Rao said. "We will use them against Pakistan. They will never suspect we have manipulated them."

"What do you think they'll do?"

"Who knows? An attack on their embassy by terrorists is one thing. If they believe Pakistan is to blame, it's another. It will be seen as betrayal, an act of war. They cannot let it pass. Whatever they do, it will make trouble for the Pakis and opportunities for us."

"What are your instructions?" Khanna asked.

"Keep monitoring events. Try to find out what the Americans and Filipinos are doing, the things we won't see on television."

"Understood."

Rao ended the conversation and set his phone down. Then he picked up the phone again and called Krivi.

"Yes."

"It's Rao," he said.

"My brother," Krivi answered.

Rao felt a glow of satisfaction, even pride. He had an important role to play in the future of India. The best part was that Krivi's group would help him achieve his revenge.

"Are you aware of what's happening in Manila?" Rao asked.

"I am."

"The Americans will soon discover evidence that Islamabad planned the attack. So far there's no reason for them to suspect Pakistan's involvement. That will change once their NSA focuses on the terrorist communications. They'll find a trail that leads straight to Islamabad."

"You seem confident."

"This kind of operation is familiar to me. The technology makes it easy."

Because of Rao, the world was already one step closer to war. Krivi was pleased that he'd judged Rao correctly.

"How can I help?" Krivi said.

"It would be good if demonstrations here in India begin to grow. Even better if they get out of hand. I can't use my own agents for that, it would be discovered."

"I'll see what I can do."

CHAPTER 19

Harker's voice sounded calm as she talked to Nick, as though it was just another day at the office. As if terrorist attacks and sending in the Marines were every day events. In Elizabeth's world, that wasn't far from the truth.

"There'll be Marines on site soon," she said. "They know the embassy detachment is dead and they're going to be pissed. If they go in, they could make a mistake. Be advised."

"Thanks for the encouragement," Nick said.

Nick stood with the others in front of the building Steph had identified as the one with the entrance to the old tunnel under the embassy. A faded sign announced that it was the Chinese Friendship Society Community Center. The door was locked. There was no one around. Everyone in the area had taken off for safer parts of town.

Nick tried the door again. It was still locked.

"Screw this," he said. "Stand back." He fired two rounds and the frame around the lock splintered. He pushed the door open and they stepped inside. Nick closed the door behind them.

Dust motes floated through beams of yellow sunlight filtering through the windows of a large, open space used for dances and meetings. One wall bore a series of faded travel posters for China and the Philippines. On another wall a cork bulletin board posted business cards and notices. They walked through the room and into a kitchen on the side of the building facing the American Embassy.

"Not much cooking," Lamont said.

Ronnie sighed and looked up at the ceiling.

"I don't see anything," Nick said. "Look for a trap door."

Stephanie's voice popped into his ear. "It should be about a third of the way along the rear wall from the end," she said.

"Which end?"

"Sorry. The bay."

"Over here, Nick." Ronnie stood in front of a large stove. Part of a metal manhole cover showed under one corner.

"Let's get this off of there." The three of them pushed against the stove. It barely moved.

"That is one heavy mother," Lamont said.

They pushed again. The stove scraped across the floor until the cover was exposed. There was an odd shaped hole on one side for a key. Nick worked two fingers into the hole and tried to lift. Nothing happened.

"It's locked. See if you can find something to pry it up."

They searched the kitchen without any luck.

"They probably lost that key fifty years ago," Ronnie said. Nick heard the distant beat of rotors. The Marine helicopters were coming in.

"Too bad we don't have a little C4," Lamont said.

"Yeah. We can't waste any more time with this. We'll do it the hard way," Nick said. He spoke into the comm link.

"Steph, send me a picture of the embassy grounds and the building where we are now."

"On the way."

Nick looked at the screen on his phone. He showed it to the others.

"We're here." He tapped the roof of a building in the picture. "It would have been nice to sneak up on them through that tunnel but it isn't going to happen."

"What's this?" Lamont asked. He pointed at the next building over. The embassy was beyond that.

"Offices," Nick said.

"And this?" Lamont pointed at a building directly behind the embassy.

"That's the Chancery," Nick said. "They may have a sentry posted there. Even if they don't, they can see it from the embassy. Hold on a moment."

He keyed the comm. "Selena, do you copy?"

Nick heard an answering cough.

"Can you see the Chancery building from where you are? Don't answer, just cough. Once for yes, twice for no."

Cough.

"Are the bad guys watching the Chancery?"

Cough.

"How many? More than one?"

Cough.

"More than three?"

Cough. Cough.

"Are you okay?"

Cough.

"Hang in there, I'm coming."

Cough.

"How is she?" Ronnie asked.

"She's good. There are two or three watching the Chancery."

They studied the picture on Nick's phone.

"We can make our way down this parking lot behind the offices. They won't see us if we stick close to the wall," Nick said.

A row of tall trees and shrubbery ran at an angle from the corner of the parking lot to the embassy.

"Those trees would give us some cover," Ronnie said. "We could use them to get over to the side of the building."

"It's not much of a plan," Nick said. "I don't see what else we could do."

"Are there windows on that side?" Lamont asked.

"Have to be. Better hope they're not looking. Any other ideas?"

"Nope," Ronnie said. Lamont shook his head.

"Let's boogie," Nick said.

They moved out into the sunlight. The block shaped building that served as office space and quarters for embassy personnel loomed on their left. At the end of the parking lot they could see where the landscaping around the embassy began. Only a corner of the building was visible from where they stood.

Nick spoke into his comm link. "Selena, we're moving in now. Be ready."

Cough.

Sudden sound drowned out thought as helicopters came in low and fast overhead. The engine notes changed as they hovered to drop the Marines.

"Go," Nick said.

They ran the length of the parking lot toward the embassy, staying next to the building wall. They reached the end of the lot and paused. There were three large trees between them and the embassy and some low shrubbery. Several windows lined the embassy wall. Anyone looking out would see them moving across the gap between the trees.

Nick wished he had more than just his pistol with him.

"We're going to need more firepower," Ronnie said. He held his Sig in both hands.

"You read my mind," Nick said. "We'll have to liberate a couple of AKs as soon as we can."

"We might get over there without being seen if we run like hell," Lamont said.

Nick thought about it. "I don't see a better way. Ronnie, you go first, then me, then Lamont. Get up against the building between the windows."

"On my way," Ronnie said.

He took off at a fast sprint. Nick gave him a lead and took off after him. He heard Lamont's footsteps pounding behind. Ronnie passed the second tree and then the third, with Nick a few steps behind. Ronnie reached the building and flattened himself against the wall between two windows. Seconds later Nick and Lamont had joined him.

Nick let out a sigh of relief.

"I'm getting too old for this stuff," he said. He kept his voice low.

"Yeah." Lamont was breathing heavily. "Tell me about it."

"What's next, Kemo Sabe?" Ronnie said.

"Whenever you start that Kemo Sabe stuff, I get worried," Nick said.

"So?"

"I haven't figured the next part out yet," Nick said.

CHAPTER 20

Omar looked at the huddled group of hostages, deciding who would be first. Two of his men had hung a black banner with white Arabic letters against one of the walls. A third man was setting up a video camera.

Selena sat on the floor next to Ambassador Cathwaite. She was unbound. The terrorists hadn't bothered to tie anyone up. Selena couldn't blame them for feeling confident. Holding AKs against unarmed civilians tended to make you feel that way. Two men watched her and the other hostages.

She read the banner. It was a verse from the Quran about slaying the enemies of Allah. Black banners with verses calling for jihad were never a good sign. Neither was the video camera.

Two of Omar's men were setting charges all around the walls. It was clear they intended to destroy the building. One of the terrorists was standing next to her. She couldn't let Nick know, not right now. Selena wondered if anyone would leave the building alive, then pushed the thought away.

Omar walked over to her. "You, journalist, get up."

She got to her feet. Omar grabbed her arm and marched her over to the video camera. He handed her a piece of paper.

"These are our demands," he said. His breath was foul with the smell of fish. "There is a transmitter on this camera. The images will be relayed on television throughout the world. Read these demands, as they are written. It is, as they say, a scoop for you. Do you understand, slut?"

"Yes." Inside, she seethed. She could kill him before he moved but it wouldn't do any good. His men would cut her down and probably kill all the other hostages as well. "I understand," she said.

The terrorist leader signaled. A bright light came on over the camera. "Begin," he said. "Read the statement."

Selena started reading the terrorist demands. Immediate release of thirty-four Abu Sayyaf prisoners being held for trial by the Philippine government. Recognition of an independent Islamic Republic on Mindanao. Reparations for past offenses by the government in the amount of $100 million, to be brought to the embassy within twelve hours. All prisoners were to be released immediately. If the release was delayed, one hostage would be executed every hour, on the hour. Any attempt to assault the embassy would result in all hostages being executed.

They were impossible demands. Selena knew they wouldn't be met. It meant they would all die if nothing happened to stop it.

She finished reading. Omar stepped in front of the camera and pushed her out of the way. "Sit down, whore," he said. Selena went back over by the ambassador and sat down.

Omar spoke to the camera.

"You need to know we are serious," he said. "I will show you how serious we are."

He pointed at one of the hostages, a local girl who worked in the mailroom. The camera followed his gesture. He signaled one of his men. "Her," he said. The man grabbed her and pulled her to her feet. He brought her over to Omar and forced her down on her knees.

"No, wait," she said. "Wait."

Omar shot her in the head in front of the camera. Gray matter and bone sprayed out over the room. The body toppled over.

"You have one hour," Omar said to the camera. "If you do not begin releasing my people I will shoot another. Next time it will be an American." He made a slashing motion across his throat. The camera light went off.

Selena felt the ambassador grip her hand.

"Bastard," Cathwaite said. "She just had a baby. Three months ago." Her voice trembled with anger. Blood spread in a wide stain under the dead girl.

Outside the embassy, Nick considered his next move. Selena's voice sounded in his earpiece. She was whispering, but Nick could hear the stress in her voice.

"Nick, do you copy?"

"Affirmative."

"There are twelve of them. They've placed charges all around. They shot a hostage."

"We're outside the building looking for a way in." He paused. "You okay?"

"Nick, these people are crazy..."

Her voice cut off.

"Selena?" he said. There was no answer.

CHAPTER 21

Lt. Colonel Kroger shielded his eyes against dust kicked up by the Sea Knight helicopters as they lifted away. Three Sikorsky CH-53 Sea Stallions came in after them and settled on the boulevard. They disgorged more Marines and half a dozen Humvees with Browning M2 .50 BMG machine guns mounted topside. Kroger believed in being prepared. From the air he'd seen a column of Philippine Army vehicles speeding down Roxas Boulevard toward the embassy. He placed some of his men and a Humvee across the Boulevard in the path of the oncoming Philippine troops. Others took up positions along the edge of the embassy grounds. Kroger had created an instant buffer zone around the embassy. No one was getting near the building without going through him.

The Philippine convoy was getting close. "Looks like we got here just in time, sir."

The speaker was his XO. Major Clifford Anderson had been Kroger's second in command for the last two years. Both men had served in Iraq and Afghanistan. Both had been under fire many times together. Kroger couldn't think of anyone he'd rather have with him in a potential firefight.

"Better get ready for an argument, Cliff," Kroger said. "The locals aren't going to be happy."

"That's too damn bad," Anderson said. They waited for the Filipinos to arrive.

The lead vehicle was a Kia 450, a medium-sized truck used for troop transport. It was followed by another half dozen similar vehicles filled with troops. Two American-made M113A2 armored vehicles brought up the rear.

"The tracks on those must be doing a real good job on that nice asphalt road," Anderson said.

"Show of force. They probably think they're going to go through the gates with them."

"That's not going to happen," Anderson said. Men wearing olive drab berets and dressed in camouflage uniforms scrambled out of the trucks. They carried modern assault rifles. An officer stepped down from the lead vehicle.

"Showtime," Kroger said. "That's the 1st Scout Rangers, if I'm not mistaken."

"Those are Steyr assault rifles they're carrying," Anderson said. "Good weapon."

"The Rangers are their elite unit," Kroger said. "They even sent a general. Let's go, Major. Time to make nice. Smile."

The two Marines walked over to the Philippine general. Kroger saluted.

"Lieutenant Colonel Kroger, sir."

The Filipino returned the salute. "I am General Narcisco. Why are you here, Colonel? I was unaware permission had been given for American troops to deploy. Your men are blocking my vehicles. I wish to pass."

"I'm afraid I cannot allow that, sir. My orders are to secure the area until the situation is resolved."

Narcisco's face tightened under his beret. "You are on Philippine territory, Colonel. You will remove yourself immediately. We will take care of this."

"Sorry, sir, I can't do that. May I remind you that the embassy is United States territory."

"Colonel, unless you wish to find yourself a lieutenant again, you will immediately get your men out of the way."

Behind General Narcisco, his troops had picked up on the hostility between the officers. They didn't look happy. It had been a long time since World War II and Americans were no longer popular in the islands. Anderson saw one of the Filipino officers give a quiet command to his sergeant. Weapons came up to port arms.

"Move out of my way, Colonel," Narcisco said.

"Sir," Anderson said.

"I see it, Major."

Kroger raised his left hand in the air in a prearranged signal. The Filipino troops found themselves staring down the barrels of Marine rifles. Kroger was bluffing. He wasn't going to fire upon troops from a friendly nation, but Narcisco didn't know that. Fifty or sixty Marines in battle dress pointing weapons at you would intimidate most people and Narcisco was no different. He looked at the faces of the men behind the rifles and saw nothing to reassure him. It was a convincing, chilling display of force.

"General," Kroger said, "my orders are to secure this area. I suggest you consult with your commanders as to the best course of action. Your troops will not be allowed to come near our embassy."

"You will regret this, Colonel."

"Perhaps I will, sir. But in the meantime I have my orders."

Narcisco looked at the rifles pointed at him and turned to the officers behind him. "Fall back and deploy the troops across the road," he said.

He stalked away toward his vehicle.

"That went well," Anderson said. "Lieutenant, sir."

Kroger laughed. "We'll let the politicians figure it out. In the meantime, I want your ideas on how we go in there without getting the hostages killed."

"Yes, sir," Anderson said.

"Get those gates open and vehicles ready to go in. If the shit hits the fan I don't want anything slowing us down."

CHAPTER 22

The taking of the embassy dominated the news. In Virginia, Elizabeth and Stephanie watched Selena reading Abu Sayyaf 's demands. Part of her team, in harm's way. They watched the hostage die.

"We have to help Nick find a way in," Elizabeth said.

Steph had put the plans of the American Embassy up on her monitor. The two women studied the image.

"Abu Sayyaf will be watching the ground floor," Elizabeth said. "I don't see how they can get in that way."

"Twelve hostiles," Stephanie said. "It's not enough to cover everything."

"The main focus has to be on the lower level."

Stephanie pointed at the plans. "Nick could get in from the roof. There's an access door and stairs to the top floor."

"That might work, but how do they get up there? There's no fire escape."

"That would be too easy, wouldn't it?"

"They could climb an outside wall." Elizabeth peered at the architectural drawings on the monitor. "There doesn't seem to be much they could use for footholds."

"The windows have blast grills over them," Stephanie said. "They can't get through those."

"The more I look at it," Elizabeth said, "it seems like the roof is the only way in. How about trees? Is there a tree they could climb to put them on the roof?"

Stephanie entered a few commands. An angled, overhead shot of the embassy grounds appeared on her monitor. She zoomed in.

"If they could get over to the opposite side of the building, there's a tree tall enough to get them onto the roof."

Elizabeth spoke into the comm link.

"Nick, do you copy?"

"Copy."

"It looks like there's only one way in. There's a tree on the south side of the building. You can climb it and get onto the roof. There's access up there."

"Copy. Climb the tree to the roof."

"It's the only way in," Harker said again.

"Copy. Out."

"Doesn't talk much, does he?" Steph said.

Elizabeth laughed.

CHAPTER 23

Selena watched Omar talking to a man carrying a heavy rifle with a telescopic sight. The man nodded. She was whispering to Nick when Omar looked her way. She stopped mid-sentence. Next to her, Ambassador Cathwaite leaned close.

"Who are you talking to?" Her voice was soft. She peered at Selena. "Is that an earpiece? You have an earpiece, don't you?"

"Yes. The rest of my team is outside."

"Your team?"

"It's a long story, Margaret."

"You, shut up." It was one of the men assigned to watch them. "No talk."

Selena took the ambassador's hand and squeezed it. The terrorist was a heavy set man with a scraggly beard and bad teeth. He looked at her, his eyes stripping away her clothes. He licked his lips and rubbed the back of his hand across his mouth.

It wasn't the first time a man had looked at her with desire. But this man's look was filled with more than lust. Selena could feel his eyes, clinging and sticky like summer heat on a humid day. It made her skin crawl.

"Selena." Nick's voice in her ear. "We're going to try and get in through the roof."

She coughed.

"Be ready," Nick said.

If only I wasn't stuck here, she thought. *If I could get up to the roof I could let them in.*

The terrorist was still looking at her. His AK hung from a strap over his right shoulder. His

fingers moved restlessly against the cold metal of
the receiver as he licked his lips again.

Selena raised her hand in the air.

"I have to use the toilet," she said.

"No toilet."

"Please." She moved on the floor as if in
discomfort. It was suggestive, a movement someone
with sex on his mind would think inviting.

"I really need to go," she said, her voice husky.
"Can't you take me?"

Next to her, the ambassador whispered, "What
are you doing?"

Selena ignored her. "Please?" she said again.
She smiled at the man as she said it and moved her
hand to her chest, under her breasts.

A crooked smile appeared on his face. "Come,"
he said. He gestured with his AK. Selena stood up.

"Where are you going?" Omar strode over.

"This one needs the toilet. She looks like she's
getting ready to piss all over the floor."

Omar laughed. "Take her." He gave his man a
careful look. "Don't be too long," he said.

"Come," the man said to Selena. He grabbed
her arm with his left hand and pulled her toward the
hall where the restrooms were. She made no
resistance. The other hostages watched them go.

They went past the body of a dead Marine.
Flies were buzzing over his open mouth. His eyes
stared at the ceiling. Selena felt cold anger wash
through her.

The restrooms were at the other end of a long
hall, next to a staircase leading to the upper floors.
The terrorist kept a grip on her arm and kicked open
the door to the restroom with his foot. He pulled her
inside the room after him.

"What's your name?" she said. She made her voice husky, inviting.

"Gibril." He licked his lips. His rifle pointed at the floor.

She moved close to him, smiling. Then she stomped down on his foot. Gibril wore sandals, but Selena had shoes with hard, flat heels. She felt the bones of his foot crunch under her shoe. Gibril howled in pain. Reflex made him double over and reach for his foot. Selena brought both her hands down on the back of his neck and brought her knee up under his chin. She heard bone crack. The rifle clattered against the tile floor and Gibril fell in a lifeless heap. She leaned over and felt for a pulse just to be sure.

The embassy had been built in a day when expensive materials were used for important buildings. The walls of the bathroom were thick stone, the door made of solid mahogany. It was like being in a soundproof room. No one outside would have heard Gibril yell.

Selena picked up the rifle. She pulled the bolt partway back to make sure it was charged. She flipped the safety off and cracked open the door. The hall was empty. She slipped out of the bathroom and started up the stairs to the roof.

CHAPTER 24

Nick and the others moved to the corner of the building and used the shrubbery between the back wall of the embassy and the Chancery as cover. They crawled past the blown out windows of the ballroom. Nick got a glimpse of the hostages sitting against a wall. He looked for Selena but didn't see her.

They made it to the south wall without being seen. The tree they needed to climb rose above the roof line. It looked like a short leap from the branches to the flat roof.

"Nick, where are you?" It was Selena's voice over the link.

"Getting ready to climb a tree."

"I'm free. There isn't much time before they know I'm gone. I'm heading to the roof."

"Got it," Nick said. "Meet you there."

Lamont had already started up the trunk with Ronnie right behind. Nick looked at the tree. The last time he'd climbed a tree, he'd been twelve years old. It was a big oak tree in their backyard. It was his refuge, the place he went to when his father came home drunk. If he could get out of the house without being noticed, he'd climb the tree and wait until the shouting stopped and his father passed out.

Then one night his sister ratted him out, one of her many betrayals. His father had beaten the hell out of him and the next day he'd cut down the tree. Nick had never forgiven her.

He started up the trunk after Ronnie. By the time he got level with the roof, Ronnie and Lamont were already over. Nick leapt and landed hard. Pain shot up his back from the jump injury he'd gotten in the Himalayas.

Ronnie saw him wince. "You all right?"

"Yeah, I'm fine." Nick ignored the pain and looked around. "Over there."

They moved to the door that led down into the building. Nick tried it. It was locked. Then he heard the lock click and the door swung open. Selena stood there, holding an AK.

"Took you long enough," she said. "We'd better hurry. They must've missed me by now."

"How do you want to play it?" Ronnie asked Nick.

"Once they figure out Selena is missing, they'll send people after her. If we can get their weapons we'll be in better shape."

"I can be bait," Selena said. "If they see me they won't shoot. They'll want to know what happened to Gibril."

"Who's Gibril?"

"This used to be his rifle."

"They see you with that, they won't ask questions." Ronnie rubbed a knuckle across his nose.

"Here." Selena handed him the AK. "Give me your pistol."

Ronnie took the rifle and handed over his Sig.

"We have to keep it quiet," Nick said. "They hear shots, they'll all come running."

Ronnie reached up behind his neck and pulled a throwing knife from a scabbard concealed under his shirt. The blade was about eight inches long, razor sharp and double-edged. It was a thing of lethal beauty, swelling out in a smooth curve and then tapering to a graceful point. The handle was a checkered extension of the surgical steel blade.

"I forgot you carried that," Nick said.

"Just get me reasonably close," Ronnie said.

"We'll clear each floor as we go," Nick said. "Most of the bad guys are going to stay down on the ground floor with the hostages. A little luck, we'll take a few out before they know what's happening."

"I'll go first," Selena said. "They're looking for me, they won't be surprised if they see me."

"They'll probably send two men. Where did you leave the guy who used to have this rifle?"

"In the bathroom on the ground floor. It's right next to the stairs."

"They could use the stairs or there's an elevator. I'd use the stairs."

"We walk out into the open, there's no way we're going to keep this quiet." Ronnie rubbed a knuckle across his large nose.

"We'll try to keep it quiet but we can't mess around. If you have to shoot, do it."

"What I'm saying, maybe Selena can draw them into a room."

"Where we're waiting for them." Nick finished the thought.

"Yep."

"Might work. I like it." He turned to Selena. "What do you think?"

"If they don't shoot first, it could work. But we'd better hurry."

Without waiting for an answer, she started down the stairs.

Nick cracked open the heavy fire door to the third floor, enough to see into the hallway beyond. There was no one there. The door opened onto a wide, carpeted hallway. The carpet was a mixed blessing. On the one hand, it muffled their

footsteps. On the other, it would be hard to hear
anyone approaching.

This part of the embassy consisted of offices, a
large storage area, a radio room and a suite that
could serve as guest quarters for VIPs. It was very
quiet. There were doors for each room, most of
them open. An old, cage-type elevator shaft with a
black lattice gate was set in the middle of the hall.
Cables hung down the shaft. The sudden whine of
machinery broke the silence. The cables in the shaft
began moving.

"Guess they didn't want to walk," Lamont said.

"They're coming here. It's what I'd do, work
from the top down." Nick looked at the open doors
along the hall. "This one will do."

They stepped into an office. Gold letters on the
door announced Alan De Witt, second commercial
attaché.

"Second attaché," Ronnie said. "Probably the
spook's lair."

The office was in the front of the building.
From the window Nick could see Roxas Boulevard
and the Marines and vehicles below. If he were in
command, he'd have a Marine sniper looking for
potential targets. He stepped back from the window.
No point in getting mistaken for a terrorist.

De Witt's desk was large and solid. A row of
locked filing cabinets took up most of one wall. An
old-fashioned carved wooden wardrobe made of
thick, dark mahogany stood by the door.

Outside the office, the clanking sound of the
elevator stopped. They heard the lattice gate open,
the sound of metal pieces banging together.

Nick signaled with his hand. Lamont ducked
down behind the desk, Ronnie to one side of the

door, Nick to the other, past the wardrobe. Nick nodded at Selena.

She put Ronnie's pistol into her waistband, behind her back and took a breath. She stepped part way into the hall as if she wasn't sure what to do. She made sure that her hands were visible and empty.

See? I'm unarmed.

Two of the terrorists stood in front of the elevator. They carried AKs. One of them shouted at her and raised his rifle. She ducked back into the office. Nick signaled her to the window. She drew the pistol and held it out of sight behind her back, just in case.

One of the terrorists called out. "You, woman, you come out now. We not hurt you."

Selena said nothing.

"You come out, or we come in." There was menace in the man's voice.

"Don't hurt me," she called. She made her voice sound frightened. If she had been in the hallway, she would have seen one of the men smile at the other. It was not a good smile.

"We not hurt," the man said.

He walked toward the office door. His companion laid a hand on his arm, a gesture of caution. The first man shrugged it off. It was only a woman. When he came to the door he paused and glanced in. He saw Selena standing in front of the window. She had her left hand held out in front of her, palm out, as if she could ward him away. She looked helpless. The Sig was in her right, behind her back.

He walked into the room, his comrade close behind. He only had time to sense movement through the air before Ronnie's knife buried itself in the side of his neck.

Even the best trained soldier takes time to react when everything goes wrong. It took the second man an instant to realize what had happened.

It was an instant too long.

Nick came at him and drove his elbow into the man's neck. He put everything he had into it, grunting as the blow landed. There was a dull, wet crunch and the terrorist collapsed like a puppet with cut strings. His feet thrashed against the floor and he made gargling, choking noises. His face turned red as he gasped for air. After a minute he stopped moving.

It had taken no more than twenty seconds to kill both of them.

"Take the guns," Nick said. "Selena, you said there were twelve, is that right?"

"Yes. Three less, now."

"Better odds, but still too many. We start shooting, hostages are going to get killed. We need to come up with a plan. "

"The leader's crazy," Selena said. "You can see it in his eyes. I think he doesn't care. He'll blow up the building and kill everyone if he thinks the game's over."

"We need a distraction," Nick said. "Something to get his attention, confuse him."

A gunshot echoed through the building. They looked at each other.

"I think they just shot another hostage," Selena said.

A second shot sounded, louder than the first, then a third.

"Shit," Ronnie said.

"That didn't sound like an AK or a pistol," Nick said.

"It was right below us," Lamont said.

Nick picked up one of the AKs. Lamont took the other.

"They don't need these anymore." He checked to see if it was loaded.

"Let's go see," Nick said.

CHAPTER 25

Ahmed entered an office on the second floor of the embassy, carrying the heavy rifle. A window faced out on Roxas Boulevard. Careful to stay out of sight, he opened the window a few inches to make room for the SV-98. He rested the end of the barrel on the sill and looked through the scope on the scene of ordered chaos below.

U.S. Marines were deployed along the fence bordering the embassy grounds. Ahmed recognized the uniforms. They had chosen their positions carefully, but not carefully enough. He had a choice of several shots. With luck, he might get two or even three before they located him.

The SV-98 was a bolt action rifle. For some that would make getting off two or three fast shots impossible but Ahmed could do it. He'd practiced making a series of quick, accurate shots. The key lay in picking targets that were close together.

Ahmed knew he probably would not leave the building alive. It was of little concern to him. His life was in the hands of God. *Insha'Allah*, he would escape to fight another day. In the meantime he would do his best to kill infidels.

There were two Humvees with .50 caliber machine guns parked beyond the embassy gates. Ahmed made an adjustment on his telescopic sight. Two men came into sharp focus, standing beyond the vehicles. They were talking. One of them was a sergeant.

Ahmed made a quick visual sweep of the street below. No one was paying any attention to him. No one was paying attention to the open window. The blast grills on the outside helped shield him from sight. The two men were still talking.

Ahmed slipped off the safety and focused on the target. He took a breath and let half of it out. His body became still and the rifle settled on the aim point. He touched the trigger. The shot blasted through the afternoon air and the man's head disappeared in a cloud of blood and bone. With practiced motion, Ahmed worked the bolt as he moved the rifle to the left and brought the scope to bear. The second man was staring down in shock at the body of his comrade. Ahmed pulled the trigger again. The Marine fell from sight.

Ahmed stepped back from the window just as one of the Humvees opened up. The .50 caliber rounds blasted into the building, chewing away the window and frame, exploding against the stone exterior, slamming into the far wall of the room. Outside, someone shouted a command. As suddenly as it had begun, the hail of bullets ceased.

Ahmed ejected the spent casing and loaded two fresh rounds. He shot the bolt home and clicked on the safety. He left the room to look for another perch.

Next time I get an officer, he thought.

He decided the top floor might give him a better angle of attack, open up new lines of sight. Ahmed walked toward the stair door at the end of the hall. He pulled the door open and Ronnie drove his knife between Ahmed's ribs. Ahmed's mouth opened to scream. The sound died in a strangled gush of blood. The rifle fell from his hand and clattered to the floor. For the few seconds of life left to him, Ahmed stared unbelieving at the man who had killed him. Then his eyes rolled up and he fell.

Ronnie pulled out his knife and wiped the blade on Ahmed's shirt.

"Leaves eight, now."

Lamont bent down and picked up the rifle. "SV-98. This is what we heard," he said. "This guy's a sniper."

"Was," Nick said. "Was a sniper. Lamont, you want to take that and give your AK to Selena?"

Lamont handed her his rifle and picked up the SV-98. He opened the bolt partway and saw that a round was loaded. He closed the bolt and flicked off the safety.

Nick looked down at Ahmed's body. "We're running out of time. The rest of them are going to start wondering about their buddies pretty soon."

"Unless they've been moved, all the hostages are in the ballroom in the back," Selena said. "There's a hall leading to it. The doors to the room are wide open. If we can get there we'd have a good field of fire. The hostages are sitting down. Only the terrorists are standing. It's easy to see who they are."

"Risky," Nick said.

"You have a better idea?"

"What about the charges they set?" Ronnie asked.

Nick said, "Did you see how they were wired, Selena?"

"They have a car battery wired up to one of those T-handle detonators like you see in the movies. The wires run from there to the main entrance, the foyer and the back room."

"Weapons?"

"All I saw were AKs. The leader has a pistol."

Nick thought a moment. "We don't have a lot of choices. If the leader is crazy like Selena says, he might do something stupid when he realizes his comrades are getting killed."

"Like blow up the embassy," Lamont said.

"Yeah. Like that. We'll do it Selena's way. We get to the ballroom and take them out. Assume anyone standing up is a hostile. Selena, where's that detonator?"

"Against the right wall, in the far corner of the room."

"Ronnie, you make that your priority. Make sure no one gets to use it. Lamont, you have the rifle with the scope. If you can get a clean shot, you take out whoever is nearest to the hostages. As soon as you can, get rid of that and grab an AK."

"Okay."

"Selena, you and I will take out as many as we can once the shooting starts."

She nodded.

"Any questions?"

"How do we get to the ballroom?" Ronnie said.

Selena wiped sweat away from her forehead with the back of her hand. "The door at the bottom of the stairs leads to a hall. That leads to a gallery that runs between the front of the building and the ballroom. The ballroom is on the left as you come out of the hall."

They followed Nick down the stairs to the ground floor. He opened the door a crack, enough to see into the hall. It was empty. Once they left the stairwell they'd be exposed, with no cover. The hallway could turn into a shooting gallery, with themselves as targets.

"I've got a bad feeling about this," Ronnie said.

Nick's ear began itching. It always did, when things were about to get difficult. His own early warning system, a psychic inheritance from his Irish grandmother. He reached up to scratch it.

"Let's do it," he said.

They moved in single file down the hall. Selena felt the adrenaline charge she loved and hated, an electric mix of excitement and fear. It made her feel alive. It gave her a high more exciting than anything else she'd ever experienced. Even jumping out of a plane didn't produce the same rush.

They made it to the end of the hall without being seen. Voices sounded around the corner from the direction of the ballroom.

"Him," a voice said. "Stand him up and bring him over to the camera. It's time."

"No!" someone said, a man.

Selena whispered. "That's the leader talking. They're going to shoot another hostage."

Nick signaled with his fingers. Three. Two. One.

They stepped into the open. The ballroom was on the left. Tall double doors opening onto the room were thrown wide. Nick saw the Chancery through the ruined back wall. A gentle, tropical breeze came through the broken windows, smelling of honeysuckle and bougainvillea and the salt water of the bay.

One of the terrorists was prodding an American man with his rifle toward a video camera set up on a tripod. A terrorist waited in front of a black banner hung on the wall, pistol in hand. Hostages huddled on the floor by the ruins of the back wall. Nick recognized the ambassador.

The foyer and entrance to the embassy were to the right. Two men stood by the doors. One of them saw Nick and the others. He raised his rifle and shouted.

Ronnie cut loose with his AK and shot him.

Nick fired and killed the other. He heard the distinctive sound of the sniper rifle Lamont carried. The heavy bullet struck one of the terrorists in the ballroom and sent him flying sideways. The man by the camera raised his pistol and let off three quick shots.

Everyone began firing at once.

One of the hostages screamed. The air filled with death, dozens of rounds whining through the air. Selena was yelling, her AK bucking in her hands. Ronnie pivoted toward the ballroom and a burst of automatic fire struck him. He cried out. Blood sprayed into the air. He fell back onto the floor. The rifle flew from his hand.

"Ronnie!" Nick yelled.

He ran forward, firing at the man who'd shot Ronnie as he went. The rifle recoiled twice in his hand, then the bolt locked back. Empty. The man with the pistol ran for the detonator next to the wall. Nick saw him reach down.

There was time for Nick to think *I should have shot him first* before the world disappeared in a violent burst of sound and light. The shock wave lifted him up and tossed him through the air. He hit the floor, hard. Light and sound faded.

Selena's voice sounded from far away, as if she were at the end of a long tunnel.

"Nick. Nick. Come on, look at me."

He opened his eyes. Dull pain radiated through his body. The air was filled with clouds of smoke and dust. Selena knelt at his side. A Marine medic leaned over him.

"Take it easy," the medic said. "You got hit with debris and you've got a concussion. You're

going to be banged up and sore but you'll be okay.
Lie there and I'll be back."

He got up and walked away.

"Stay awake," Selena said.

He had a terrible headache. He tried to
remember what had happened. Then he had it.

"Ronnie. He got hit."

"He's still alive but it's bad," she said. "The
ambassador and most of the hostages are dead.
Lamont is okay. So am I."

"What about the terrorists?"

"All dead."

"I screwed up," Nick said. "I should've figured
out another way to go after them."

"There wasn't any other way. There was no
way to stop them from killing more people without
exposing ourselves. It's not your fault."

Nick could feel himself drifting away. He
gripped her hand.

"I screwed up," he said again. Then he slipped
into black, churning nothingness.

CHAPTER 26

Nick lay between crisp, white sheets in a hospital bed on Clark Air Force Base. His body was covered with bruises. He had a relentless headache that sent spots dancing before his eyes. His old wounds ached with dull, throbbing pain that clawed deep into his body.

Pointless. The word echoed in his mind.

The embassy was in ruins. Most of the hostages were dead. The American ambassador was dead. All of the terrorists were dead. Ronnie was fighting for his life. And for what? What had any of it accomplished?

He'd gone over what had happened again and again. Each time he came to the same conclusion, but it didn't help. There was nothing else he could have done. There wasn't any other way to get to that ballroom. There wasn't any way to rescue the hostages without getting in a firefight. It felt as though a relentless, dark force had wrapped itself around him like a cloud.

You should have shot the man with the pistol first. It's your fault.

He told himself the feeling would pass, that in a day or two things would seem almost normal.

It wasn't the first time he'd told himself that. It was a familiar, inner lie.

Pointless.

He'd spent his adult life telling himself that what he did had a purpose. That it made a difference. He'd taken an oath to defend his country. He'd honored that oath, even when there were times it seemed to him his country was wrong. It was a matter of integrity, of honor. Now it had all brought him here, to a hospital bed far from home.

He'd been lying in a hospital bed when Harker offered him a job with the Project. He'd thought it would be different. A new start. A better way to serve his country. But it was the same old story. It was like the game where you hit a target with a hammer and a new one popped up on another part of the board. There was always another target to hit. No matter what he did, no matter where he went, there was always another enemy ready to take the place of the last one. There would always be another enemy. It was a war he could never win.

Selena came into the room.

"Hey." She pulled up a chair next to his bed.

"Hey. How are you doing?"

"I'm the one that's supposed to ask that," she said. "So, how are you doing?"

"I've got a hell of a headache. I get dizzy if I stand up too fast." He looked away for a moment then turned back. "I keep thinking about Ronnie."

"I know. I do, too."

"I don't know if I can keep doing this," Nick said. "I used to think I was fighting for something that had meaning. I don't think like that now."

"Because of Ronnie?"

"It's more than that. What we do seems meaningless. I don't know what I'm fighting for anymore."

Selena heard a note in his voice she'd never heard before. It made her uneasy. Nick was one of the most confident men she had ever known, but he didn't sound that way now. She chose her words with care.

"I've thought about this a lot," she said. "What we're fighting for. I think it's what Lincoln called increased devotion."

"What do you mean, increased devotion?"

"It's what Lincoln said at Gettysburg. I don't remember the exact words, but he was talking about the men who'd died on the battlefield and about taking increased devotion to the cause they died for. He said that they didn't die for the North or the South but for the idea of freedom. So the nation wouldn't perish."

Nick was silent. Then he said, "I'm not so sure what happened in the embassy was about freedom."

"What else would you call it? Abu Sayyaf and the other extremist groups hate the whole idea of freedom. They're the enemy of freedom. I'd say stopping them and everyone just like them is a job with plenty of meaning."

"Christ, Selena. Next thing you're going to tell me is that somebody has to do it."

Suddenly she was angry. She stood up. "That's right, somebody has to do it. You're angry about Ronnie, I get that, but don't you dare tell me that what we do has no meaning."

She stalked from the room.

CHAPTER 27

The private terminal at Geneva International Airport was reserved for the kinds of people who could afford private jets and who demanded discretion and privacy. Switzerland had a high regard for those who required such services. Entry into the country was made as painless as possible for men like Krivi. Formalities like passport control were cursory and courteous. A customs officer met Krivi at the foot of the steps as he descended from his Gulfstream. He saluted and stamped Krivi's passport. The blacktop pavement under the plane glistened from an afternoon shower that had left shallow puddles of water reflecting the pure blue of the Swiss sky.

A liveried chauffeur and a black Mercedes limousine waited nearby. The chauffeur took Krivi's bag and held the door open. Johannes Gutenberg greeted Krivi from the back seat.

"My friend, welcome."

"Hello, Johannes."

The limo pulled away. Gutenberg pressed a button and a smoked partition of thick glass slid up behind the driver. The interior of the car smelled of leather and a hint of Gutenberg's expensive cologne. Krivi settled back in the comfortable seat. He was tired after the flight. As much as he hated to admit it, he was beginning to feel his age.

Gutenberg said, "Things seem to be going well."

"In general, yes. The Americans are incensed. It won't be long before they find convincing evidence that Pakistan was behind the attack. Rao has done a good job of misdirection. There is an unexpected complication, however."

"Oh?"

"There is always an unexpected complication," Krivi said. "There were members of the American Project at the embassy. They almost succeeded in stopping the attack."

In the past, the Project had created real trouble for the organization. The fact that there were now seven board members instead of nine was a direct result of their interference.

"They can't know anything," Gutenberg said.

"No. Even so, it would be unwise to ignore them."

"What action do you suggest?"

"Nothing at the moment. If we go after them now, it will only draw attention. Besides, it may not be necessary. If it becomes necessary we'll eliminate them."

"Perhaps Secretary Rao may prove useful in that respect," Gutenberg said.

For a few moments the men were quiet, watching the streets of Geneva pass by. They took the road along the Rhone. The city began to give way to the countryside. Gutenberg's chalet was several miles outside of the city limits.

Gutenberg broke the silence. "Rao still thinks you represent some Hindu society?"

Krivi nodded. "The Eye of Shiva," he said. "In Hindu mythology, Shiva's third eye has the power to shatter the unrighteous with divine fire. Rao is obsessed with the concept. He hopes for the return of a jewel stolen centuries ago that formed the eye of an idol. It fits his longing for revenge."

"Speaking of divine fire, have you approached him yet?"

"About the missiles? Not yet, but I am sure there won't be a problem. His hatred of Pakistan runs deep. He sees me as his benefactor. The drugs I've given him make him grateful to me. They also make him susceptible to ideas that fulfill his need for revenge."

"When do you plan to approach him?"

"I'm flying back to India tomorrow, after our meeting. One of Kamarov's subsidiaries in Mumbai makes the control systems and guidance modules for the Agni III missiles. He's bringing a card to the meeting programmed with the launch and targeting codes. It will be a simple matter for Rao to insert the card on site and launch. He'll think the missile is going to hit Islamabad."

"But it won't, will it?"

"No," Krivi said. "The target is Chengdu. The Bank of China has located the majority of their servers there, as well as their gold reserves. Destruction of the city will cripple China's financial system."

The car slowed for an ornate iron gate set in a high, stone wall. The gate swung open as they approached and they turned onto a curved drive paved with gray flagstones. The drive ended at a circular courtyard in front of an elegant 18th century chalet. The mansion sat on a spit of land jutting out into the River Rhone. A fountain in the courtyard rained a constant spray of water on laughing nymphs frolicking with Pan.

A crest carved in stone marked the wall above the entrance to the chalet. It showed a central, radiant eye against the background of a nine-pointed star. A Latin inscription encircled the eye in raised letters.

AETERNA EST ORDO NOVUS

For an observer who understood Latin, the meaning was clear.

THE NEW ORDER IS FOREVER

Both Krivi and Gutenberg wore identical gold rings that repeated the motif. A tall, blond woman waved at them from the open door of the chalet as they got out of the limousine.

"Marta is looking forward to your visit," Gutenberg said. "She had the chef prepare a special meal for us tonight."

"Are the others here yet?"

"Hugh de Guillame flew in this afternoon from Paris. Thorvaldson and Halifax arrived this morning. Mitchell's flight from Washington was delayed but he should get here later tonight. I'm afraid he'll miss dinner."

"Kamarov?"

"Delayed in Moscow. He should get here after dessert."

"It's been quite a while since we all met face to face," Krivi said. "I'm looking forward to it."

"I thought it best," Gutenberg said. "We're entering a critical phase of our plans. Being together in the same room brings out thinking you can't get in a teleconference."

"That's true," Krivi said. "I confess I'm not looking forward to Kamarov's bad digestion."

"That man releases enough gas to float the Hindenburg," Gutenberg said.

Krivi laughed. The two men went into the chateau.

CHAPTER 28

Four days after the attack on the embassy, the
Project team assembled in Harker's office. Sunlight
streaming through the windows couldn't dispel the
feeling in the room. Ronnie had been transferred
back to the states and was in the intensive care unit
at Bethesda. His absence hung over all of them.
Even the cat knew something was wrong. Burps
kept going from room the room looking for him.

A folder with an intelligence update from NSA
lay on Elizabeth's desk. It put a different spin on
Manila. She looked at Selena and Ronnie and Nick
and paused, searching for the right words.

"Ronnie getting hit is a blow to all of us but we
have to stay focused. This isn't over yet. Before
we're done we may get a chance for payback."

Nick looked as though he hadn't slept for a
week. There were dark shadows under his eyes. His
lips were compressed in a thin line.

"What kind of payback?" he said.

She tapped the folder on her desk. "NSA thinks
the attack on the embassy was more than just an
Abu Sayyaf operation. So do I."

"What do you mean, more?" Lamont asked.

"Abu Sayyaf had help from ISOK."

"You mean weapons?" Selena asked. "We
already knew ISOK was giving them money."

"That's another issue. We'll talk about that
later," Elizabeth said. "This report says it was ISOK
behind the embassy seizure all along. They planned
the attack, using Abu Sayyaf as a surrogate."

"What's the Intel that backs that up?" Lamont
said.

"Three cell phone calls between Abdul Afridi, the leader of ISOK and Omar Madid, the terrorist who led the attack and shot the hostages."

Selena picked a bit of lint off her skirt. "That doesn't make sense. ISOK wants India out of Kashmir, that's their focus. Why attack our embassy in the Philippines?"

"Are they allied with Al Qaeda?" Lamont asked. "That might explain it."

Elizabeth said, "I don't think this has anything to do with Al Qaeda."

"What's Rice going to do?" Selena asked.

"He hasn't decided yet. I've never known him to be this angry. Ambassador Cathwaite was a personal friend of his. I talked with him yesterday. What complicates things is Pakistan."

"Pakistan?" Nick said. "How do they come into it?"

Elizabeth picked up her pen and set it down again. She was trying to break her habit of tapping it on the desktop.

"ISOK wouldn't attack us without permission from Islamabad. If they planned it, it means Pakistan has declared a covert war on us."

"Not much new about that," Lamont said. "They've been lying to us and helping our enemies for years."

"Yes, but we ignored it because we wanted access through their border with Afghanistan. This is different. Politically, it's a perfect storm. The media, Congress and everyone else wants to know who's responsible. Everyone is calling for retaliation. Suppose it gets out that Pakistan used a proxy to blow up our embassy and kill one of our ambassadors? It could trigger a war. If a war starts, it would end up involving the entire Muslim world."

"You said *if* it's true. That ISOK is behind the attack," Nick said. "Does that mean you have doubts?"

"Something about this doesn't feel right," Elizabeth said, "even though we know ISOK is in bed with Abu Sayyaf."

"So where does the doubt come in?" Lamont asked.

"Like Selena said, it doesn't make sense. Why would Pakistan tell ISOK to help Abu Sayyaf attack our embassy? It doesn't get them anything except trouble. It's a major incident that guarantees retaliation when we find out Islamabad is behind it."

"Abu Sayyaf wanted their prisoners released," Nick said. "It could be Pakistan has nothing to do with it."

"The cell phone intercepts between ISOK and Omar Madid are damning," Elizabeth said. "It's the classic smoking gun. The calls leave no doubt that the attack is being carried out in return for ISOK providing funds for their so-called Islamic revolution."

"That seems clear enough," Selena said.

"That's the problem. It's too clear, too pat. ISOK and Abu Sayyaf have been around a long time. They aren't amateurs in the terrorist game. Both have years of experience avoiding detection by our surveillance. They practice strict communication discipline and they're good at it. They don't use cell phones that can be tracked. Then all of a sudden we find these convenient intercepts and a trail a mile wide pointing straight back to ISOK and Islamabad."

"You think it's a set up." Selena sat up straighter in her chair.

141

"My intuition says yes, it's a set up. Someone wants us to think ISOK and Pakistan are behind the attack. I think the calls are fake."

Elizabeth's intuition was one of her major strengths. She was seldom wrong. It was eerily accurate, almost a sixth sense. When it kicked in she'd feel an electric tingling all over her skin. She'd learned long ago to pay attention when she had that feeling. She had it now.

"Who would have the resources to fake those calls and not get caught?" Lamont asked.

"That's the magic word, Lamont. Resources. It takes a lot of sophistication to set up an operation like this."

"Qui bono?" Selena said. "Who benefits?"

"Someone who doesn't like Pakistan," Nick said.

"Lots of people don't like Pakistan." Elizabeth looked at them. "There's one obvious answer."

"India," Selena said.

Elizabeth said, "Lots of things seem off about this. Two days before they're supposed to mastermind an attack on our embassy, ISOK blows up the Indian Embassy in Manila. Why? Manila is a long way from Kashmir and there are plenty of prime targets closer to home. Attacking the Indian Embassy in another country would be a major operation in itself. It's a real stretch for an organization that's basically local. Then two days later they get their good friends in Abu Sayyaf to take us on? I don't think so."

"You think the Indian Embassy explosion was part of a set up as well?" Selena said.

"I think it could be."

"Are you saying that the same person or persons is behind both attacks?" Nick asked.

"If I'm right, that's the only explanation that fits."

"What's the payoff?" Nick tugged on his ear. "Being pissed at Pakistan isn't enough of a reason. There has to be more to it than that."

"Why don't we do the assumption thing?" Selena said. "Brainstorm it."

Elizabeth put her pen down. "It's worked before. What's our first assumption?"

Stephanie had been quiet. Now she said, "That it's a set up, like you said. A false flag operation to make us and everyone else think Pakistan is responsible."

"We're back to who benefits," Selena said.

"Does Pakistan gain anything from this?" Lamont asked.

"I don't see how," Harker said. "On the contrary."

"Then assumption number two has to be that the Pakis aren't behind it. If not them, who is it?"

"Someone who wants us to think Pakistan killed our ambassador," Nick said.

Selena heard the energy in his voice and smiled to herself. It was the first time he'd sounded normal since Ronnie had been hit.

"Don't forget the Indian Embassy bombing," Lamont said. "They want us to think Pakistan is behind that too."

"This is a real can of worms," Selena said. "It's making my head spin."

"Yeah," Lamont said.

Elizabeth glanced at her watch. "Let's take a break."

There was a refrigerator and a kitchen on the floor below Harker's office. Nick, Selena and Lamont went down a spiral staircase to what had once been a large living room when the house had been in civilian hands. It was now the operations center. Lamont headed for the bathroom. Nick and Selena went into the kitchen. Nick reached into the refrigerator and grabbed two bottles of water and handed one to Selena. He opened his bottle and took a drink.

Selena said, "If Elizabeth is right, whoever is behind this wasn't killed at the embassy. He's still out there."

Nick's expression was grim. Selena had only seen that look a few times before. It meant he'd made a decision and nothing would stop him from following through on it. She had an idea about what he was going to say next.

"I don't care who's behind it," Nick said. "Ronnie's hanging by a thread because of this asshole, whoever he is. When I find him, I'm going to kill him. If there's more than one, I'll kill them too."

"What if Elizabeth doesn't send us after him? Or them, as the case may be?"

"Then I'll do it on my own."

"Do what on your own?" Lamont came over. He took a bottle of juice from the refrigerator.

Selena said, "Find whoever set up the attack and kill him."

"Might not be easy," Lamont said. "Harker may have other ideas."

"I'll cross that bridge if I come to it," Nick said.

"You can't do it alone."

"It could turn out to somebody protected," Nick said.

"What do you mean, protected?" Selena sipped her water.

"Somebody high up in the Pakistani government. Or in India."

"That could be a problem," Lamont said.

Nick said nothing.

"We're good at solving problems," Selena said.

"That's right," Lamont said.

Nick looked at them. "What are you saying?"

Lamont finished his juice and set the empty bottle in a case stacked by the refrigerator.

"Like I said, you can't do it alone."

"And three are better than one at solving problems," Selena said.

"You know what you're saying? We could get killed. We could get thrown in a federal Super Max for the rest of our lives."

"What else is new?" Lamont said.

"We can't let whoever it is get away with it," Selena said. "Besides Ronnie, there are those dead Marines. And Margaret. I didn't know her well but I liked her."

Nick looked at them. "Am I right in thinking this? Whatever else happens, we find out who did this, we take him down?"

"Agreed," Selena said.

"I'm in," Lamont said.

Nick held out his hand, palm down. Lamont placed his hand over Nick's. Selena placed hers over both of theirs.

"For Ronnie," Nick said.

Selena and Lamont both spoke at once.

"For Ronnie."

CHAPTER 29

"Where were we?" Elizabeth said.

"That it's a set up. An unknown person or persons with resources wants us to think Pakistan is behind the attacks on the embassies," Stephanie said.

"Not just any resources," Nick said. "Who has the ability to manipulate cell phone intercepts and conversations?"

"That's easy," Lamont said. "An intelligence agency. Like NSA or Langley."

"They're not behind it," Elizabeth said.

"I didn't say they were. There are plenty of others who could do it."

Harker toyed with her pen. "I think you're right."

"Who are we talking about?" Nick asked. "China? Russia?"

Selena brushed the back of her hand across her forehead. "Remember I asked earlier who benefits? We haven't answered that question. What will happen because of the attacks? What's the benefit and to whom? That could tell us who's behind it."

Elizabeth said, "Blowing up the embassies doesn't accomplish anything except get a lot of people angry. It's like poking a stick in the eye of India and America. Both countries have to respond and they have to do it soon. The public is screaming for someone to blame. They want revenge."

So do I, Selena thought. Lamont was looking at his fingernails. Nick was silent. All of them were thinking the same thing. *For Ronnie.*

Stephanie's computer beeped. She looked at the screen.

"Oh, oh."

"I don't like it when you say that," Elizabeth said. "What's happening?"

"The NSA report's been leaked. It's gone viral."

Elizabeth picked up the report and set it back down again. "This report makes it look like Pakistan is to blame. It's going to create a lot of pressure on Rice to strike at them. The sabers are going to come out."

"This can't be a coincidence," Selena said. "Now we know who benefits. Someone who wants to make a lot of trouble for Pakistan, even start a war."

"It can't be the Indian government," Elizabeth said. "Their Prime Minister has gone out of the way to avoid provoking Pakistan. It's made him unpopular and it's probably going to cost him the next election."

"Who's the opposition over there?" Nick wanted to know.

"The right wing. It's Hindu and nationalistic and bitterly opposed to Pakistan."

"It might not be the government," Selena said, "but it could be a group inside the government. We said it could be an agency. How about India's intelligence agency?"

"You're talking about a right wing conspiracy to drag India into a war," Stephanie said.

Selena nodded. "And us right along with it."

"Déjà vu all over again," Elizabeth said. "We've been here before."

"Why is there always some lunatic who wants to start a war?" Nick said.

"If there wasn't one, we'd all be out of a job," Elizabeth said.

"What's the next step?" Selena asked.

"I have the records of the intercepted calls," Steph said. "I've been developing a program to pinpoint where a call comes from when it's encrypted in a microburst or there's no GPS info. It's got some bugs but I might be able to narrow down the source some more."

"Outstanding," Nick said. "Nail the bastard down."

"I'll try. I can't guarantee anything."

"All right," Elizabeth said. "Steph, see what you can find out. We can't do anything without more information."

She picked up the report again and set it off to the side.

Steph cleared her throat. "About that coin Nick found in the Philippines," she said. "I did some research on it."

"Go on," Elizabeth said.

"It comes from the early sixteenth century. It's rare, worth thousands. Coincidentally, three of them turned up at an auction in Hong Kong two weeks ago. They went for 22K as a lot."

"I don't believe in coincidences," Elizabeth said.

"Abu Sayyaf had a dozen more besides the one I brought back," Nick said. "Some were bigger. They'd be worth more than a hundred grand."

"That would buy a lot of things that go boom," Lamont said.

"It's strange that a bunch of rare coins like those would turn up in the hands of terrorists," Nick said. "Where would they come from?"

Selena looked thoughtful. "There's one possibility that would explain it," she said. It's pretty far-fetched, though."

"What's that?"

"Who is it that runs ISOK again?" Selena asked.

"Abdul Afridi," Elizabeth said.

"Afridi could have stumbled on some of the lost treasure of the Mughal emperors."

Nick raised an eyebrow. "What lost treasure?"

"I never heard about a Mughal treasure," Steph said.

"The Mughals again," Lamont said.

"The Mughal Empire was richer than Rome," Selena said. "In 1739 a Persian king named Nader Shah invaded India and sacked the treasury at Delhi. Accounts from the time say he set off for home with a train of elephants and pack animals that stretched for a hundred miles. All loaded down with treasure."

Lamont whistled. "You're making it up."

"No, it's true. After he got back home, no one had to pay taxes for three years."

"Too bad that guy's dead," Lamont said. "He'd make a good president."

"Are you done?" Elizabeth said.

"Sorry."

"How do we know the treasure really existed?" Nick said.

"Because of the Peacock Throne and the Koh-I-Noor diamond. They were part of the Mughal treasury. The diamond is one of the British crown jewels. That's the reason we know the treasure is real and not a myth. The throne was made of solid gold and decorated with diamonds, pearls, rubies and sapphires. One of the stones on the throne was known as the Timur ruby. That's another one of the crown jewels. A second large ruby was called the Eye of Shiva by the Hindus. It was supposed to have sacred powers. That's lost."

"Where's the throne now?"

"Nobody knows," Selena said. "Nader Shah started back with it toward Persia and that's the last anyone saw of it. The treasure caravan got caught in an early winter storm somewhere in Afghanistan. There's one account that claims the throne and several pack animals bearing chests of gold and jewels were swept over the side of a mountain by an avalanche. People have been looking for it ever since. It's worth hundreds of millions of dollars, if it still exists."

"That's a great story but what does it have to do with the coins I found in the Philippines?" Nick said.

"What are the chances of more than a dozen valuable coins from the sixteenth century turning up in the hands of a bunch of terrorists?" Selena said.

"Slim to none," Stephanie said.

Selena nodded. "What if that story is true and Afridi found some of the gold that was swept away? The coins are almost unheard of and they're from the right time frame. If Afridi found that treasure, the coins make sense. Maybe that should be our next assumption."

"We're getting off the track," Nick said. "The coins don't explain the attacks, or why someone would want to start a war."

Elizabeth looked at Stephanie. "Steph, this program you're working on. How soon can you get it working on those calls between Abu Sayyaf and Afridi?"

"It's hard to say. I need time to tweak it. It might only take a few hours but it could be longer."

"Then you'd better get going," Elizabeth said.

CHAPTER 30

Morning sun streamed through the windows of Ashok Rao's office. Rao sat at his desk, reading the morning briefs. The military had gone to high alert. Troop buildups had begun along the border. It looked more and more as if war was coming. His plan was working.

The NSA memo had been a godsend. Rao had leaked it to the Indian press with predictable results. The Prime Minister had been forced to make a public statement blaming Pakistan for the bombing of the embassy in Manila. Islamabad denied involvement with ISOK or any other terrorist group and accused India of trying to provoke a war. Since everyone knew Pakistan's intelligence services backed the Islamic State of Kashmir, every denial reinforced the idea that they were responsible.

Rao pulled open a desk drawer, took out two of Krivi's tablets and swallowed them dry. He rubbed his hand across the top of his head. The headaches were happening more often but the pills helped. Krivi had called yesterday and asked for a meeting today in the park near the temple.

Rao had gathered information about Krivi. He'd come up with a reclusive, self-made billionaire, a successful business man from Mumbai who controlled a global pharmaceutical empire based in Switzerland. That explained the pills and it explained the money. Rao always felt better if he had an explanation.

On the other hand, he'd found no information about a society called the Eye of Shiva. That was odd. Right wing groups and secret societies were popular in India and watched as a matter of policy. No group could remain hidden from the kind of scrutiny Rao could bring to bear. Yet he'd found nothing.

Rao had hoped to meet others in the group. When he'd asked about it, Krivi had reminded him of the need for secrecy. It was like the old Communist model, Krivi had said, each cell isolated so no one person could betray more than a few members of the movement. Rao was too important, Krivi had said. It was better if he remained in the shadows.

Rao had stopped looking. There were bigger things to occupy his attention. Until war started, chance and circumstance could derail the plan. No matter how well an operation had been thought out or executed there were always unknown factors that caused problems.

Like the Project, for one thing. Most people had never heard of Elizabeth Harker's unit but Rao was a high-ranking intelligence officer. It was his job to know about things like that. He had no reason to think they suspected what he was doing. All the same, he wasn't going to make the mistake of underestimating them.

He had to keep an eye on them. Harker's people had almost screwed everything up at the embassy. One of her men had been badly wounded and Rao's sources said he was going to die. His comrades would look for vengeance. Rao understood vengeance. If Harker learned of his involvement it would create a complication he didn't need.

Then there were those gold coins found during that raid in the Philippines.

I don't know enough about the coins, he thought.

He called Prakash Khanna in Manila on his encrypted satellite phone.

"I want to talk about the gold recovered from the Abu Sayyaf camp," Rao said.

"Everyone has been curious about that."

"Tell me about the coins."

"They're unusual," Khanna said.

"You've seen them?".

"Not the coins themselves. I have a contact inside Philippines special operations. He obtained pictures for me."

"What can you tell me about them?"

"They're from the Mughal Empire, minted during the sixteenth century," Khanna said. "I'm told they're quite rare and in excellent condition. Uncirculated."

"How could they be that old and be uncirculated?"

"If they'd been minted and immediately set aside, it's possible."

Rao felt a surge of adrenaline. There was only one place where an emperor's coinage could be set aside.

The treasury.

Rao kept his voice calm. Inside, he was shaking.

"It's certain they are authentic?"

"Yes. Why are you asking?"

"ISOK had to get them from somewhere. I want to follow the money trail."

Rao wasn't going to tell Khanna he suspected the coins might have come from the Mughal hoard, or that they might lead him to the Eye. He changed the subject.

"What is Manila doing about the attack?"

"President Navarro is demanding more American aid to fight the Muslim insurgency in Mindanao," Khanna said. "The Americans are unhappy with him. They've given him millions of dollars to fight Abu Sayyaf and all they've got to show for it is the ruins of their embassy. Rice is playing hardball. If Navarro wants more money, he's going to have to make concessions about American bases here."

"That's about what I'd expected," Rao said.

"Is there anything else?" Khanna asked.

Khanna had initiative and intelligence and he knew how to follow orders. Rao decided that he'd be more useful here in India.

"You've done well, Prakash. Come home. I'll send your replacement."

"I won't be sorry to leave," Khanna said. "It's become an uncomfortable country for foreigners."

Rao ended the call. His pulse pounded as he thought about the coins and what it might mean.

History recorded that the treasure had been loaded on the backs of elephants and other beasts for transport back to Persia. Most of the treasure had reached its destination. The key word was *most.* No record existed of the throne ever reaching Persia. Some famous gems from the treasury had never resurfaced, among them the Eye of Shiva. Somewhere between India and Persia, the throne and the gems had disappeared. There was a discredited account from the time that claimed the throne and several chests of gold and jewels had been lost in the mountains between Afghanistan and what was now Pakistan.

What if the account is true? Rao thought. *If Afridi found some of the coins lost when the trail collapsed he might have found the jewel as well.*

Only Afridi knew where he'd gotten the coins. The only way to find out where they were was to interrogate him. It would be difficult to capture Afridi but not impossible. An opportunity would arise.

A sudden headache and wave of nausea sent Rao scurrying to the washroom. He leaned over the bowl and threw up his breakfast. It was a reminder that whatever he decided to do about Afridi, it would have to be soon.

He told his assistant he'd be gone the rest of the day. He hailed a cab on Lodhi Road and not long after was walking toward the bench where Krivi waited for him.

"You seem pale, my friend," Krivi said, concern written on his face. "Are you all right?"

"I'm fine. A little nausea earlier. I'm fine now."

"I have something to help with that," Krivi said. He took a bottle of white pills from his jacket pocket. "These will keep the nausea down and give you an energy boost."

Rao took the bottle. "Thank you. Is that why you wanted to meet? To give me these?"

"Partly. I wanted to give you this as well."

Krivi withdrew a clear plastic envelope containing a blue card from his jacket pocket. The card had a magnetic stripe on it, like a credit card, only this card was bigger. Rao recognized the crossed swords and three headed lion of the Indian Army printed on the corner.

"Do you know what this is?" Krivi asked.

Rao felt a chill of recognition. "It looks like a code card, one that could be used to launch one of our missiles."

Krivi nodded. "That is exactly what it is."

"How did you get that?" Rao asked. In spite of himself he was shocked.

"It doesn't matter. This card contains guidance data for an Agni III missile. The target is Islamabad."

Krivi handed the envelope and card to Rao.

"What do you want me to do with it?" Rao said. He already knew the answer.

"I want you to use it. It will only work with the Agni III. A shorter range missile might have been better, but this was the best I could do."

Agni III had a range of up to 5000 kilometers, overkill for a nearby target like Islamabad. It carried a nuclear warhead. Rao's mind was a jumble of thoughts.

"When? How? I hadn't planned on this."

"You'll know the right time to do it," Krivi said. "When the war starts, we can't risk a first strike from Pakistan. You know that Lanka will never launch first. By the time he realizes Pakistan's missiles are in the air, it will be too late. We must not let that happen."

India had an avowed policy of no first strike. Rao thought it a foolish policy that encouraged a potential enemy to deliver a first, fatal blow. Pakistan had enough missiles to destroy India. If India used her nuclear arsenal, Pakistan would cease to exist except as a radioactive wasteland. The threat of mutual assured destruction had so far kept the two countries from each other's throats.

Rao's mind was already thinking of how it might be done. A vision of a mushroom cloud rising over Islamabad filled his mind's eye.

Revenge.

"The codes change on a regular basis," Rao said. "How long is this good for?"

"Until the end of this month," Krivi said.

CHAPTER 31

It was a beautiful October day, the kind of day that marked cooler weather and the onset of Indian Summer. Elizabeth was holding the regular morning briefing. The team sat in their usual semi-circle in front of her desk. The cat lay on his back in a patch of sunlight coming through the French doors to the patio, snoring.

Harker's black suit jacket was draped over the back of her chair. She wore a white silk blouse with a Mao collar and black pearl buttons.

"Ronnie is still in intensive care in an induced coma," she said. "He's stable. It's about the best we can hope for at the moment. Now we're going to move on. I want to find out who pulled the strings that got him shot. Steph thinks she has something. I'll let her brief you."

"My new program is up and running," Stephanie said. "There are still a few bugs but it gives us more capability. For the moment, it's working fine."

"What did you find out?" Nick's voice was tinged with impatience.

Stephanie was annoyed. "I'm getting to it."

"Sorry."

"First, the call from the American Embassy to Abu Khan is a dead end. It came from an office phone on the third floor. Anyone could have used it when no one else was around."

Stephanie paused and took a sip of coffee from a mug bearing the logo of the Oakland Raiders.

"The intercepted calls between ISOK and the terrorists in the embassy are a different story," she said. "The records show the calls coming from Pakistan. We know Afridi hides out in Pakistan and we know where his base is. I wanted to confirm it was him, so I went looking for the exact location of the phone that made the calls."

She touched a key on her laptop. The office wall monitor came to life with an aerial view of a large city. She touched another key and the picture zoomed in on the roof of a tall building set back from a pleasant, tree-lined street. The roof of the building was studded with antennas and satellite dishes.

"This is what I found. Doesn't look much like Pakistan, does it? The calls came from here."

"Where is it?" Nick asked.

"New Delhi." Steph sat back, looking pleased with herself. She waited.

Nick looked confused. "Why would Afridi be in New Delhi?"

"I have a better question," Selena said. "What building is that?"

"It's the headquarters of the Research and Analysis Wing, India's CIA," Stephanie said.

"Holy shit," Lamont said. "Spooks are behind this?"

"I'm pretty certain Afridi isn't hanging out in the headquarters of RAW making phone calls."

"If it wasn't Afridi, who was it?" Nick asked.

"I don't know," Steph said. "All I can tell you is that those calls originated somewhere in that building."

Harker took a sip from a bottle of water on her desk.

"I guess we were right," she said.

"About what?"

"That it could be an intelligence agency making it look like Pakistan ordered the attacks. RAW's involvement changes everything," she said. "It makes things a lot more complicated."

"You think?" Lamont said.

Harker gave him a warning look. "Someone in that building has gone to a lot of trouble to make it look like ISOK and Pakistan are responsible for what's happened."

"It can't be a low level official," Nick said. "It has to be someone who can use serious agency resources without anyone questioning what he's doing."

"And who can keep it hidden," Lamont said.

"It's their CIA," Steph said. "Everyone who works there keeps things hidden."

"What does it take to fake cell phone calls like that?" Nick said.

"Planting a call is easy, if you know what you're doing," Steph said. "Making it look like this is a different story. Even the NSA thinks those calls came from Pakistan."

"How high up do you think it goes?" Selena asked Elizabeth.

"Hard to tell. I don't think it's the man who runs the agency. He's a liberal, an appointee of the Prime Minister. The PM is afraid of getting into an armed conflict with Pakistan. The last thing either of them wants is a war."

Nick scratched his ear. "Steph, you tracked the phone. Can you call it?"

Stephanie looked surprised. She began fiddling with the bracelets circling her left wrist.

"I never thought of that. Yes, if it still exists and it's turned on."

"So why don't we call and see who answers?" Nick said. "How long will it take you to do it?"

"I can do it right now."

Elizabeth said, "Hold on, Nick. Let's talk about it first. What would be the point in calling him?"

"Aside from finding out who answers? We could rattle the bastard's cage. "

"Why?"

"Why not? If he knows we're on to him, he may make a mistake that could expose him."

"I don't think we should call him," Selena said. "He's smart, he won't rattle easily. All it would do is make him more dangerous."

"We have to find out who he is," Nick said.

"You think I don't know that?"

Harker reached for her pen. "Steph, can you intercept calls made on that phone?"

"Sure. Now that I've broken the encryption, his phone is mine. Anything he says can be understood."

"Good. Set it up."

Nick looked uncomfortable. "I didn't think of that. I should have."

"You're letting your feelings get the best of you," Elizabeth said. "You're upset about Ronnie and you want to strike back. We all want to take this man down. I need to know you can keep a clear head about this."

"I understand," Nick said. "You don't have to worry about it."

Selena heard him say the words but she wasn't sure he meant it.

"We need an operational name for him," Elizabeth said. "Until we know more, we'll call him Cobra."

"Are you going to tell the president about this?" Stephanie asked.

"Yes, but not yet. We need to know who Cobra is before I go to him."

CHAPTER 32

The Hazratbal Mosque was a magnificent building on the shores of Lake Dal in the city of Srinagar. The mosque was built entirely of white marble and was famous for a shrine housing a true hair of the prophet Mohammed. That put it high on the list of pilgrimage destinations for devout Muslims.

Abdul Afridi was under no illusions about his chances if he strayed far or long from his protected compound in Pakistan. He was marked for assassination. He couldn't risk the journey to Mecca required of the faithful. Until the day came when he could make the Hajj, Afridi had vowed to visit Hazratbal and view the relic of the Prophet once a year as an act of devotion. He'd slipped in and out of Kashmir many times without being detected.

The hair of the Prophet could only be viewed on a few special days. One was fast approaching and Afridi had decided to go, in spite of the increased attention focused on him since the attacks in the Philippines.

It was widely believed that he was responsible. The attacks staged in his name had created problems for him, but whoever was behind it had done him a favor. His status among the jihadists had skyrocketed. His reputation had never been so high. Everyone thought he was lying when he denied involvement. Recruitment was up. Donations were pouring in.

They were needed, the gold was almost gone.

Afridi thought back on the day Allah had led him to the coins.

He'd been traveling back to his compound in Pakistan with Abu Khan after meeting with the Taliban leaders in Kandahar. The American drones still targeted vehicles in Taliban territory and they'd gone on foot, accompanied by a mule to carry supplies. Their weapons were hidden. From the air, they were just two more Afghani peasants.

They weren't far from the border with Pakistan, where his men would meet him with vehicles to take them the rest of the way. It was late in the day and Afridi had begun to think about making camp for the night.

Afridi and Khan were walking at the bottom of a canyon, following the bed of an ancient watercourse. The ground underneath was a mixture of gravel, rock and coarse sand. Steep rock walls rose above them for thousands of feet on either side.

The mule began tossing his head and braying, pulling on the rope halter Khan used to lead him.

"Stupid beast," Kahn said. He struck the mule with a stick and yanked on the halter. "I'll be glad when we're rid of you."

Overhead a flock of birds took flight, wings beating frantically against the thin mountain air.

The ground trembled beneath their feet. Kahn and Afridi looked at one another. Earthquakes were common in this region. Both spoke at once.

"Earthquake."

"Get away from the walls."

The mule broke free of Khan's hold and ran down the canyon. Stones began shaking loose from above, bouncing around them. The ground bucked and heaved underfoot. Afridi struggled to keep upright. A low, menacing rumble echoed down the defile, vibrating against the rock walls of the canyon. Ahead, the ancient river bed widened out into a broad, open area.

"Run for it," Khan shouted.

They staggered in a shambling run toward the protection of open space. Ahead, a boulder tumbled from high above and struck the crazed mule, crushing the helpless animal beneath its weight. A stone struck Afridi on his shoulder and knocked him to his knees. He cried out in pain, got up and kept running. They passed the twitching body of the mule and stumbled onto the wide part of the canyon floor. When they reached the center, they stopped and waited for the tremor to pass. After what seemed a long time, it subsided.

A second tremor began, stronger than the first. The air filled with dust and the sound of mountains moving. Afridi fell to the ground and prayed that none of the falling rock would crush him like the mule. Through the dust and flying debris he watched a waterfall of rock collapse onto the path ahead.

The earth stopped moving.

Khan raised himself up on his hands and knees and said, "Do you think it's over?"

"Insha'Allah it is over."

Afridi got to his feet. The old riverbed was littered with stones and boulders, some bigger than the one that had killed the unfortunate mule.

"What's that?" Kahn said. He pointed at a white, curved object sticking up out of loose rocks at the side of the canyon.

They walked closer until they could see what it was. There was more than one.

"Bones," Afridi said. "Big ones. They look like ribs."

"Only one animal big enough to have ribs like that," Kahn said. "Elephant."

"These have been here a long time." Afridi looked around. "The earthquake uncovered them."

"How did they get here?"

Afridi looked toward the sky. "There used to be a trail up there, a route to India. Nobody's used it for a long time. It's unsafe, the rock is loose. The elephant could have fallen from there."

"Nobody uses elephants anymore."

Afridi shrugged. "As I said, no one has used that trail for a long time."

He knelt down over the bones. A dark shape stuck out from under the pile of rocks.

"What's that?" Khan said.

"It looks like a box," Afridi said.

The two men cleared rocks away. The box was dark with age, made of hard wood. It had rusted hinges and an elaborate iron padlock. The lid was studded with tarnished brass and bound with straps of rotting leather.

"Old," Khan said. "It must've been on the elephant's back."

He used the butt of his AK to break the lock away from the box and lifted the lid. Yellow metal gleamed up at him. Khan reached into the box and picked up a coin.

"Gold," he said softly. "The shahada is written upon it."

"That can be no accident," Afridi said. His voice was touched with reverence. "Allah has smiled upon us. This will bring many fighters to our side."

"And many enemies," Khan said, "if they learn of this."

Both men had the same thought. "It must be part of Nader Shah's treasure," Afridi said.

"He's supposed to have come this way," Khan said.

"Only you and I must know of it."

"With the mule dead, there's too much for us to carry away."

"We'll take what we can and hide the rest."

The pile of rocks that had hidden the remains of the elephant was large. It sat at the bottom of a long scar carved out of the canyon wall where the trail had collapsed centuries before. Only the outer layer of the pile had been disturbed by the earthquake. Afridi wondered what else might be under those rocks. Without men and tools to move the boulders, it was impossible to know.

They walked back to the body of the mule and salvaged enough food and firewood for a meal.

"Come, brother," Afridi said. "It's time for the evening prayer. Let us give thanks for Allah's blessing. Tomorrow is soon enough to conceal what we have found."

The next morning they covered up all signs of the elephant bones and set off for home. If there was anything else under those rocks, it wasn't going anywhere. There was time to plan how it might be done.

Afridi's thoughts came back to the present. The gold from the box was almost gone. It was time to see if there was more. He decided to clear away the rock fall. Afridi had chosen a new lieutenant to replace Khan, Ibrahim Sayeed. Sayeed would pick men who could be trusted from Afridi's fighters.

Afridi stepped outside his whitewashed house. The view from his walled compound looked up on

the snow-covered peaks of the Hindu Kush. A chill
in the air hinted at the coming winter. Overhead, the
sky was a thin, clear blue. He could hear the women
gossiping in the community kitchen across the way.

The peace of the day shattered as a jet fighter
passed low overhead, on its way back to the
Pakistani airbase bordering his compound. Afridi
didn't mind the loud noise of planes overhead. The
location next to the airbase was the reason the
Americans and the Indians had avoided targeting
him with their drones. They knew where he was and
couldn't do a thing about it.

Ibrahim Sayeed sat on a chair on the hard
packed earth, cleaning his rifle. He rose as Afridi
came over.

"*Salaam aleikum.*"

"*Aleikum salaam,*" Afridi replied. He touched
his chest. "We are going to Srinagar. I must visit
Hazratbal and fulfill my vow. "

"Is that wise?" Sayeed said. "With the
increased surveillance it will be difficult."

"*Insha'Allah,* our enemies will not find us."

Sayeed placed his hand over his heart in
acknowledgment.

"When do you wish to leave?"

"In three days' time. Inform our friends in
Srinagar."

"Will you at least disguise yourself this time?"
Sayeed said. His voice was filled with concern.

Afridi had never made much effort in the past
to alter his appearance on one of these journeys. If
Allah wanted to hand him over to his enemies, there
was nothing to be done about it. Nonetheless, it
wasn't necessary to tempt fate out of pride. It would
encourage Sayeed if Afridi listened to him.

"If you think it is the best thing," Afridi said.

"I do."

Afridi nodded his assent.

"Everything will be ready."

Sayeed picked up his rifle and walked away to begin preparations. Afridi went back into his hut, unaware the conversation had been overheard.

Everyone thought Wahid Malik a dedicated fighter, committed to the cause. The truth was somewhat different. Malik worked for Ashok Rao, with orders to avoid all contact unless he had information of vital importance. What Malik had just heard more than qualified. Here in Pakistan, Afridi was beyond the reach of the agency. Once he left the country, he was vulnerable. In Srinagar he could be taken.

It would be difficult to get the information out without being discovered. Wahid had no radio. A radio could be found and implicate him. He would have to find a way to leave the compound without being caught and questioned.

Inside his house, Afridi unrolled his prayer rug and turned toward Mecca. He longed to make the Hajj and circle the sacred *Kaaba*. Until that time came, he would fulfill his vow to visit the relic of the Prophet.

Outside, dark clouds were forming over the mountains. A storm was coming.

CHAPTER 33

Nick looked through the glass of the cubicle in ICU and felt his stomach clench. Ronnie's skin was a pale yellow-brown, like weak sun on a desert plain. A bank of monitors over his head traced the electronic fragility of his life. A bag of clear liquid hung from a rack, feeding into his veins.

"It's a miracle he's still alive."

The speaker was Ronnie's doctor. She was a tall redhead with clear blue eyes and pale skin. Nick guessed her age at around forty. The name tag on her white lab coat identified her as Evelyn Fairchild, M.D.

"Were you with him when he was shot?" she said. "If you're the one who kept him from bleeding out, you saved his life."

"I was there. It wasn't me that saved him."

"One of the bullets just missed the heart and exited his back. A little to the left and that would've been it. Another round destroyed his spleen. We removed that."

"You took out his spleen?"

"What was left of it," she said. "He can live without it."

She waited to see if Nick was going to say anything else. When he didn't, she continued.

"A third bullet perforated the lower abdomen. We had to go in and clean him out. He lost about a foot of intestine but we were able to reattach the two ends. If he recovers, he'll have normal intestinal function."

"If he recovers?" Nick said.

"I won't kid you," she said. "It could go either way. We were able to repair the injuries but his body was badly traumatized. We're keeping him sedated to help the natural healing process."

"Shit," Nick said.

"Yes." She waited for the question she knew was coming.

"When will we know?" Nick asked.

"I can't say. He's stable and his EEG is normal. That's good. He's in excellent condition, aside from his injuries. I don't think there's any neurological damage from hydrostatic shock but we won't know for sure until he wakes up. That's one of the major concerns. I think there's every reason to be hopeful but that's all I can tell you."

Hydrostatic shock was bad news. When a bullet struck a living body, it sent pressure waves throughout the fluid in the tissues. It was hydrostatic shock that knocked down big game when shot. It could scramble the brain.

"Thanks for not sugarcoating it. Can I go in and talk to him?"

Doctor Fairchild nodded. "You can, but he won't respond. Five minutes, no more." She reached into a box on the nurse's station and took out a disposable face mask. "Wear this," she said.

Nick put on the mask and entered the cubicle. It was quiet there, except for the monotonous hum of air conditioning and the beeping of the machines monitoring Ronnie's vital signs. Green and red and yellow digital blips moved across the screens above Ronnie's head.

"Hey, amigo," Nick said.

His stomach twisted into knots as he looked at his friend. He'd never felt so helpless.

"You gotta quit laying around like this. Everybody misses you. Selena said for me to give you a kiss for her but I figured you wouldn't mind if I just told you about it instead."

Nick reached out and took Ronnie's hand in both of his, careful not to disturb the IV needle taped to his arm. The skin was cool, unresponsive to his touch.

"The guy who shot you is history," Nick said. "It turns out somebody else set the whole thing up. We're going to find out who it is and then we're going after him. I wish you could go with us. I wanted you to know we're going to get the bastard."

He squeezed the limp hand. "Stay with us, Ronnie. We need you. We miss you."

Nick felt moisture on his cheek. He wiped it away with the back of his hand.

"I have to go. I'll come back as soon as I can."

Nick got up and left the room. He tossed the mask in a wastebasket as he went out.

He didn't look back.

CHAPTER 34

In Virginia, Stephanie studied the latest satellite intelligence from Pakistan. The troop buildup on both sides of the border with India had increased since the last overpass. The main concentration of Indian forces was in Kashmir. A drive west from Kashmir would threaten Islamabad. Both sides were moving heavy armor to the border. The largest tank battle since World War II had been fought between Pakistan and India in 1965. Three of the four wars the two nations had fought since the partition of India had begun in Kashmir. History seemed ready to repeat itself. What was different this time was that both sides had nuclear weapons.

Stephanie's computer alerted her to a call from Cobra's encrypted phone. An automatic recording began. She picked up her laptop and went into Elizabeth's office.

"Cobra is making a call."

"Let's hear it," Elizabeth said.

Stephanie pressed a key. The sound of the call being dialed came through the speakers. The tone sounded distant. Atmospherics hissed around it. Someone answered.

"What language is that?" Elizabeth asked.

"Hindi, I think. We'll have Selena listen to it."

It was frustrating to hear and not understand what was being said. The conversation lasted less than a minute before Cobra disconnected.

"There were a couple of words I understood," Elizabeth said. "Afridi and Srinagar."

"I heard them too."

"Where's Selena?"

"Everyone's downstairs," Steph said. "I'll go get them."

She got up and went down the spiral stair to the lower level. The stairs opened onto the ops center. To the left were the computers, given a room of their own. To the right were the gym, the armory and the shooting range. Steph heard gunfire and headed to the right.

Nick, Selena and Lamont stood at separate firing stations, practicing with their pistols. Steph picked up plugs from a bucket near the door and stuck them in her ears. Three Sig .40 caliber pistols firing at once made a lot of noise. All three shooters wore noise canceling ear protectors and tinted shooting glasses.

Steph looked down range. The targets were man sized silhouettes. On all three, neat groups of bullet holes had punched through the head and heart areas. The slide on Nick's pistol locked back and he ejected the magazine. As he reached for another, he saw Steph standing by the entrance. She pointed at the ceiling. He waited until the others finished firing.

"Cease-fire," he said in a loud voice. He took off the ear protectors. Selena and Lamont followed suit.

"Elizabeth wants us upstairs," Steph said. "Cobra used his phone. We need Selena to tell us what he said."

"Secure the weapons," Nick said. "We'll clean them later. Let's go hear what this creep says."

Fresh mags went in the guns from force of habit. An empty gun was no more useful than a baseball and harder to throw. The pistols went into their holsters. Everyone went back upstairs.

When they were settled in front of her desk, Elizabeth played the recording.

"Cobra is talking with a man named Ijay. He's giving him orders," Selena said. She listened to the recording, face tight with concentration. No one interrupted. It came to the end.

"Play it again. I think I've got it but my Hindi is a little rusty."

Stephanie played the recording again.

"Oh, boy," Selena said.

"I think he mentioned Afridi," Elizabeth said.

"He did. He told Ijay, whoever he is, that Afridi is planning to visit a mosque in Srinagar next week. Cobra wants Ijay to kidnap him and take him to a safe house."

"How does he know about the visit?"

"Afridi has a viper in his little terrorist band of brothers. Someone betrayed him."

"Why does Cobra want him?" Nick asked.

"He wants to question him. Then he's going to kill him."

"Mm." Harker picked up her pen. "Tells us something about Cobra. Question Afridi about what? Did he say?"

"He wants to know where Afridi got the gold to support Abu Sayyaf."

"The gold?" Nick said. "Not many people even know about that. Did you get Cobra's name?"

"No," Selena said. "Ijay never mentioned it. Anyone Cobra calls on that phone must know who he is. But I have an idea how we might ID him."

"What do you have in mind?"

"Cobra wants to question Afridi in person. He's going to meet Ijay after he grabs him."

"When?" Nick asked.

Selena smiled. "Three days from now."

"You're thinking we spot Afridi and watch for Cobra to try and grab him."

"Yes."

"Why don't we turn the tables on them?" Lamont said. "When Cobra shows up, we do the grabbing. Him and Afridi too."

"Two for the price of one," Nick said. "I like it. What do you think, Director?"

"It has possibilities," Elizabeth said, "but there are two problems that I can see. Afridi is one of them. Our primary objective is Cobra. Afridi isn't the one who put Ronnie in a hospital. As much as I'd like to get rid of him, he's a secondary target and he's bound to have bodyguards. He'll be at a mosque. You go after him there and you run the risk of setting off a riot. Kashmir is always on edge. The whole area could explode with very little provocation."

Nick said, "You said two problems. What's the other?"

"We have to consider the political implications. All we know about Cobra is that he's high up in India's intelligence agency. What do you think will happen if you grab him and he turns out to be important, like Langley's deputy director?"

"That's easy. The shit will hit the fan."

"It will. And eventually it will all land right here, on us."

Nick threw up his hands in frustration. "So what do you want us to do?"

"I want you to observe what happens between him and Afridi. I want you to get pictures so we can find out who he is. Then I can decide the next step."

"He said he was going to kill Afridi," Selena said.

Elizabeth looked at her and raised an eyebrow. "Your point being?"

"You don't have a problem with that?"

There was a note of surprise in Selena's voice.

"Why should I? Afridi's group has killed hundreds of innocent people. He's a jihadist who wants to establish an Islamic state in Kashmir. He's demonstrated that he'll do anything to achieve that end. Don't forget, the explosives that blew up the embassy and the AK that shot Ronnie were probably purchased with money that came from him."

"I still think we should at least try for Cobra," Nick said. "He wants to know where Afridi got the money and so do we. If we can take him without a problem, we ought to do it. Cobra's gone rogue. He gave up his protection when he set up those attacks in the Philippines."

Harker considered. "What would you do with him?"

"We need a safe house in Srinagar," Nick said. "A nice quiet place where we can ask him a few questions. He doesn't have to know who's doing the asking."

There was a hard quality in his voice that made Selena glad it wasn't her he was talking about.

"There's no time to set that up," Lamont said.

"Lucas could help." The bracelets on Stephanie's wrist made tiny metallic sounds as she twisted them.

Lucas Monroe worked for the Director of the CIA and was Stephanie's lover. If Langley had a safe house in Srinagar, Lucas could find out where it was. Elizabeth had a good relationship with DCI Clarence Hood. Revealing the safe house location would require his okay. He didn't have to know exactly why she needed the house. In fact, he would probably prefer not to know. Elizabeth made a decision.

"That's a good idea, Steph. You talk with Lucas and I'll call Hood. I'd be surprised if Langley doesn't have a safe location over there."

"Then it's a go," Nick said.

Elizabeth nodded. "Be careful, Nick. Don't create a problem for us. If you succeed in getting Cobra, try not to hurt him."

"What about transportation?"

"I'll get you a Gulfstream. You can take weapons and fly right into Srinagar."

"What's our cover when the Indians want to know what we're doing there?" Lamont asked.

Elizabeth thought for a moment. "We could use the film company ploy."

"Cool," Lamont said. "I always wanted to be in movies."

CHAPTER 35

Hood gave them use of a CIA safe house in
Srinagar. The team would pose as a Canadian film
company making a PBS documentary about
Kashmir. Their Canadian passports were real. The
names on the passports were not.

Their ride was a Gulfstream V, courtesy of a
DEA seizure from one of the Colombian drug
cartels. The interior of the plane was decorated with
hand-painted murals of happy workers harvesting
coca leaves under a sunny sky. Dominating the
forward bulkhead was a panel picturing a stocky
man with a white shirt and a black mustache. He
had a broad smile, large square teeth and black eyes
that reminded Nick of a snake. He stood next to a
silver Bentley parked in front of a palatial mansion,
handing out candy to a flock of excited children.
Nick figured it was a portrait of the plane's previous
owner.

It was a big plane for just three passengers, but
it had the range and speed they needed. Inside, it
was like a luxury hotel. The seats were wide and
comfortable. There were beds in the rear cabin. The
center cabin sported a dining table, couch and bar.
Polished rosewood accents were everywhere.

They took seats in the front cabin. The flight
plan called for refueling in Anchorage and then a
direct shot over the North Pole. Arrival in Srinagar
was set for some time the next afternoon.

Two hours into the flight, Lamont headed to the
back of the plane and lay down on one of the
comfortable beds. In a little while, they heard him
snoring.

Selena sat next to Nick. She was doing her best to read an article about the Mongolian language in the time of Genghis Khan but her mind kept wandering. A lot had changed over the past months. Before joining the Project she would have found the paper stimulating. Not today, though. Today the paper seemed to her as dead as the great Khan. She found herself looking at the painting on the cockpit bulkhead, where the mustachioed drug lord leered at her.

"That man's picture gives me the creeps," she said.

"Not exactly Santa Claus, is he?" Nick said.

"I wonder what happened to him?"

"*El Patron* used to run one of the big cartels down in Columbia."

"Used to?"

"One of his rivals put a bomb under that fancy car."

"Whoever it was, I think they did everyone a favor," she said.

Nick looked out the window. There was nothing to see but an ocean of cloud passing beneath them. His mind drifted with the drone of the engines. He thought about Selena. Both of them had been keeping away from talk about marriage. The more they avoided the subject, the more it occupied his mind. He was tired of thinking about it.

"How do you think it's going to play out?" she asked.

"Are you talking about Cobra?"

"What else would I be talking about?"

"I can think of several things," Nick said. "The conversation we haven't been having, for one."

"Which conversation is that?"

"How many of them are there?"

"I don't know, why don't you tell me?"

Nick felt himself starting to get angry. Why couldn't she just give him a straight answer?

"Damn it, Selena. You know which one. The one about how we are or we aren't engaged."

"Oh. That one."

"Yes, that one."

"When I asked how you thought it was going to play out, I was thinking about Srinagar," she said. "But since you brought up the *other* conversation, I suppose we can talk about that."

Nick's face closed down. Selena knew she was being bitchy. She could feel the urge to start an argument with him. They hadn't talked about getting married since it came up in their hotel room in Manila. They'd left it hanging. Then Ronnie had been wounded and she'd gotten angry at Nick in the hospital. Since then Nick had been keeping to himself in his apartment. Most of the time they only saw each other at work.

Damn it, she thought, *why do I always end up in this place when I think about getting married to him?*

She loved him. But that day in the jewelry store she'd backed off, fast. She still hadn't figured out why she was pushing him away. It was as if something was knocking on a door inside her mind, demanding attention. She didn't want to open the door.

She took a deep breath. "I'm sorry. I don't know why I said that."

"Why did you say yes when we were on that island? Since then it seems like you really meant no."

She heard a new tone of resignation in his voice. It made her uneasy.

"I said yes because it seemed right."

"So what changed? It sounds like you don't think it's right anymore."

"No, I don't think that," she said. "I mean, I still think it's right. Something keeps getting in the way, but I'm not sure what it is. We talked about one of us getting killed, but I don't think that's it, not anymore. I don't know."

"It feels like you're always trying to pick a fight," he said.

Selena decided to say nothing.

"You have to stop doing that," he said. "I really hate it."

She started to get angry again. Who the hell was he to tell her that she had to do anything?

"I think that can be arranged."

Selena got up and moved to an empty seat across the aisle and began reading her article. She couldn't concentrate. After a few minutes she gave up pretending to read and stared out the window.

A half hour before they were due to land in Anchorage, Lamont emerged from the rear of the plane yawning and stretching. He looked at Nick and Selena sitting apart. The feeling of tension in the cabin was like a cloud.

"What did I miss?" he said.

CHAPTER 36

Lohendra Bhagati's job was to watch people. He'd been in the national police before being recruited by India's intelligence agency. He was a fervent nationalist, a factor that weighed heavily in favor of his selection. What had ensured it was an eidetic memory for faces. Once Bhagati saw a face, he never forgot it. He'd spent endless hours reviewing photographs and film of every person in RAW's database that might pose a threat of any kind to mother India. That included terrorists like Abdul Afridi. It also included pictures of known intelligence agents from other countries. Bhagati's boss reported to Ashok Rao.

Bhagati sat at a small metal table at a tea stall in the Srinagar airport and watched people coming out of the secured area. It was a boring job but the strong, black tea helped keep him alert.

Three foreigners came into view, pushing a cart filled with black equipment boxes. Two men, one black and one white, accompanied by a tall woman with reddish blond hair and unusual violet eyes. The white man was about six feet tall, muscular, with short black hair and intense gray eyes. The other man was smaller, wiry and tense. A distinctive scar marked his face.

The woman and black man were unfamiliar. The third man triggered the part of Bhagati's mind that remembered people he'd seen but never met. Within seconds he had it.

Nicholas Carter, Bhagati thought. *He was the one in Jerusalem, with their president. He works for an American intelligence unit.*

A few years before, Carter had been caught on live television protecting the U.S. president during an assassination attempt. The event had been seen worldwide. The two people with him must also be spies, probably part of the same unit. Why were they here, in Kashmir?

Bhagati got up from the table and followed them through the airport. They stopped at an automobile rental counter. The woman talked to the agent behind the counter while the other two waited. She finished the transaction and all three headed for the rental parking lot. Bhagati watched them go.

When they'd left the terminal building, Bhagati walked over to the rental agent and showed his identification. She looked nervous. People tended to do that when they saw the wreath and three headed lion on Bhagati's credentials that identified him as an agent of the Research and Analysis Wing.

"The foreign woman who was just here, the American. What vehicle did she take?"

"You mean the Canadian woman?"

"Canadian?"

"Yes." The clerk showed him the rental agreement. It was with Sarah Thompson of Toronto. Payment had been with a Visa card.

"She's part of a film crew. They rented a van, a blue Toyota."

"I'll take this," Bhagati said. He folded the paper and put it in his jacket pocket.

"We're supposed to keep that," she said. "What do I tell my manager?"

"Tell him to keep his mouth shut about it," Bhagati said. "That goes for you, too. Understand?"

The clerk looked in Bhagati's eyes and nodded.

Bhagati walked away from the counter and took out his phone. His boss would want to know about this.

Nick and the others walked through the terminal building toward the exit for the rental car area, pushing the equipment boxes in a rented luggage cart. The atmosphere in the terminal wasn't reassuring. Srinagar airport was considered a prime terrorist target and the rhetoric between Pakistan and India was becoming more heated every day. Soldiers in full battle dress were stationed at regular intervals around the terminal, armed with automatic weapons.

"What's that they're carrying?" Lamont asked. "Looks nasty."

Nick waited until they were past one of the soldiers before he answered.

"Those are Kalantaks, the lightweight version of their INAS assault rifle," Nick said. "Used for close quarter combat. It takes the 5.56 NATO round. These guys must be from one of their elite units."

"Seems like there are quite a few of them," Selena said.

"The way things are heating up between India and Pakistan, I'm not surprised. This airport is new. It's supposed to be a showcase for progress and development. That makes it a good target, along with the crowds of people."

They found their rental and loaded the gear. The truck was well used but it had a brand new, large screen GPS on the dash.

"Who's driving?" Selena said.

They pulled out of the airport with Selena behind the wheel.

CHAPTER 37

Stephanie came into Elizabeth's office.

"Cobra just called his man, Ijay. He knows Nick and the others are in Srinagar. Their cover's blown."

Elizabeth had been reviewing a CRITIC brief destined for the president's desk. She set it down, took off the glasses she used for reading and rubbed the bridge of her nose.

"That didn't take long. It might even be a record. How did he find out?"

"Nick and the others were spotted coming through the airport. Cobra is still in New Delhi. He told Ijay to put eyes on their van."

"There's more, isn't there?" Elizabeth said.

Stephanie nodded. "Cobra wants Ijay to neutralize the team. That was the exact word. Neutralize."

"Mm. Anything else?"

"Cobra's not coming to Srinagar until Ijay has Afridi. He wants Nick and the others out of the way before that. He told Ijay to take care of things right away."

"What did Ijay say?"

"That his leopards were ready."

"Leopards?"

Stephanie shrugged. "That's what he said."

Elizabeth had a brief mental picture of a half dozen leopards leaping out at the team, snarling, claws extended, tails twitching.

"It has to be a code name," Stephanie said.

"Or a unit designation. Steph, see if you can find a reference to an Indian unit with that name or nickname. We don't know who Cobra is but perhaps we can find out who he's talking to. When is Cobra going to be there?"

"He didn't say, but it has to be soon. We have to give Nick a heads up."

"I'll do it now."

Elizabeth touched a button on her desk. The satellite call would come over the speakers in the room. They heard Nick pick up.

"Yes, Director."

The connection was poor, distorted by atmospherics and static. It sounded like they were in a vehicle.

"Where are you, Nick?"

"In a rental van that smells like curry, headed for the safe house."

"Cobra knows you're in Srinagar."

"How?"

"You were seen at the airport. It tells us that Cobra has a network of agents out there. That might help us narrow down who he is. Meanwhile, we have a problem. Remember, he was talking to a man called Ijay?"

"Yes."

"Ijay is in Srinagar. Cobra told him to neutralize you."

"Neuter me?" The speaker crackled.

Stephanie snorted, suppressed a laugh.

"Neutralize, Nick, neutralize. Ijay told Cobra he'd use his leopards, whoever they are. He intends to take the three of you out. Permanently."

"Is Cobra in Srinagar?" Nick asked.

"Not yet. He wants Ijay to take care of you before he gets there."

"If they spotted us at the airport, they probably know what we're driving."

"How far away are you from the safe house?"

"Hard to say. The traffic's lousy and it's on the other side of Lake Dal."

Selena was driving. A gravel truck coming in the opposite direction pulled out into her lane, passing a slow-moving car. The truck was painted in psychedelic red, yellow and orange colors. The gigantic chrome grill was wreathed in garlands of artificial flowers. A fringe of colored, knitted balls dangled inside the cab across the top of the windshield. BABA GANESH was painted across the bumper and the top of the cab in yellow letters a foot high.

The truck bore down on them. Selena could see the driver's face through the mud splattered windshield, grim and determined. His horn bellowed. The windows of the van shook from the sound.

"Shit," Lamont said.

Nick gripped the phone, his eyes riveted on the oncoming truck. Selena yanked the wheel. The van veered onto the narrow shoulder, where a deep ditch paralleled the road. The wheels of the van rode the crumbling edge of the ditch. The truck roared by, horn blasting, taking her side mirror with it. Selena steered back onto the pavement. She clenched the wheel, her knuckles white.

Nick let out a long breath.

"Crazy bastard," Lamont said.

"Nick? Are you still there?" Elizabeth's voice. "What was that sound?"

"Yeah. Still here. Barely."

"What happened?"

"Never mind, it's not important."

"It was only a few minutes ago when Cobra called," Elizabeth said. "Ijay won't have had time

yet to mount an operation against you. You should
be able to get where you're going before anything
happens."

"I'm glad to hear it."

"Call me when you reach the safe house."

"Roger that." Nick broke the connection.

In Virginia, Elizabeth turned to Stephanie.

"Let's talk about Afridi. Cobra said he was
coming to Srinagar because he wanted to visit a
mosque. Which mosque? Why would he do that and
why now?"

Stephanie said, "I think I know. There's an
important mosque in Srinagar that has a relic of
Mohammed. It's locked up most of the time, except
for a few days a year when they bring it out for
viewing. The next time it can be seen is tomorrow.
We know Afridi is a true believer. I think he's
making a pilgrimage to see the relic. For him, it
would be an act of devotion. Why else would he put
himself at such high risk?"

"That makes sense," Elizabeth said. "If he's
going to be at the mosque, Ijay will be there looking
for him."

"Cobra said something else but I don't know
what he meant."

"What's that?"

"He said that everything was set with the
Army."

"That doesn't sound good, whatever it means,"
Elizabeth said.

"If I'm right, at least we know where Ijay will
be and when." Steph brushed away a fly. The
bracelets on her left wrist jingled.

"Good work," Elizabeth said. "That will help
Nick."

"He's going to need all the help he can get."

"If we can identify Ijay, we might be able to pinpoint Cobra. See if you can find out about those leopards."

"I'm on it." Steph headed for her office.

An hour and twenty minutes later in Kashmir, Selena drove the van along a narrow track that ended at the lake and the agency safe house. They got out and looked at their temporary home.

"This is it?" Lamont said. "Hell, makes me feel right at home."

The safe house was a flat roofed houseboat made of dark wood. It was pulled up onto the northern shore of Lake Dal in a secluded cove. The hull rested on two thick timbers with curved ends. An ornately carved wooden railing ran around the deck. A second railing paralleled it along the roof line. There was a large water tank on the roof. Tall, arched windows lined the sides. The boat was large, sixty feet long or better. At one time it had been painted in bright colors but that had been long ago. The paint was peeling and the boat looked in need of repair.

"I don't think I'd want to be out on the lake with that if a big storm blew in," Selena said. She looked up at the sky. It was dark and overcast. The air smelled of rain.

Lamont looked at the boat and shook his head. "Safe house. Only Langley could come up with this."

"Think of it as your tax dollars at work," Nick said.

He picked up his travel bag and climbed a sagging set of stairs onto the porch by the entrance.

"Let me guess," Lamont said. "The key's under the flowerpot."

"You're almost right."

Nick took a rusted skeleton key from under a wooden carving on the railing. He unlocked the door and stepped through into a narrow passage. The air smelled of damp and mold. Doors on either side opened into four small rooms. The passage ended in a large living area that took up the rest of the interior space.

Selena saw something scuttle away out of sight as she walked into the room. A small galley was set to the side with a gas stove, a sink and a propane powered refrigerator. The end of the boat featured a door and two wide, latticed windows that looked out over Lake Dal. Snowcapped mountains ringed the lake.

Selena went to the sink and turned on a tap. There was a gurgling noise and thick, brown liquid ran out of the faucet.

"I guess they don't have much use for a safe house out this way. Not exactly the Hilton." She turned off the tap.

"Yeah, but it's got a nice view," Lamont said.

"I think there are rats in here," Selena said.

"What about the stuff in the van?" Lamont asked

Nick said, "Get the guns and leave the rest where it is."

"You think this guy Ijay knows where we are?"

"Whether he does or not, we need to be ready for him."

Mist began rising from the surface of Lake Dal, turning the lights of Srinagar on the far shore into a soft glow.

CHAPTER 38

President James Rice sat behind Teddy
Roosevelt's desk in the Oval Office, meeting with
General Holden from the Joint Chiefs and the
Secretary of State, Edgar Silverby. Tension was
escalating between Pakistan and India. An
emergency session of the UN Security Council was
set for the next day.

Outside the bullet proof windows of the Oval
Office, the day shone with the luminous quality of
fall. Rice wished he was home in Vermont, with
nothing more important to do than rake leaves and
watch the colors turn.

Public anger over the embassy attack was
running high and Rice was under a lot of pressure to
do something about it. What he was supposed to do
or how he was supposed to do it was conveniently
left unsaid. Politically speaking, the situation was
more toxic than Chernobyl.

The media was having a field day fanning the
outrage. The hawks in the Senate wanted the White
House to send advisors and advanced missile
defense systems to India. They were pushing for
drone strikes against Pakistan as an initial statement
of American anger. Even the doves were screaming
for tough sanctions.

While the politicians postured for their
constituents, the situation between India and
Pakistan continued to deteriorate. There had been
clashes along the border with Kashmir and
casualties on both sides. What had happened at the
American Embassy was no longer Rice's biggest

concern. The events in Manila were overshadowed by a larger danger.

"Just spit it out, general," Rice said. "Are they, or are they not going to war?"

"It's hard to say, sir. But in my opinion, yes, they are. The troop buildups along the border are significant."

Rice turned to Silverby. "What do you think, Ed? Is there any hope of a diplomatic solution?"

"I hate to say it but I don't think so, Mister President. I agree with General Holden. New Delhi and Islamabad have recalled their ambassadors and broken off relations. I'm getting stonewalled by both sides. Pakistan's Foreign Minister warned me that there could be an unfortunate escalation in terrorist activities if we help India."

Rice suppressed his anger. "He actually said that?"

"Yes, Mister President."

"The man is an idiot if he thinks threatening us is going to make any difference. At least we know where they stand. What about the U.N. emergency meeting?"

Silverby made a dismissive gesture. "We have to go through the motions but it's a waste of time. It's not going to affect anything unless Pakistan admits responsibility for the attacks and offers reparations. You can be certain that's not going to happen. Russia will block any of our initiatives. On the bright side, we might have support from China for a change. They don't like what's happening."

Holden cleared his throat. "Mister President, there is a potentially serious complication. India has modified their latest ICBM to deploy multiple reentry warheads. It's called the Agni VI."

"India has MIRVS? When did this happen?"

"They've been working on it for several years. The latest intelligence indicates that several of the new missiles are ready to go into service."

"Does that mean they are not yet on line?"

"We're not certain, sir. What makes a bad situation worse is that the Agni VI is fired from a portable launcher. Launch time is almost nothing. The multiple warheads tilt the balance of power in India's favor. It gives them the potential to knock out the Pakis before they can get off a shot."

Rice looked at General Holden with concern. "Pakistan is one of the most paranoid countries in the world," he said. "If they think India is going to deploy that missile, it could provoke a first strike."

"Sir, we are maintaining 24/7 surveillance on the missile facilities in both countries," Holden said. "We know the location of the new Indian missiles. If they bring them out of their tunnels, we'll know about it. Once they do that, if they do that, they could launch within minutes. Pakistan has its own satellite surveillance and I'd be surprised if they didn't have an eye on the site. They'll see the same thing we do. I think if those missiles come into the open, we're looking at nuclear war on the subcontinent."

Holden's words hung heavy in the air.

Rice steepled his hands together. "What is your recommendation, General?"

"Mister President, this is a very volatile situation. I recommend we go to DEFCON 2 immediately. DEFCON 3 for our units in the Asian region."

"That will escalate tensions in the area," Rice said.

"Yes, sir, but raising the defense condition level now saves valuable time if it becomes necessary to go further. If war begins, it will happen very quickly."

"Sir, I think a higher state of readiness for our forces in the area would be expected," Silverby said. "It's no secret that this latest showdown holds the potential for nuclear confrontation. China is as worried about this as we are. After all, it's happening on their doorstep."

Holden nodded agreement. "There are signs of military preparations on the Chinese side of the border. They're worried, all right. The Agni VI is highly sophisticated but some of India's older missiles aren't very accurate. It wouldn't take much for one of them to end up in China if they fire them at Pakistan."

Rice turned to his Secretary of State. "Ed, I want you to get on the horn with the Chinese Foreign Minister and work out a mutually acceptable position to present at the U.N. Emphasize that we're willing to cooperate with Beijing to keep this from escalating. The Russians have been supplying heavy weapons to India that we wouldn't sell them, so however you word it, try not to piss them off. Run it by me when you've worked it out."

"Yes, Mister President."

"General, go ahead and implement your recommendations for DEFCON status. Inform the rest of the Chiefs that I want a meeting tonight at 2100 in the situation room. I want to see alternate scenarios for our military response in the event things get out of hand."

"Yes, sir."

Rice stood. Holden and Silverby rose with him.

"Thank you, gentlemen."

When they were gone, Rice walked over and looked out over the White House lawn. The Secret Service didn't like him doing that, even with the bullet proof windows. Rice absentmindedly rubbed his chest, where he'd taken a bullet during the last assassination attempt.

Rice held the record for assassination attempts on American presidents. Everyone who made it to the Oval Office faced the threat of assassination. Plots were uncovered and stopped on a daily basis. Most of them amounted to nothing, idle threats, drunken plans, the ramblings of men with a grudge to bear. But with Rice there had been four near misses. All of them had scarred him in some way.

He'd come into office hoping he could do good for the country. Instead, he'd spent most of his time dealing with problems caused by men seeking power and wealth or by fanatics who believed God had given them a mission to conquer the world and destroy the United States.

Rice was worried about what was happening on the subcontinent. Pakistan and India had already fought four wars and the hatred between them was virulent and deep. Horrific atrocities between Hindus and Muslims had scarred the collective soul of the two nations for centuries. It was an unbridgeable chasm, exploited by religious leaders and opportunistic politicians on both sides. Rice thought there was a good chance a war would go nuclear.

He was supposed to be the most powerful leader in the world, but he was helpless to do much about nuclear weapons in the hands of people driven by ego and religious dogma.

Sometimes power was little more than an illusion.

CHAPTER 39

"What's the plan?" Lamont said.

The three of them huddled around a glowing heater fed by a large propane tank. Outside the houseboat, it was cold and dark. Heavy fog had drifted in off the lake soon after the sun disappeared behind the mountains. The fog sucked up sound and light. It felt as though the world was rolled up in a thick, wet sock.

"We have to assume Cobra's guy is coming after us," Nick said.

"Ijay," Selena said, "and his leopards."

"Right. We don't know how many he has in his zoo but I doubt that it's more than a half-dozen at the most."

"He has to find us first," Lamont said.

"I don't think that's going to be a problem for him. For one thing, that van has a GPS that lets the rental company know where it is. All he has to do is tie into that and he'll know exactly where we are. Here."

"So much for this being a safe house," Selena said. "We should just go back into town and rent a hotel room. Somewhere with hot water and a bed and no rats."

"For now, this is perfect," Nick said. "We're isolated, away from the city. It's darker than the inside of the devil's closet out there, there's no one nearby and the fog will muffle any noise. It's a lot easier to deal with a problem here than in the middle of town where there are cops and witnesses."

"You want to set a trap for him?" Selena asked.

"That's exactly what I want to do. Ijay has no reason to think we know he's coming. He won't expect us to be waiting for him."

"When do you think he'll come?" Lamont said.

"If I were him, I'd wait until later. After midnight for sure. By then we'd probably be asleep."

"Since we have nothing to worry about because no one knows we're here," Selena said.

"That's right."

"Gonna be a problem for them to see the boat in this stuff," Lamont said.

"We'll leave a light on for them," Nick said.

CHAPTER 40

Ijay stood next to a tree, motionless in the fog. Drops of condensation formed on his armored vest. His breath misted in the night air, blending seamlessly with the fog. Anyone seeing him might have thought he was part of the tree. He was dressed all in black. He wore a black ski mask over his face. The skin around his eyes was darkened with camouflage paint. He'd brought four of his team with him, now hidden in the fog.

Everyone was in position. He'd go in the front with two of his men. If the Americans tried to retreat out the back toward the lake, the other two would cut them down.

The houseboat was no more than a black shape in the swirling darkness. A dim light showed through one of the windows. The soft lapping of shallow waves on the shore and the smell of decaying vegetation on the beach were the only indication of the lake, invisible in the night. Every sound was muffled by the fog.

Ijay smiled to himself. There were only three of them, these American spies. Careless spies. The light in the window showed they were unaware of their danger. By the time they realized what was happening, it would be over. He flicked the safety off on his silenced MSMC.

Ijay liked the weapon. It was Indian made, based on the Israeli Uzi. It had been designed to overcome the failures of the INAS carbine carried by the regular forces. It took a 5.56 X 30mm cartridge and put out over 700 rounds a minute. You didn't want to be in front of it when it went off.

He gave the signal to move in. His men mounted the steps in single file, silent as their leopard namesake. They took up position on each side of the door at the end of the boat. Ijay followed them onto the porch. The first man's name was Arjuna, named for the hero of the Bhagavad-Gita. Arjuna eased up the latch on the door. It lifted with a dull click. He looked a question at Ijay, who nodded.

Arjuna opened the door, making no sound. He moved into the dark interior, his finger on the trigger, followed by the second man. Ijay brought up the rear. A glow of light showed at the end of the hall. There was a faint smell of propane in the air. In the darkness at his feet, Arjuna didn't see a thin wire stretched at ankle height across the passage. He tripped on the wire.

On the other side of the flimsy wall separating one of the bedrooms from the hallway, there was a bright arc of electricity. Lamont had left the valve on the propane tank open and rigged a detonator. Gas filling the room ignited and exploded.

Arjuna was engulfed in a hellish blue ball of flame. The force of the blast smashed the second man to the side and threw Ijay backward through the open door and off the porch. His clothes were on fire. He tore the burning mask off his face and rolled on the ground, back and forth until the flames were out.

The explosion had blown a hole through the roof of the houseboat. Fresh air rushed in and fed the flames consuming the old, dry wood. The fire roared out into the night and shot upward in a blazing column. The fog turned red and yellow with reflected light.

Ijay scrambled to his feet, stunned, trying to make sense of what had just happened. His weapon was somewhere inside the inferno, ripped out of his hands by the blast. He heard shouts and pistol shots at the other end of the houseboat. There was a short, quiet stutter of machine gun fire, then more shots.

Silence in his earpiece.

If his men were still alive, they'd be talking to him. He felt the beginnings of rage but pushed it down. Now wasn't the time. He'd made a mistake with these Americans. He'd underestimated them. It wouldn't happen again.

Ijay backed away into the fog, turned and ran.

Nick and Selena skirted the blazing houseboat and met Lamont at the van.

"I think one of them got away," Lamont said.

"That IED of yours worked like a champ," Nick said, "but it started a hell of a fire."

The houseboat was engulfed in flame. The big timbers underneath the boat began to burn. The fire roared and crackled and clawed at the air. They backed away from the heat.

"I need to talk with Harker," Nick said.

Nick touched the transmitter in his ear. "Director, you copy?"

"Copy, Nick. Go ahead."

Her voice was clear and strong. *Satellite must be right overhead*, Nick thought.

"We have a problem. Cobra's team tried to take us out."

"Are you all right?"

"Yeah."

"What's the problem?"

"We're fine but Langley is going to need another safe house. All this one is good for is toasting marshmallows."

"There's a fire?"

The remains of the burning roof folded inward and collapsed, sending a fiery column of sparks into the air. Nick watched the flames rise into the night.

"You could say that. One of them got away."

"All right," Elizabeth said. "Nothing's changed. We still need Cobra if you can get him. Find a place to stay."

"Roger that. Out."

"What now?" Selena said.

"Now we look for a hotel and get some sleep."

"You're not worried about Cobra finding us?"

"He already did. They're not going to try anything else tonight. There's no point in keeping out of sight now that Cobra knows who we are. Afridi will be at that mosque tomorrow and we're going to be there looking for him. Now we need to get out of here before somebody gets curious about this fire."

They got into the van, turned around and bumped out the dirt track until they came to the highway. Behind them, all that could be seen of the burning houseboat was a deep, orange glow in the fog.

Selena drove, remembering a hotel they'd driven by in Srinagar that might do. She really wanted a shower. Her mind went back to the lake and the firefight, a brief, surreal moment of utter violence. Wrapped in the fog, it had been like shooting at black ghosts in a dream world where nothing was real. It was real enough, though. She'd seen her bullets take down one of the black figures. With a start, she realized she was more concerned with finding a hotel with hot water and a soft bed then she was about the man she'd just killed.

She wasn't sure what that said about her.
Whatever it was, she didn't much like it.

CHAPTER 41

Abdul Afridi and Ibrahim Sayeed were just two more bearded men wearing turbans and robes in a crowd of thousands. The high dome and graceful minaret of the Hazratbal Mosque stood silhouetted against snowcapped mountains and a storm lit sky filled with dark clouds.

All eyes were turned toward a high balcony, where the chief cleric of the mosque would emerge with the relic of the Prophet. The crowd was silent, waiting for the moment. A sudden burst of sunlight struck the white marble building with translucent light, just as a bearded man wearing a white turban and dressed in a black robe embroidered with gold appeared on the balcony. For Afridi, it was a sign God was pleased with this gathering of His followers.

A vast, collective sigh rose from the crowd. The cleric paused for effect, then held up a tapered crystal and silver container in his right hand. A green, woven cord attached to the container wrapped around his little finger. Two silver and green enamel teardrop shapes scribed with holy scripture trailed from the cord.

Afridi held up his open hands toward the relic and prayed for Allah's blessing. Next to him, Sayeed's eyes moved constantly, searching the crowd for potential threats.

Nick had parked some distance away on the main access road leading toward the mosque. He scanned the crowd through binoculars. A picture of their quarry was pinned to the dash.

"This is impossible," he said. "We'll never be able to pick Afridi out in the middle of that. He could be anybody."

"Let's think about it," Selena said. "Afridi is somewhere in that crowd right now. If Ijay wasn't killed last night, he'll be here somewhere. But I don't think he'll try anything with all these people around."

"No, I don't think he would."

"That means he'll wait until Afridi leaves and try to get him somewhere else."

"Makes sense," Nick said.

"If you were Afridi, would you put yourself in the middle of all that?" Lamont asked.

"I hate crowds," Nick said. "I'm the wrong guy to ask."

"If I were him, I'd hang out on the edge where I could get away fast. He'll probably be one of the first to leave. That's our best chance to spot him."

Nick panned the binoculars past the crowd and adjusted the focus. Beyond the mosque was a wide, barren area with a few houses.

"Trouble," he said. "A convoy of army trucks just pulled up. Soldiers are getting out." He paused. "They're in full battle dress."

"Armed?" Lamont asked.

"Take a look." Nick handed him the binoculars.

"Assault rifles," Lamont said. "They're forming up. Looks like two or three hundred men. That's a lot of firepower."

Nick's ear began itching. He reached up to scratch it. "I've got a bad feeling about this. The crowd's peaceful. Why bring in the military?"

"They're advancing toward the crowd," Lamont said.

Nick was behind the wheel. They were facing
the mosque. He looked in the rearview mirror and
saw more troops approaching.

"Time to boogie, boys and girls. This is going
bad, fast." He started the van and turned around,
ready to drive away.

"Too late," Selena said.

An officer broke away from the troops coming
up the road. He held up his hand and signaled them
to the side. Nick pulled over. He left the engine
running and rolled down his window.

"You are in a restricted zone. What are you
doing here?" the officer said. His voice was
unfriendly.

"I didn't know we weren't supposed to be here,"
Nick said. "We're making a documentary film about
Srinagar."

"Where are your cameras?"

"In the back. We were getting set to film the
crowd and the mosque. Waiting for the light to be
right."

The soldiers moved past the van. They looked
determined. Their assault rifles were held in the
ready position. Nick saw that the safeties were off.

"You took no pictures?"

"No."

"Filming is not permitted here. You will leave
immediately." He put his hand on his holstered
pistol.

"Nick, let's go finish that segment about the
antiques market," Selena said.

"Listen to the woman," the Indian officer said.
"Leave. Don't come back here."

Nick didn't like his tone. He was about to say
something when Selena gripped his arm, hard. She

shook her head. He put the van in gear and began to move away.

Lamont watched the mosque recede in the side mirror. "They're closing on the crowd," he said.

Everyone was looking at the relic. The cleric suddenly looked out past the crowd. Sayeed turned to see what he was looking at and saw the line of soldiers. He put his hand on Afridi's shoulder.

"Abdul."

Afridi turned, annoyed, his prayers interrupted.

"Soldiers," Sayeed said, his voice quiet.

Afridi looked at the soldiers advancing in a tight line, weapons at port arms.

"Dogs," he hissed. His face was angry.

"When they reach the crowd there will be panic," Sayeed said. "That will be our best chance to escape."

He slipped a long dagger from his sleeve and held it down by his side in his right hand. Afridi nodded and drew his own. Allah would forgive the shedding of blood at this holy site. It was permitted in defense of the faith against the infidel. Whatever happened here today, it was on the heads of these Indian vermin.

The soldiers were almost upon the worshipers. Voices rose in alarm. People started to turn around. With no warning, the soldiers attacked. They used their rifles as clubs, striking out at anyone in their path, driving viciously into the crowd. Afridi saw an old man go down, blood gushing from his forehead. He heard screams from the other side of the compound, where the women had gathered separately from the men.

"Abdul," Sayeed said, "over there."

The formation began to break up as the soldiers plunged into the crowd. A small gap appeared in the line and Afridi and Sayeed started for the opening. They pushed against the current of people trying to get away.

A shot sounded, flat and harsh, echoing from the marble walls of the mosque. A low moan swept through the crowd. For an instant, there was silence. Then someone shouted in a voice filled with rage and anguish.

"Allahu Akbar! Allahu Akbar!" God is Great!

Words that had echoed over the centuries. Words that had soaked a quarter of the earth in blood.

The mob awoke. Thousands of voices took up the cry. In seconds, the lawn in front of the mosque turned into a churning mass of people. Soldiers began to go down under a storm of kicks and curses as the crowd surged forward. More shots were fired. The sound grew into a constant, rippling crackle.

Afridi and Sayeed were surrounded by panicked and angry men. Two soldiers blocked Afridi's way. He ran his knife into the stomach of one and ripped upward. Bright red blood gushed out and the man screamed. Sayeed's dagger flashed in the sunlight and another Indian fell. Then the two men were through the line and running for their lives.

Nick turned off the exit road and started back into the city. Trucks filled with police sped past them, sirens blaring. Lamont was in the back of the van, watching through the binoculars.

"The soldiers are firing into the crowd," he said. "It's a massacre."

"Whoever sent them in has got a lot of explaining to do," Selena said.

"Why do that?" Lamont asked. "Those people weren't hurting anybody."

"It's a deliberate provocation." Nick swerved to avoid a man on a bicycle. "How do you think this will go down in Pakistan? Indian troops attacking unarmed Muslim worshipers?"

"Maybe Cobra's behind it," Lamont said.

"If he wants a war, he's got it. It can't be stopped after this. The only question is whether or not it goes nuclear."

"Why would he think India could win a nuclear war?" Selena asked. "It's crazy."

"People like him think they're smart enough to control the outcome," Nick said. "They never think the missiles will fall on them. Or else they think they've figured out how to survive and that means they win."

"What if Cobra isn't motivated by winning?" Selena said.

"What else would it be?"

"Hate. Revenge. Religion. Love."

"How do you get love in there?" Lamont asked.

"Shakespeare did it all the time. Love and hate are just flip sides of the same feeling."

Nick thought about what she had just said. If you didn't care about winning, you had nothing to lose. An enemy with nothing to lose was the most dangerous kind of opponent. An enemy with nothing to lose who wanted a nuclear war and the ability to make it happen was a nightmare.

More trucks filled with troops sped past them, heading toward the mosque.

"What's our next move?" Lamont said.

"Time to bring Harker up to date and see what she wants us to do."

Nick touched the transceiver in his ear. "Director, you copy?"

"Copy, Nick. Go ahead."

"Things are going south over here."

He told her about the attack at the mosque.

"Any sign of Afridi or Cobra?" Elizabeth said.

"Negative."

"Where are you now?"

"Heading back to our hotel."

"This changes everything," Harker said. "It makes war between Pakistan and India a certainty."

"I thought the same thing."

"Keep trying to find Afridi."

"We need more Intel or we'll never find him."

"I'll see what I can do," Elizabeth said. "Be ready to get out of there in case things start to heat up."

"I think they already have," Nick said.

CHAPTER 42

The threat of war had sent tourists and businessmen packing, leaving a glut of rooms in Srinagar. The hotel they'd settled on was nearly empty. They had the entire top floor to themselves.

Selena stepped from the shower and began drying off. She wrapped a towel around her hair and walked across her room to the window, leaving damp footprints on the wood floor. It was raining, a steady, depressing rain that fell from skies thick with gray cloud. Selena looked out over Lake Dal and watched the rain.

Nick and Lamont were in rooms to either side of hers. She didn't feel like dealing with her feelings about Nick right now. They were all tired and separate rooms had seemed like a good idea. Nick hadn't argued about it. She was grateful for that. At the same time, it made her feel sad.

There was a soft noise behind her. She turned her head in time to see a silent, dark shape coming at her. There was a gleam of steel in his left hand. He wore a black ski mask. She could see his eyes, black pupils wide, intent on murder.

Years of Korean martial arts training and conditioned reflexes took over. She spun and blocked the knife thrust and kicked out. The blow landed off-center. Her attacker stumbled and recovered. He turned and came at her again. She pulled the towel from her hair and whipped it around his arm, pivoted and pulled him past. The knife sliced along her ribs under her breast as he went by, a sharp clean pain. The front of her body was suddenly slick with blood.

She held onto the end of the towel and jerked hard and leapt into the air. She struck him in the chest with one of her feet. Something cracked. He grunted and staggered back. She landed and pulled down and around and back, twisting his arm into an impossible angle. The shoulder joint gave way and he let out a muffled scream of pain. The knife clattered across the floor. She pivoted to land a kick to his spine and slipped in her blood on the polished floor.

She landed hard on her hip. Pain shot down her leg. Her attacker scrambled for the knife and she swung her leg and tripped him. He landed on his back. She rolled and brought the hard edge of her rigid hand down on his throat. A choking, gurgling noise came from his mouth. Blood ran over his lips.

She rolled away and got to her feet, breathing hard, and watched him die.

A fist pounded on the door.

"Selena. Selena, open up." Nick's voice.

She went to the door and unlocked it.

Nick and Lamont were in the hallway. Nick saw the blood.

"You're hurt."

"I'm all right," Selena said. "I think."

He looked beyond her at the motionless figure on the floor.

"Lamont, watch the hall. There could be more of these guys."

"I'll be right outside," Lamont said.

Nick stepped into the room and closed the door behind him. He guided her over to the bed.

"Sit down."

Nick saw a hotel bathrobe hanging by the bathroom door. He took it and draped it over her. Red spots began to appear through the white cloth.

He went into the bathroom and got some towels. He wet one, came back out, opened her robe and gently began cleaning away the blood. He held a dry towel against the wound until the bleeding slowed. The cut was eight or nine inches long, the flesh laid open in a wide gash.

"It's nasty, but it's not too deep," he said. "It needs stitches."

"There's a kit in my belt pack."

He found the kit. He cleaned the wound with disinfectant and sprinkled antibiotic powder on it.

"This will hurt."

Nick began stitching the edges of the wound together. She winced as he worked.

"What happened?"

"I'd just come out of the shower and I was watching the rain. I heard a noise. When I looked, I saw him coming at me. He must've been hiding in the closet. He was good, he almost had me. I hurt him but he kept coming."

"He must be one of Cobra's men."

Selena began shivering. "I feel cold," she said.

The shivering turned into shaking. Her whole body shook. Nick put his arms around her and held her close.

"I...don't know...why..."

"Shh," he said, "shh. It's all right. It's just a reaction, it'll pass soon."

He held her for what seemed like a long time before the shaking stopped.

CHAPTER 43

Stephanie came into Elizabeth's office, her face flushed with excitement.

"Cobra," she said. "I've got him. I hacked into RAW's computers and took a look at their personnel files. Then I pulled a record of all the phones issued by the agency and referenced it against that list and Cobra's encrypted number. Cobra's information was behind four layers of security. He's the Secretary for Special Operations at RAW, the equivalent of our DCNS. His name is Ashok Rao."

"That explains how he had the resources needed to fake those calls," Elizabeth said.

"I also found out who Ijay is. He commands a black ops unit that works under Rao. He has birthmarks that remind people of the spots of a leopard. That's how his group got their name."

"Very poetic. I wouldn't be surprised if it turned out that they were the ones who blew up the Indian Embassy in Manila."

"It might be hard to prove that."

"We have a bigger problem to worry about," Elizabeth said. She briefed Stephanie on what Nick had told her about the Hazratbal mosque.

"Nick said it was a massacre. Automatic weapons turned against unarmed civilians."

"It must be what Cobra meant in that phone call," Stephanie said, "about the Army being ready."

Elizabeth shook her head in disgust. "He has to be stopped. It's too late to prevent a war. Indian soldiers firing on Muslims at a holy shrine is the last straw."

"What are you going to do about Rao?"

"I'm going to tell Rice what we found out and let him decide. Without presidential authorization he's untouchable. I can't do anything right now except let Nick know who he is."

She picked up her pen and set it down again.

"Rao is trying to start a war. Why?"

"His file was extensive," Stephanie said. "He's a Hindu nationalist and was an active field agent in Afghanistan for several years before he was singled out for promotion. His wife and son were killed in a terrorist attack by Afridi's group. He blames Pakistan and he hates Muslims."

"Lots of people in India hate Muslims and Pakistan too. They don't try to start a war because of it. Rao may be psychotic."

"If he's crazy, he's doing a good job of hiding it," Stephanie said. "The only medical notes in his file are routine. His psych profile shows tendencies toward violence and paranoia but that wouldn't be unusual for a field operative. "

"Anything else?"

"He has a high IQ. He comes from an acceptable caste for his position, but he's risen as high as he's going to. It's a little unusual that he got that far, which says a lot about his ability. He's also a devotee of Shiva. That's not unusual in India."

"How old is he?"

"That's another thing," Steph said. "Rao is sixty-one. He's facing involuntary retirement next year."

"So if he doesn't act now, he'll lose access to the resources he's using to stir up trouble."

"That's right."

"Steph, you just painted a picture of a dangerous man."

"We already knew he was dangerous," Steph said.

"Yes, but he sounds like he's more than just paranoid and violent. He could be delusional. What kind of person sends soldiers with loaded weapons against a peaceful crowd?"

"You're saying he's a psycho?"

"I think he may be," Elizabeth said.

Steph said nothing.

"The president is going to love this," Elizabeth said.

"When are you going to tell him?"

"Today. We need to take this man off the board before he does any more damage."

CHAPTER 44

On the ride over to the White House Elizabeth thought about what she was going to tell Rice about Ashok Rao. She was convinced it was Rao and not Pakistan that had planned the attacks against India and the U.S. in Manila. There was enough evidence for her. Would it be enough to convince Rice to take action?

She watched Washington's cityscape pass by. She passed the Smithsonian. Large signs proclaimed an exhibition about ancient navies and warships. It made her think of her father and something he'd said to her. She'd been around twelve years old.

Judge Harker liked to build ships in a bottle. It could take him a year or more to complete a single ship. When the model was ready, the masts and broad yards were folded down and in, so that the hull could be slipped through an opening just wide enough to accept it.

Elizabeth had been watching him get ready to install his latest creation, a miniature version of Admiral Nelson's flagship, the 104 gun HMS Victory. It was a masterpiece, the jewel of his collection. The canvas sails were white and crisp, the paint work bright, the black cannons run out and ready for action. A tiny figure of Nelson in his blue and gold uniform stood on the quarterdeck.

"Daddy, don't you ever get worried that you'll break it when you put it in the bottle?"

"In the beginning, I did, when I first started building them."

"But not now?"

He smiled. "No, pumpkin."

"Why don't you worry?"

"Because I trust that I know what I'm doing."

"My teacher was talking about certainty in class today. Is trusting yourself the same as having certainty?" Elizabeth asked.

Her father had laid his tools down and looked at her.

"That's a very good question. I'd say that they're almost the same but not quite. Sometimes you have to act as if you're certain about something because you trust your judgment and knowledge."

"Even when you're not certain?" Elizabeth had said.

"Even when you're not."

She had to trust her judgment, even though she couldn't be one hundred percent certain she was right. If Pakistan had planned and executed the attack on the American Embassy, they had become an active enemy. If that was the case, any strategy Rice formed to deal with the crisis on the subcontinent had to take that into account. The intelligence she was bringing to him challenged the assumption of Pakistan's guilt. It could change the entire U.S. position regarding Pakistan and India.

An aide escorted Elizabeth into the Oval Office. President Rice sat behind his desk. With him in the room was Clarence Hood, Director of the CIA. Both men rose when Elizabeth entered the room.

"Director. Thank you for being so prompt. Please, take a seat."

That was Rice's way, to thank people for doing what was expected of them. As if she would ever be late for an appointment with him.

"Thank you, Mister President. Hello, Clarence."

"Elizabeth."

Rice sat and Hood followed. Elizabeth chose a peach-colored upholstered chair in front of the president's desk.

Clarence Hood was tall and almost thin. He looked tired, his skin color a little too close a match for his light gray suit. His eyes were rimmed with red, the product of stress and late hours. Elizabeth liked him. In the shadow world they both worked in, he had earned her respect.

Rice looked even more worn out than Hood, almost exhausted. Without the makeup that made him appear robust for the cameras, his face was pale and lined, unhealthy looking. The strain he was under was evident.

"You said you had disturbing information concerning India and Pakistan," Rice said. "I thought it might be a good idea if Clarence sat in on this meeting."

"Yes, sir," Elizabeth began. She plunged in.

"Sir, I believe that the embassy attacks in Manila were a false flag operation conceived and executed by a rogue official high up in India's intelligence agency. I am also convinced that the same individual instigated the riot in Srinagar at the mosque. All of these acts were carefully planned as provocations to push India and Pakistan into war."

The effect of her words was shock. She might as well have thrown a dead fish onto the president's desk.

Rice sat up straighter in his chair. "You have proof of this, Director?"

"Yes, sir, or I would not be sitting here."

"Go on."

Elizabeth proceeded to brief the two men on what she had learned. When she was done, Rice looked at the DCI.

"Did you have any indication of this, Clarence?"

"No, sir. But what Director Harker has said ties together some loose ends. The assault on the Indian embassy has never made sense as an operation by ISOK. It's too far from their home base. It makes a lot of sense if it was a false flag op designed to move Indian public opinion and political will toward war with Pakistan. I admit it never occurred to me that anyone except Abu Sayyaf was behind the attack on our own embassy. They certainly had enough reasons."

"I believe they *were* planning the attack," Elizabeth said. "I think that Cobra used it as an opportunity to point the finger at Islamabad."

"Cobra?" Rice said.

"Sorry, sir. My codename for Ashok Rao."

"This is a real mess, Director."

"Yes, Mister President."

"Clarence, what kind of a relationship does Langley have with India's intelligence agency?"

"It's mixed, Mister President. To be blunt, we haven't always told the Indians everything we knew about what was going on in Pakistan. We needed access for our supply route into Afghanistan. Self interest dictated how much we decided to tell New Delhi about what Islamabad was up to."

"You mean they don't trust us," Rice said.

"Yes, sir. That about sums it up."

"They're not going to be happy if we tell them that their Secretary of Special Operations is a traitor."

"No, sir, I don't imagine they will."

Rice turned his attention to Elizabeth. His blue eyes bored into her.

"Director, how certain are you about this?"

"The phone calls are damning, Mister President. I'm as certain as I can be. This man is to a great degree responsible for what's happening over there."

"What action would you recommend?"

"He has to be neutralized before he does any more damage," Elizabeth said. "We should let Gupta know what we've found out."

"Gupta?" Rice said.

"The Secretary of the Research and Intelligence Wing, Mister President." Hood said. "I've met him. He won't believe us, not without hard evidence."

"I have the recordings of Rao's phone conversations," Elizabeth said.

Hood seemed doubtful. "It might be enough. On the other hand, our past history with the Indians regarding Pakistan doesn't lend us a lot of credibility. As you pointed out, phone conversations can be false."

"He must be neutralized," Elizabeth said again.

"You've made your position clear, Director," Rice said. His voice bore an unspoken warning. *Don't push it.*

They waited for him to speak.

"This is intolerable," he said. "I expect war to start at any moment over there, and you're telling me it's all because of one man who wants revenge for a terrorist attack that killed his family?"

"Yes, Mister President," Elizabeth said. "Although he may not be acting alone. He seems to have extensive resources. I'm not sure where they come from, but it isn't from his government."

"A conspiracy, then?"

"It's possible."

As she said it, a thought occurred to her.

Could it be AEON? It can't be, not again.

AEON was a secret organization of wealthy men with roots going back to the time of the Templars. For AEON, the world existed to be exploited and controlled.

Elizabeth had thought them defeated. Even as she told herself it couldn't be, she knew it was possible. She kept the thought to herself.

"Sir, my team is in Kashmir as we speak. There may be an opportunity to intercept Rao and question him. But I need your permission."

"That's refreshing, Director. You usually don't ask."

Elizabeth flushed. "You usually don't want to know, sir."

Oh, oh, Hood thought. *Rice won't like that.*

Before the president could respond, Hood interrupted.

"Mister President, I think Director Harker's idea has merit. I'll do my best to convince Gupta that Rao has gone rogue, but there's no guarantee he'll believe me. Langley has a few assets in Kashmir. Director Harker and I can work out a joint operation to, ah, persuade Rao to talk with us. If you give us the okay, we can get on it right away. Things are moving quickly over there."

Rice gave Harker a calculating look. "We haven't gone after a high ranking intelligence officer since the Cold War," Rice said. "That was against an enemy. India is an ally."

"India may be, but Ashok Rao isn't," Elizabeth said. "Sir, this is what you hired me to do."

There were few people Rice trusted in the snake pit of Washington's intelligence community and few who would stand up to him. Harker and Hood were among those few.

Hell, I have to trust someone, he thought. *She's right, I hired her to tell me the truth, even if I didn't like what she told me. If the Indians or the Pakis bring out those missiles...*

"All right," he said. "But Director..."

"Sir?"

"Under no circumstances are you to use severe methods of interrogation. You get what we need in a civilized manner or we'll turn him over to the Indians and let them deal with it. Is that clear?"

"Perfectly clear, Mister President."

CHAPTER 45

After she'd left the White House, Elizabeth called Nick in Srinagar. He told her about the attack in Selena's room.

"Selena's all right?"

"She's fine. A little shook up. Knives are up close and personal. It's worse than being shot at from a distance. "

"No sign of Afridi?" she asked.

"None. It was always a long shot."

"We have to assume that he's gone."

"The cops are unhappy about the man Selena killed," Nick said. "They're treating it like a terrorist attack on a tourist but they're suspicious by nature. They told us not to leave the city while they investigate. They took our passports. What do you want us to do?"

"The Indians have temporarily closed the airport. The whole country is gearing up for war. You'd be stuck there anyway."

"What about Cobra?"

"That's what I'm calling about," Elizabeth said. "We found out who he is. He's an important officer in India's intelligence agency, the equivalent of our DCNS."

"That explains a lot," Nick said. "He could make it look like Pakistan was behind what happened in Manila. But it doesn't explain why."

"He's a fanatic," Elizabeth said, "a Hindu fundamentalist who hates Pakistan. It's personal with him. His family was killed during a terrorist attack by Afridi's group. Islamabad was behind it."

"Ah."

"I think he's responsible for the riot at the mosque. If his goal was to provoke a war between India and Pakistan, it looks like he's succeeded. Both sides are moving tanks and artillery to the border."

"If it's personal, that tells us why he's after Afridi," Nick said. He thought for a moment. "Afridi is a fanatic just like Cobra. Those Indian soldiers were after him. I think he's going to want payback. His credibility is at stake."

"What do you mean?"

"Isn't he the big cheese in the jihadist movement in Kashmir? He has to do something in retaliation for what happened at the mosque. We know where Afridi's compound is, don't we?"

"Yes. It's not that far from you, across the border in Pakistan. It's next to an airbase."

"Can you put surveillance on it?"

"I already have. Why?"

"Whatever Afridi does, I don't think Cobra is going to give up. If he comes after him again it could give us another chance at him."

"You'll be happy to hear that the president agrees with you. We've got a green light to go after Cobra."

"A sanction?"

"No, Nick. Interrogation only. Strictly by the rules. You can't hurt him. Rice was adamant."

"Damn it, Director, this isn't a time to play politics. This guy is responsible for the deaths of a lot of people. He put Ronnie in the hospital. He's trying to start a war. What's it going to take to get him out of the picture?"

Elizabeth heard the anger in Nick's voice.

"I understand, Nick. Cobra will get what's coming to him but you have to be patient."

In Srinagar, Nick took a deep breath. "What about Afridi?"

"He's a different story. If you have a chance to get him, take it."

"Cobra's a pro. If we do get him, it won't be easy to get him to talk."

"I'm sure you'll find a way. But I mean it, when I say you have to play by the rules. You'll have some help."

"What do you mean?" Nick asked.

"This is a joint op with Langley. Hood was there when I spoke with Rice."

"Director..."

"It's not debatable, Nick. Think about it. You say Cobra might go after Afridi. Afridi is in Pakistan. How do you intend to get there if Cobra shows up?"

Nick said nothing.

"That's what I thought. Take down this number. The asset's name is Jeb."

"Jeb?"

"That's what Clarence said." Elizabeth read off a twelve digit code. "Call it at 1400 your time."

"How do I know I'm talking to the right guy?" Nick said.

"Don't laugh," Harker said. "There's a recognition phrase."

"And?"

"When he answers you say, *the water in the river is not very good to drink.*"

"You're kidding."

"No. And then he says, *that's because the women wash their clothes in it.*"

"I don't believe this."

"Hood's agent must have a sense of humor. Or he's just paranoid."

"Or maybe Langley thinks it's 1950." Nick paused. "How's Ronnie doing?"

"He's stable, his vitals are good. No real change."

"I'll tell the others."

"Set up a meeting with Langley's agent. Try and stay out of trouble. If Cobra makes a move, I'll let you know."

CHAPTER 46

Nick called the number Harker had given him. Selena and Lamont waited with him. Nick had the phone on speaker.

"Yeah."

The voice on the phone sounded like gravel.

Nick said, "The water in the river isn't very good to drink."

"No shit," the voice said. "They told you to use that old chestnut?"

Nick felt like an idiot. "You want to give me the response before I hang up?"

"Yeah, okay. It's because the women wash their clothes in it."

"Where can we meet?" Nick asked.

"There's a place right on the river downtown called the China House. Lousy food, but they've got cold beer and we can watch the boats go by. You know where it is?"

"No."

Nick listened to the directions.

"Two hours."

"How do I know who you are?"

"I'll be the guy in the cowboy hat."

The line went dead.

"He hung up," Nick said.

"Cold beer," Lamont said. "Guy sounded like he'd already had a few."

Two hours later, they were sitting on a scarred wooden deck overhanging the Jhelum river at the China House. The water flowed past twenty feet below, broad and cloudy and brown. Bits of debris and garbage floated by on the surface. A light breeze brought a faint smell of sewage from the water. It had stopped raining. A faded red awning over the deck sheltered them from the glare of the sun.

The river was busy with river taxis and boats that looked too fragile to handle the passengers they carried. The boats were long and pointed at each end, narrow, with broad sun canopies that made them look top heavy. The gunwales were inches above the surface of the water. *I wouldn't want to be in one of those if a strong wind came up*, Selena thought.

The waiter brought three large bottles of Kingfisher beer. Lamont poured some into a glass and tasted it.

"Not bad," he said. "Strong. Like a Bud on steroids."

"Here comes the cowboy," Selena said. "Bet he calls himself that."

"Kind of old," Lamont said.

Langley's asset was somewhere in his late sixties. He was about five ten, with a lean, gnarled look. He needed a shave. His hat was a brown Stetson, stained with sweat. He wore a khaki colored shirt, dark pants and heavy brown work boots. He moved with confidence, but Nick saw him tilt a little as he approached.

The man sat down across from Nick and reached across with his hand.

"Jeb Akron. Most people call me Cowboy."

Selena looked at Nick. *See?*

Akron's grip was strong. His hand was rough in Nick's grip.

"I'm Nick. This is Selena and Lamont."

A waiter appeared unbidden with a bottle of Kingfisher covered with drops of condensation. He set it down in front of Akron.

"Nice to see you, Mister Cowboy," the waiter said.

"You, too, Choy. Thanks."

"Your favorite spot?" Nick said.

"I come here a lot."

Akron took a long swallow from the bottle. Selena looked at Nick and raised an eyebrow.

"I think this is a mistake," Nick said.

"You ought to think again," Akron said. "You want help from the big dog in Virginia, I'm it. Don't let this fool you." He picked up the bottle and gestured vaguely with it. "It's what they expect to see."

"Who?" Nick saw that Akron's eyes were clear and focused. They weren't the eyes of a man who'd had too much to drink.

"You think three foreigners visiting Srinagar when a war's about to start aren't an item of interest to the security forces here?" Akron said. "Two of them are watching us from the other end of the deck. Their buddies are probably going through your rooms right now. Not to mention that little incident at your hotel."

"You know about that?"

He took out an old style steel Zippo cigarette lighter and lit an unfiltered cigarette. He set the lighter upright on the table. It bore the globe and anchor of the Marine Corps.

"We are Langley. We know all," Akron said. "Don't worry, they can't hear what we're saying. That's more than a lighter."

"You were a Marine?"

"Yup. Still am."

"Vietnam?"

"That's right. I was a WO. I flew choppers. Two tours."

Nick's estimation of Akron went up. The casualty rate for helicopter pilots in Vietnam was staggering. Akron had to know what he was doing and he had to be damned lucky.

"What were you told about us?" Nick asked.

"You might need a lift somewhere. Maybe over the border."

"It could get hairy," Nick said.

"Your point?"

"We don't know where we're going yet, but we will. Once we do, how do you plan to get us there?"

"I've got a Huey," Akron said.

"What's a Huey?" Selena asked.

Akron looked at her, then at Nick. "Why is she here?" he said.

Nick put his hand on Selena's arm before she could say anything.

"Sometimes you need to get past what you think you see," Nick said to Akron. "Like what I'm trying to do with you right now. Trust me, you want her on your side. What she doesn't know about helicopters isn't a problem. If it is, we're done here."

Lamont said, "A Huey is a chopper, Selena. They used them for everything in Vietnam. Suits an old guy like him." He looked at Akron. It wasn't a friendly look.

Akron looked at the three of them.

"Okay," he said. "Sorry. No offense meant."

"Selena?" Nick said.

She was annoyed. Akron came across as one of those macho males who figured women were no use except in the kitchen or in bed. Still playing warrior when he should be playing golf somewhere. Or whatever old warriors did.

"He meant it, but it doesn't matter," she said. "As long as he can do his job."

CHAPTER 47

Selena lay with her arm across Nick's chest. They listened to the sound of tanks rumbling by outside the hotel.

"I wish we were back home," she said. "It's not much fun waiting for something to happen."

"If I had a dollar for all the times I sat around waiting for something to happen, I could retire."

"You know, we could," Selena said.

"Could what?"

"Retire. I've got more than enough money, you know that."

"And then what would we do? Buy a house in the country? Go fishing?"

"We could buy a yacht. Sail around the world."

"Are you serious?"

She sighed. "No, I'm not serious. You think I'd want to watch you pace the deck all day with nothing to do?"

"I've been thinking," he said.

"About what?"

"Us."

"What about us?"

Outside, they heard shouting. Another tank went by, the treads making a rhythmic, steady clanking noise on the pavement.

"Do you still want to get married?" he said.

There it was. The question she'd been dreading.

"Do you?"

"Don't do that," he said.

"Do what?"

"Answer the question with another."

"But I need to know."

Selena got up. The bandage on her side where she'd been cut was white in the moonlight coming into the room. She wrapped a robe around herself and went to the window. She looked out at the armor going by below, the soulless machines of war. Men in green uniforms walked in the dark alongside the tanks, stretched out in endless lines on either side of the highway. Marching toward an enemy.

"Sometimes I wish I smoked," she said.

"We could start," Nick said. "I don't think we need to worry much about the effects."

She looked at him. He lay on his side, his head propped up on one elbow.

"That's the whole problem, right there," she said.

Nick sat up, pushed a pillow behind him. "You think I might get killed."

"Or I might. Isn't that what you meant? About effects?"

"We wouldn't be the first people to worry about what was going to happen," Nick said. "Sometimes I think that, yeah. Mostly I don't. If I did, I couldn't do what we do."

She went over to the bed and sat down.

"Damn it," she said. "Most people who talk about getting married are worried about giving up personal space, where they'll live, things like that. You and I, though? We wonder if the other person is going to get blown up or shot. You have to admit, sometimes the odds are stacked against us."

"There aren't any guarantees for anyone, no matter what. Anything could happen."

"Please don't say we could be walking down the street and get hit with a meteor."

Nick laughed. Then he got serious. "You haven't answered my question. Do you still want to get married?"

Selena looked down at the covers and plucked at the sheet. "You know I love you," she said.

His face closed down. "Guess I've got my answer."

"I didn't say no."

"You didn't say yes, either."

"Why can't we leave it like it is for now?" she said. "It's worked pretty well."

"What are you afraid of?"

"I'm not afraid. It's just that the whole world seems ready to go over the cliff and we're sitting right on the edge. It doesn't feel like a good time to make plans for the long run."

"Like getting married."

"Like that."

"But you're not saying no?"

"No."

Inside, Nick relaxed a little. He wasn't sure why. Because she hadn't said no or because it meant he didn't have to take that last step.

"Come back to bed," he said.

CHAPTER 48

Abdul Afridi was angry. The slaughter at the mosque was an offense against God. It demanded retribution. He would restrain himself no longer.

Until now he'd avoided attacking targets his ISI handlers told him were off-limits. He'd kept within the constraints imposed upon him by Pakistan as conditions for receiving their money and protection. Well, the mountains offered many places he could go where Islamabad's protection was unnecessary. Pakistani money was no longer relevant. Their leaders were corrupt. He owed Islamabad nothing.

Afridi was convinced that more gold lay in the bottom of that Afghan canyon, along with whatever was left of the Peacock Throne. The elephant bones were the clue, even more than the coins. The throne had been large, made of solid gold and decorated with precious jewels. It would've been too heavy to move intact. It would have been broken down into smaller pieces, the kind of weight pack animals could handle. If he could recover even one of those pieces, the gold would buy all the explosives and weapons needed to bring down a reign of death on the Indians.

It was just after the morning prayer on the second day after he'd returned with Sayeed from Srinagar. The trucks and men were ready.

"Everything is set, Abdul," Sayeed said.

Afridi nodded approval. "You have all the tools? The explosives if we need them?"

"Everything. God willing, we will be there by tomorrow evening."

A dozen men waited by the vehicles. Three of the trucks mounted Russian KPV heavy machine guns. The KPVs fired a devastating 14.5 millimeter armor piercing round. They could shoot down low-flying aircraft and shred anything up to 3000 meters away. Two more Toyotas sported American M-60 light machine guns. He'd decided to take the quick way into Afghanistan through the Khyber pass. He'd been through many times before. There wouldn't be a problem at the border crossing, even with the guns. If he tried to take the alternate road south and west from Jamrud Fort, he'd end up in the tribal areas and certain trouble.

Everyone carried personal weapons. AKs, pistols and carbines wouldn't get a second glance from the crossing guards. A sixth truck carried the tools. Afridi hoped to fill it with treasure. He climbed into the lead vehicle. The convoy set off for the nearby mountains.

High overhead, a Global Hawk made lazy circles in the sky. Images of the vehicles streamed back to Beale Air Force Base in California. From there, the video was relayed to a list of intelligence agencies that included Langley and the Project.

It was seven at night in Virginia. Elizabeth had been alerted to the activity at Afridi's base. Now she watched the video feed with Stephanie. A string of vehicles left the compound, passed by the Pakistani air base and headed west.

"Where are they going?" Stephanie asked.

"I don't know. On that route, I'd say Afghanistan. There isn't much on the Paki side to interest them."

Stephanie got up. "I'd better make some coffee. This could take a while."

Elizabeth watched the convoy. The video was clear and detailed. She could make out the features of a man riding in the bed of the lead truck. His beard was full and black. He wore a skull cap and long robe. His baggy pants billowed around his legs as the truck sped along, trailing dust in a long cloud. A second man sat with his back against the side of the truck bed, arms clasped about his knees.

Where was Afridi going?

Stephanie came back into the room with two steaming cups. She handed one to Elizabeth.

"Black, no sugar," she said.

"Thanks." Elizabeth blew on the coffee and took a careful sip.

"Do you think Ronnie is going to make it?" Stephanie asked.

"He's tough. If anyone can survive that, he can."

"Nick and Ronnie have been friends for a long time. If Ronnie dies..."

She left the thought unfinished.

"Let's not go there," Elizabeth said. "We have to wait and see if nature will do the job."

Stephanie pointed at the screen. "They've turned onto the N5, headed for the Khyber Pass. The only place that road goes is Afghanistan."

"As we thought."

"Look at those guns. Why head into Afghanistan ready for a fight? Afridi is allied with the Taliban."

"Not with all of them," Elizabeth said. "That area by the border is under the control of a group unfriendly to everyone. They're Shinwari. Afridi is Pashtun like them but it won't make any difference. He's not one of them."

"Do we have any troops there?" Stephanie asked.

"Not any more. Security was handed over to the Afghans months ago. It never was a safe area and no one has ever been able to pacify it. It's not that far from Kabul but it might as well be on the moon, in terms of control from the capitol."

Elizabeth peered at the image. "What's he got in that last truck?"

Stephanie made an adjustment and the satellite picture zoomed in on the vehicle.

"Tools. Shovels, picks." Warning markings were visible on one of the boxes. "I think the crates are explosives."

"Tools? Why would he take tools into Afghanistan?"

"To dig something up?"

"He could have hidden supplies across the border, but I don't know why he'd do that. His handlers in Pakistan wouldn't care what he stockpiled on their territory."

"They're stopping," Stephanie said.

The driver got out of the lead vehicle and walked to the side of the road and began relieving himself.

"Men have it so damn easy," Stephanie said.

CHAPTER 49

Krivi and Rao sat in the back of a cafe in New Delhi. Krivi held a brown pill bottle in his right hand.

"This is a new medication our laboratory has developed," Krivi said. "It is experimental, but we are seeing excellent results. It will stop further growth of the tumor."

"Stop the growth?"

"Animal results are very positive."

"It hasn't been tested on humans?"

"Does it matter?" Krivi said. "What have you got to lose?"

"Give me the pills."

Krivi set the bottle down on the table.

"It may make you feel light-headed but the feeling will pass. Take four of them once a day for the next three days, then every other day. More will be delivered to you."

"Thank you."

"My sources say you were responsible for the riot in Srinagar," Krivi said. "Is it true?"

"It wasn't difficult. Everyone was already on edge. I told the commander of the garrison I had definite intelligence the Muslims were going to riot after the evening prayer. I suggested he take strong measures to disperse the gathering."

"It was well done." Krivi paused. "Have you decided on a plan?"

"For the missiles? Not yet."

"Remember, the codes are only good until the end of the month."

Rao made a dismissive gesture. "There's still time."

Krivi knew Rao was on edge. He needed a diversion to keep him busy until it was time to send the missile on its way.

"Afridi has left his compound," Krivi said.

Rao tensed at the mention of his enemy.

"Where is he going?"

"West, toward Afghanistan. He has a dozen men with him. What's interesting is that he has taken tools with him."

"Tools?"

"Shovels and picks, the kind of thing you need to dig. Do you remember when we first met at the temple?" Krivi said.

"Of course."

"I said that few dreamed of returning the Eye of Shiva to its rightful place."

"Yes. I wondered how you knew I wanted that."

"I think our enemy knows where part of the Mughal treasure is hidden and he's going after it. What if the Eye is part of that?"

The Eye! Rao's heart skipped a beat.

"It's possible," Rao said. His voice betrayed his excitement. "Afridi had gold coins, old ones. I wanted to find out where they came from before I killed him. I thought they might lead to the Eye. If it's there, we must recover it."

Krivi nodded, looking serious. "It would be a great service to Lord Shiva."

"I'll need his exact location."

"When he gets to where he's going I'll be able to give it to you," Krivi said.

"If he finds the Eye, I will take it from him. With his life."

Rao's face was ugly with hatred. Krivi stood, clasped his hands together and bowed slightly.

"Namaste," he said. "Wait for my call." He turned and left the cafe.

Rao considered the problem. Only two things mattered. Retrieving the jewel, if it could be found, and killing Afridi. Once he knew where Afridi was he'd send Ijay after him. Ijay was still in Srinagar, waiting for instructions.

Rao poured bottled water into a glass and took his first dose of the new medicine Krivi had brought.

CHAPTER 50

Stephanie and Elizabeth were in Steph's office when her computer beeped. "Cobra is using his phone," she said.

She turned on the speaker. They listened to the call ringing. Someone answered. Rao began speaking.

"Hindi, again," Elizabeth said.

The conversation lasted about a minute. When it was over, Elizabeth called Nick.

"Yes, Director."

"Nick, Cobra just made a call. Put Selena on and I'll play it for her."

"She's right here."

Selena came on the line.

"Cobra made a call," Elizabeth said. "I need you to tell us what he said."

"Okay."

Stephanie played the call.

In Srinagar, Selena said, "Run it one more time."

Stephanie did.

"He's talking to the same man as before," Selena said, "Ijay. Is Afridi on the move?"

"Yes."

"Cobra is waiting to hear exactly where Afridi is going. Once he knows, he's sending Ijay after him."

"Waiting to hear from whom?"

"He didn't say."

"What will he do if they catch him?" Elizabeth asked.

"He didn't say that either. But my guess is he wants to kill him."

"Let me speak with Nick."

When Nick took the phone, Elizabeth said, "Afridi has left his compound. He's traveling in a convoy headed for Afghanistan. Selena will brief you on the call from Cobra. We'll watch Afridi from here. Once we know where he's going or what he's doing, I'll let you know. There's not much you can do at the moment."

Nick said, "There are troops everywhere and the Indians are moving heavy armor. The desk clerk said that the roads out of town are packed with people leaving the city. What's happening?"

"India and Pakistan are about to get into it," Elizabeth said. "It looks like the curtain's going up any time and Srinagar is stage center. War between those two always seems to kick off in Kashmir."

"You know," Nick said, "when I was a kid I read about the Vale of Kashmir. It sounded like one of the most beautiful places in the world. Magical, like a fairy tale for real. I always wanted to go there."

"Well," Elizabeth said, "it looks like you got your wish."

"Yeah. But in the descriptions I read people were admiring the scenery, they weren't getting ready to kill each other."

"Did you hook up with Langley's asset?"

"Yes."

"You don't sound enthusiastic."

"He's an old guy," Nick said. "It's hard to think he'll be much use if we get into it with Afridi or anyone else."

"Hood says he's one of the best," Elizabeth said. "He got a Navy Cross in Vietnam. They almost gave him a CMO."

"That makes me feel a lot better knowing that. You'd never guess by looking at him."

"You know I don't like to tell you how to do your job," Elizabeth said.

"That means you're about to," Nick said. "What is it?"

"I want you to wait and see what happens between Cobra and Afridi. There's no need for you to get mixed up in the middle of that. One of them is going to come out on top. Wait and see which one and go from there."

"Where is Afridi now?"

Elizabeth looked at the monitor and the image of Afridi's convoy.

"He's in the Khyber Pass, about to cross into Afghanistan."

CHAPTER 51

The Khyber Pass was a major gateway between West and East. The old Silk Road connecting the Mediterranean to China had come through the pass. Invading armies seeking to plunder the riches that lay beyond the snow-capped peaks had fought and died by the thousands in the narrow defile. In the days of Marco Polo and the trade caravans the route had been little more than a steep and difficult, rocky trail. Now there was a modern, blacktop highway. The camels had given way to trucks and armored personnel carriers.

Afridi signaled a stop when they reached the summit. They were still five kilometers inside Pakistan. Around them the market center of Landi Khotal bustled with tradesmen and trucks bearing goods from both sides of the mountains. Merchants eyed the heavily armed pickups and gave them a wide berth.

Afridi got out to stretch and look out over the view. The day was clear, the sky cloudless. A constant wind blew through the pass, bringing with it the smell of dust and spices and the passage of time. To the west, a long series of switchbacks descended to the brown landscape of the arid Lowyah Dakkah plain in Afghanistan. To the east, the plains of Peshawar were turning green after the passing of the monsoon rains.

Afridi thought of his ancestors, warriors among the invading hoards from the west, a scourge upon the Hindu unbelievers.

With God's help, I will raise a new scourge upon them, he thought.

All that was needed was a spark to ignite the wrath of the faithful. That, and the weapons to arm them. The spark had been struck at the mosque in Srinagar. Afridi intended to fan it into flames. The weapons waited only for gold to buy them. Gold that lay in a forgotten canyon, mixed with the bones of elephants.

After the men had refreshed themselves, Afridi ordered everyone back into the trucks. They headed toward Afghanistan.

Once down from the pass, the convoy turned south and then back into the mountains, following the alternate route Afridi had taken on foot months before. An hour before dark, they arrived in the canyon where he'd found the coins.

Everything was as it had been. The scar left by the landslide that sent the elephant to its doom was a gray line down the side of the mountain. At it's foot, the huge pile of rock and debris lay where it had fallen centuries ago.

"Post sentries," Afridi said to Sayeed. "The Shinwari will know we're here. They need to see we're ready for them if they try anything."

"The men are hungry."

"Let them eat while it's still light. No fires. Split everyone into two groups. Feed one, while the rest stand guard. Then the other. We'll begin clearing the rocks tomorrow."

"*Insha'Allah*," Sayeed said. He walked away and began giving the orders.

Afridi sat down on a rock, took out a copy of the Qur'an and began reading. He didn't know he was being observed or he would have been less tranquil as he studied the Book.

On the other side of the Khyber Pass in New Delhi, Rao's phone alerted him to a call.

"I have Afridi's location," Krivi said. "He's just west of the Khyber Pass in Afghanistan, this side of Kabul."

"What's he doing there?" Rao asked.

"Nothing, yet. Setting up his camp. Do you have a satellite over the area?"

Rao made a quick check. "Yes."

Krivi gave Rao the coordinates.

Rao brought the area up on his monitor. The light would soon be gone but there was still enough to see Afridi reading a book.

"I see him," Rao said. Bile rose in his throat at the sight of his enemy.

"Can you get to him there?"

Rao thought about it. The only way was to send Ijay and the Leopards in by helicopter. It meant flying across Pakistan from Kashmir, through the mountain valleys. A night mission was bad enough in itself. With Islamabad alert on the eve of war, there was a high risk of failure. The chances were good Ijay would be intercepted.

On the other hand, Ijay had one of only two Rudra attack helicopters modified with experimental stealth technology. Even the Americans didn't have anything like it. The technology was untested in combat, but field tests had gone well. If anyone could get through Pakistan's air defenses, Ijay could.

Rao made up his mind. "Yes. I can get to him."

"How can I help?" Krivi said.

"You seem to have a lot of resources," Rao said.

"A few."

"My team will have to cross Pakistani air space. Can you distract their defenses tomorrow evening, if I tell you when?"

"Where will the flight originate?"

"From Poonch. It's near the border, west of Srinagar."

"I'll see what I can do and call you back," Krivi said.

Fifteen minutes later, Rao's phone rang.

"You have a corridor one mile wide west of Poonch and across to Afghanistan from 2000 to 0600 tomorrow," Krivi said. "Tell your pilot to stay low and inside the corridor. He may still run into problems."

"Good," Rao said. "That should be enough time."

CHAPTER 52

In the morning, Afridi set his men to work moving rocks. It was tedious, hard labor. After several hours had passed, Afridi was beginning to doubt there was more to find. Then one of the men shouted. He pointed at a large, yellowed bone in the debris. They found more bones and the remains of a wooden pack cradle, still tacked with rotted bits of leather. Then an iron box about a foot square.

Afridi stood next to Sayeed, looking down at the box. His men gathered around him, waiting. A rusted lock held the top shut with a metal clasp. Afridi broke the lock away with the butt of his rifle. He lifted the lid.

A collective gasp came from the men. The chest was filled with jewels that shone with brilliant colors in the bright morning sun.

Sayeed sucked in his breath at the sight of so much wealth.

"God is Great," he said.

"Allah has blessed our cause," Afridi said. He looked at the sky. "Come, brothers, we must pray and give thanks."

After the prayer, Afridi picked up the chest with the jewels and took it over to one of the trucks while the men continued digging. He sat on the worn seat in the cab and looked through the gems. Sunlight poured through the windshield onto the stones. Afridi had never seen such beauty. Diamonds. Sapphires as large as bird eggs. Stones of yellow, red, green and blue, rough cut and polished. At the bottom of the chest, buried under smaller stones, something glowed blood red. Afridi reached in and grasped it and took out a ruby so big he could barely get his fingers around it. It was as big as his palm, heavy in his hand. It swirled with color as it caught the rays of the sun, changing from a fiery glow to a deep red and back again.

A jewel for a king, he thought. *Or a caliph.*

In the next few hours they found the remains of two more beasts and six more of the iron chests. Two of the chests had broken open where they'd fallen and spilled hundreds of gold coins under the stones. Three other chests held shaped pieces of reddish gold set with precious stones.

Afridi held one of the heavy pieces in his hands and hefted it. *From the Peacock Throne*, he thought. *Enough gold to build an army.*

He kept the men working for the rest of the day but they found nothing more. Afridi called a halt to the digging. It was enough. It would soon be dark and the road was dangerous at night, plagued by bandits. Afridi decided to leave early the next morning. He called the men to him.

Afridi went to each man and gave him ten gold coins. It was more wealth than any of them had ever seen or could hope to earn in three lifetimes. One coin would feed a family for a year or more, a village for many months. Any man would be tempted by such riches as they'd found. Afridi knew that a man who had riches was much less likely to give in to temptation.

"God has said to be generous and to reward the worthy," Afridi said. "You are faithful men and you have earned this gift. We will take the rest and use it to bring death upon the infidels."

His fighters shouted and brandished their rifles. *"Allahu Akbar! Allahu Akbar!"*

"Park the trucks facing out. Man the guns and post sentries," Afridi said to Sayeed. "Then we eat."

"The men have worked hard," Sayeed said. "Hot food would be good and the night is cold."

Afridi nodded. "Build a fire under that ledge." He pointed toward a nearby rocky overhang. "Not a big one."

Sayeed said, "Do you expect trouble?".

"Always. I don't think the tribesmen will do anything, not against those guns. If they were, we'd already know. I worry more about the American satellites."

An hour later the camp was settled for the night. The men not standing guard sat around the small fire. The flames cast shadows and light against the canyon wall. The heat of the day faded and the temperature plummeted. Overhead, the sky was deep black and filled with stars.

Afridi wrapped himself in his cloak and lay down on the hard earth, his rifle beside him. Once, when he was younger, the ground would have felt almost as soft as a bed, a place just to rest. But he was older now. It was a long time before he drifted into an uneasy doze.

The sound of helicopter rotors drawing near woke him.

Instantly, he was up and shouting. He grabbed his AK.

"Wake up! Wake up!"

The rotors became a roar overhead. The canyon floor flooded with bright, white light. Clouds of dust rose from the beating blades as a half dozen men dressed in black dropped on long lines into the clearing.

Afridi raised his rifle and shot one of the dangling figures. The man fell from the line and hit the ground. A burst from one of his comrades slammed into Afridi's chest, knocking him to the ground. He was aware of pain. He couldn't breathe. He heard the rapid *tacktacktack* of automatic weapons, the screams of men dying, the indifferent beat of the helicopter blades. His last thought was of the giant, blood red stone he'd found among the jewels.

CHAPTER 53

It was evening in Virginia and day in Afghanistan. The satellite Elizabeth used to observe Afridi came into range. The black and white image was crisp and clear. It wasn't what Elizabeth expected to see.

"What on earth..." she said.

"What happened?" Stephanie asked. "It looks like they're all dead."

Afridi's campground was destroyed. Elizabeth counted thirteen bodies sprawled on the canyon floor. The trucks had been torched, leaving charred hulks. A thin column of black smoke lazed into the sky from one of them.

"People coming," Stephanie said. She pointed to a group of bearded men approaching in a battered pickup. A machine gun was mounted in the back.

"Tribesmen," Elizabeth said. "Probably Shinwari. They must have seen the smoke and decided to take a look."

Stephanie zoomed in on a bearded corpse lying on his back. His mouth was open, his eyes staring at the sky. The front of his light colored shirt was dark with dried blood. A rifle lay on the ground next to him.

"That's Afridi," Stephanie said.

"It wasn't the tribesmen," Elizabeth said. "They're just showing up."

"That leaves Cobra's man."

"Ijay. I guess Cobra decided he didn't want to hear whatever it was Afridi had to say."

"I wish all these people would just kill each other off," Stephanie said. "It would save us a lot of trouble."

"That's a bit bloodthirsty, Steph. Anyway, Afridi isn't a problem anymore."

"I rest my case."

"We've still got Cobra to deal with. I'd better let Nick know about Afridi."

"Look at that mound of rocks," Stephanie said. She pointed at the stones and dirt Afridi's men had moved and piled to the side. "That's some serious labor."

"They were looking for something. We still don't know what."

"If they found anything, Cobra has it now."

On screen, the tribesmen had gotten out of their truck and were fanning out through the site. Elizabeth called Nick.

"Director."

"Afridi's dead," Elizabeth said. "So are all the men he had with him."

"Where do I send the flowers?"

"Very funny, Nick. It looks like Cobra caught Afridi and his men by surprise. There's no one there now, except the locals."

"So we don't need an insertion into Afghanistan or Pakistan after all," Nick said. "I'm not sorry to hear that. I wasn't looking forward to it."

"If I didn't know better, I'd say you were getting soft," Elizabeth said.

"You don't give me the chance."

Elizabeth laughed. "I don't want you to get bored."

"What's next?"

"We still have Cobra to deal with."

"Where is he now?"

Stephanie had been listening to the conversation. She pulled up a map on her monitor. Rao's phone was marked by a blinking red dot.

"I've got a lock on his phone," Stephanie said. "He's not that far from you, on a road that goes to a town southwest of Srinagar called Poonch. It's right on the control line, near the border with Pakistan. Ijay would have needed to use a helicopter to get to Afridi. There's an airstrip in Poonch, the only one in the region. I think Cobra is going to meet him there."

"I don't know what this guy looks like," Nick said.

"I can fix that," Stephanie said. She called up a photo of Rao, hacked from his file on the Research Wing servers. "I'm sending a picture now."

Nick looked at the photo. Cobra was an innocuous looking man for someone who had caused so much trouble. There was something hidden in his eyes. Nick had seen it before, in the eyes of men for whom everything was a means to an end. It was the look of a man with no conscience.

"What do you want us to do?" Nick said.

"Go get him," Elizabeth said. "Find out what Afridi was doing in Afghanistan. Cobra went to a lot of trouble to track him down and kill him."

"I'll let you know if his location changes," Stephanie said.

"Copy that," Nick said.

CHAPTER 54

Nick and Selena rode in the front seat of the rental van, Lamont in back. Nick was behind the wheel. Black travel cases loaded with film gear and marked with the logo of the bogus Canadian film company took up most of the cargo space behind Lamont. Their pistols were out of sight.

"Check point coming up," Lamont said.

Concrete barriers placed in a staggered pattern across the pavement blocked the way. Four soldiers in Indian uniforms and carrying INSAS assault rifles waited by a covered truck parked at the side of the road. One of the soldiers stepped out and held up his hand to stop.

The soldiers looked nervous.

"Itchy fingers," Lamont said, as Nick slowed. "Don't piss them off."

Selena said, "Let me do the talking."

Nick came to a stop and rolled down his window. The soldier who approached had two red and gold chevrons on his shoulder boards. A corporal. The man was young, no more than twenty at most. He eyed the foreign faces with suspicion.

"This is restricted area," he said. His English was awkward, heavily accented. "Who are you? Why you come here?"

Nick said, "We're a film crew from Canada, making a documentary on Kashmir."

"No filming here. Turn around."

Selena leaned across Nick and began speaking Hindi. The soldier looked surprised. He answered her and held out his hand.

"He wants to see our passports," Selena said.

They handed over the passports. The soldier looked at each photo, comparing the pictures to the people.

Selena said, "Give him the letter."

Part of their cover was an official looking letter written in Hindi and English from the Indian Ministry of Culture, giving them permission to film anywhere in Indian Kashmir. It instructed anyone who read it to provide full cooperation to the distinguished Canadian film crew. It was signed by the minister himself. The letter had been provided courtesy of Langley's clandestine ops division. Even the minister would think it was his signature.

A second soldier came over to the van. This man had three stripes on his shoulder. The corporal gestured at the van and said something. The sergeant took the documents and studied them.

"You speak Hindi?" he said to Nick.

"Not me. She does." He nodded at Selena.

"Give me the key to the back of the van."

"It's unlocked," Nick said.

The sergeant barked out a command. A third soldier opened the doors and began looking in the cases. Lights. Sound gear. A computer. He held up an expensive steady cam.

"Please be careful with that," Nick said. If they did a personal search they'd find the guns. That wouldn't go over well.

The soldier finished searching and shook his head. He got out of the van and closed the doors.

"Why are you going to Poonch?" the sergeant asked.

Nick didn't have a story ready. He was about to make one up when Selena began talking to the sergeant in Hindi. She spoke for a minute before the sergeant replied. The conversation went back and forth. Nick had no idea what they were talking about.

The sergeant handed the passports and letter back to Nick.

"You may go. Be careful. There are reports of infiltrators from Pakistan. They will not treat you well if they see you."

"Thank you, Sergeant," Nick said.

The sergeant stepped back and saluted. Nick put the van in gear and they eased around the barriers.

Nick turned to Selena. "What did you tell him?"

"I told him we wanted to film the spot where the courageous Indian Army and proud people of the area held back the Pakistani hoards in 1947 and saved the nation."

"Did you really say that?"

"More or less. Not quite so dramatically."

"What's Poonch got to do with saving the nation?"

"The Kashmir Valley is a major corridor for invasion from Pakistan and Poonch is on a natural strategic choke point. When war started in 1947 there wasn't any airport. Civilian refugees hacked out a dirt runway in six days while a small unit of the Indian Army held the Pakis off. Once the strip was done, reinforcements and supplies could be airlifted in to block the invasion."

"Saving the nation," Nick said.

"Exactly."

Poonch was a city of about 500,000 people. They passed a large mosque on the side of a hill overlooking the city.

"Most of the people here are Muslim," Selena said. "The boundary line runs right through the city."

"Hindus and Muslims," Nick said. "You'd think after a thousand years or so they'd would learn to get along."

"Religion divides everything in India and Pakistan," Selena said.

A marker told them they were on the Surankote Daraba Road. They passed a turnoff with a sign in English, Arabic and Hindi pointing the way to the airstrip. Tall hills surrounded the strip on three sides. They could see the fortified control line between Indian and Pakistani Kashmir, snaking along a hill on the other side of the field. Guard posts and bunkers bristled on the hillside. High barriers of rolled wire in two rows with a narrow dirt path between them marked the line.

"I spy a helicopter," Lamont said.

"Yup. Looks nasty. What is that, a 20mm sticking out in front?" Nick said.

"Looks like it. Rocket pods, too."

Selena had binoculars on the chopper. "People standing around. Sentries on the perimeter. Looks like an elite unit, everyone is armed and wearing black uniforms. Wait a minute."

Selena adjusted the binoculars. "There's a car turning onto the strip."

She watched. The car came to a stop and a man in civilian clothes got out and walked toward the chopper.

"It's Cobra."

"Jackpot," Lamont said.

Nick drove pulled to the side of the road and parked where they could see the helicopter through the trees.

"Now what?" Selena asked.
"Now we wait for Cobra's next move."

CHAPTER 55

Rao turned off the road and onto the landing strip. Ijay's helicopter sat part way down from the end. Four men armed with Kalantak micro assault rifles were stationed around the perimeter.

Ijay's bird was a Rudra Class attack helicopter, named for the Vedic god of the tempest. The aircraft looked the part, lethal and black. Four long blades stretched out over the center of a wide body that could carry twelve heavily armed soldiers. A long-barreled 20mm cannon stuck out like a spear from a chin mounted gun turret in front. Pods mounted out to the sides carried antitank and antiaircraft missiles. The Rudra was a fast attack helicopter designed to put the fear of God in an enemy tanker, right before he got to meet his god in person. The sophisticated systems of the bird placed it with the best of its kind, anywhere in the world. The new radar evading technology on this one put it in a class of its own.

Ijay stood outside the craft talking with several of his men. As he pulled up and parked, Rao could see the pilot and another crewman in the cockpit. It looked as though the pilot was angry. As Rao got out of the car, Ijay broke away from the group and came forward to meet him.

"Ijay," Rao said.

"Sir." Ijay saluted.

"Where is Afridi?"

"Dead. As are all his men. Two of mine were killed. This man has been costly."

Rao thought of Lakshmi and his son, dead on that station platform all those years ago because of

Afridi. He wished he had Afridi's corpse at his feet. He would urinate on him, kick him, spit on his face. He wished Lakshmi and Arjuna were here with him, to feel his revenge. But they were not, and all he felt was a numb recognition that his enemy was dead at last. Somehow he'd thought it would be more intense, more satisfying.

"Sir?" Ijay was looking at him.

"Sorry, I was thinking," Rao said. "I'm sorry about your men."

Ijay nodded.

"Tell me what happened," Rao said.

Ijay described the flight across Pakistan and the brief battle for the camp, the death of Afridi. Then he told Rao what they had found.

"We recovered several boxes of gold and one of precious stones," he said. "Old coins. Pieces of gold, finely worked."

"It's all part of the Mughal treasure stolen during the sack of Delhi," Rao said. "We'll use some of it to compensate the families of your men who were killed. Did you look through the box with the jewels?"

"No. We were busy."

"Let me see it."

"It's inside."

The two men walked over to the helicopter. Rao heard cursing, a steady stream of muttered blasphemies.

"That's the pilot you hear," Ijay said. "There's an electrical problem. We almost crashed when we came in and now we can't take off until it's fixed. It's probably a problem with the new gear. We'll find it, but it might take a while."

They climbed into the helicopter. There was a faint, acrid smell of burned insulation in the air.

Two black body bags lay at the rear, uneven shapes in the gloom of the interior. The co-pilot had a panel off the side of the cabin, studying the wiring. The boxes from Afridi's campsite were stored under an aluminum bench seat. Ijay pulled one out.

Rao opened the lid.

Ijay said, "I've never seen anything like what's in this box. Never."

Rao pushed aside several stones and saw the Eye.

At last!

He drew the Eye from the box and held it up to the light coming through the open door. His hand trembled.

"We'll use some of the gold to compensate the families of your men. I'll turn the rest of it in," Rao said. "Except for this. This belongs in the temple."

"It's beautiful," Ijay said.

"Do you know the prophecy about the Eye of Shiva?"

"Every good Hindu knows the prophecy," Ijay said. He quoted: *"When the Eye is returned, my enemies will be consumed in the divine fire."*

"That's right."

"That is the Eye?" There was awe in Ijay's voice.

"Yes. You've served Lord Shiva by bringing this back to Mother India."

"You knew it was there?"

"I had hoped it was. I suspected Afridi had found the Mughal treasure, or some part of it. This was meant to be."

"Karma," Ijay said.

Rao nodded. "I'm going to take this to the temple in New Delhi. Bring everything back to base once you've completed repairs."

Ijay saluted. "Sir."

Rao got back into his car. He felt one of the headaches starting. Eating seemed to help and he could take some of Krivi's pills. He decided to stop at a restaurant he'd noticed in town. After hundreds of years, a few more minutes before the Eye was returned wouldn't matter.

Selena had been watching. Now she lowered the binoculars. "Cobra's getting in his car."

Nick said. "We can't take him here. Those guys are Special Forces. There's no cover and we're outgunned. We wouldn't have a chance."

Lamont swatted at a fly buzzing in the van. "What do you want to do?"

"He has to be going back to Srinagar. There's only one road, the way we came in. He has to go that way. We'll get ahead of him and wait."

"Then what?" Selena asked.

"We ambush him, force him off the road. Once we're out of the city and past that checkpoint, there are long stretches of highway where we could do it."

"You ever do anything like that before?" Selena asked.

"In Iraq. Of course, we had armored vehicles there. Made it easier."

"He's driving a Jaguar. If he wants to ditch us, he'll leave this heap in the dust," Lamont said.

"Then we'll make sure he doesn't get the chance."

Nick started the van and pulled out after their quarry. The Jaguar was already far ahead. They entered the city. Soon they were crawling in heavy traffic, stuck behind a large truck belching black smoke. There was no opening to pass.

Nick couldn't see Cobra's car ahead.

"This traffic sucks," he said. "We're going to lose him."

Suddenly Selena pointed off to the side. "There's the Jag."

The Jaguar was parked outside a restaurant.

"Looks like we caught a break," Lamont said.

"Let's hope he takes his time."

The truck in front turned off into a side street. Nick dodged a three wheeled motor bike loaded down with a family of four and a goat and picked up speed. In another ten minutes they reached the outskirts of town.

Different sentries manned the checkpoint. They passed through with no problem and half an hour later were parked on the side of the road in the shade of a cluster of trees, waiting for Cobra.

Dusty fields lined the road on both sides. The sun lit the countryside with a luminous quality of light Nick had never seen anywhere else in the world. In the distance, a man walked behind a plow pulled by a hump-backed ox. It was a scene that hadn't changed much in thousands of years.

Nick chose a place for the ambush where the road rose and made a blind turn into a sharp curve before it opened out onto a long straightaway. He parked the van halfway around the curve under some trees. Nick's plan was to pull onto the road in front of Rao's car as he slowed down in the turn.

He called Harker.

"Director, we're going for Cobra. Have you got us on satellite?"

"Affirmative, Nick. We have a clear view of the area and GPS signals from you and Cobra."

In Virginia, Stephanie and Elizabeth watched the vehicles and the colored dots that marked their location. Nick's dot was stationary. Cobra's moved at a high rate toward the ambush.

"He's moving right along," Elizabeth said. "He must be doing close to a hundred."

"On this road that's suicide," Nick said. "He might save us a lot of trouble and take himself out."

"Everyone drives like that here," Stephanie said. "India has a lot or traffic accidents."

"He'll have to slow down for the curve. Let me know when he's close."

"Not long," Elizabeth said. "Less than two minutes."

"Any other vehicles coming?"

Elizabeth looked at the live image. The highway was clear, except for the dark shape of Rao's Jaguar speeding along the road toward the curve.

"Negative. Nothing either way."

Nick drove onto the highway and blocked it. They got out of the van.

"What if he doesn't stop?" Selena asked.

"He has to or he'll turn that fancy car into scrap metal."

They heard the sound of the Jaguar's engine approaching, a deep, throaty sound.

"Here he comes," Nick said. "Get out of sight. I'll pretend I'm fixing a flat."

Inside the Jaguar, Rao was floating on Krivi's pills. The car's expensive sound system played soft music, counterpoint to the steady purr of the powerful engine. Rao loved his car, the fine leather, the polished wood accents. It was a joy to drive, fast and responsive. Now that it was owned and built in India, driving a Jaguar had become a matter of national pride as well as status.

Rao had the transmission in manual mode. He liked the feeling of controlling the shifts instead of letting the computer do it for him. He geared down as the curve approached and crested the rise. A blue van blocked most of the highway. At the rear of the truck a man knelt by the tire. He looked up and waved at Rao to stop.

As Rao hit the brakes, his mind registered alarm. A white man. He looked familiar. Then Rao remembered where he'd seen him.

In a file in his office.

Carter!

Rao shifted down, whipped the wheel over and punched the accelerator. The rear end skidded toward the van, then he was off the highway onto the hard packed earth of the field. The low-slung car bottomed out in a cloud of red dust, fishtailing and scraping. Rao spun the wheel again and was back on the road and moving away. He shifted up and floored it.

"Shit!" Nick yelled. He pulled out his pistol and fired half a dozen rounds at the Jaguar as it sped away. In seconds, it was a speck in the distance.

"That went well," Selena said.

CHAPTER 56

Rao's heart pounded against his ribs. The pleasant calm of the pills had vanished. His hands shook as he gripped the steering wheel. He could feel vibration in the wheel that hadn't been there before. It sounded like something had come loose underneath. The ride felt harsh. He looked at the gauges. He was doing over 200 kph. Except for the vibration and a loud exhaust, everything seemed normal. The van and the curve vanished in his rear view mirror.

Then he laughed. He hadn't felt alive like this since Afghanistan. It made him realize how dull he'd become, how he missed the edginess that made life interesting. It had slipped away, somewhere in that office high above Lodhi Road. What had Krivi said that day in the cafe?

"What have you got to lose?"

The answer was simple. Nothing. *Nothing to lose.* It didn't matter whether or not he succeeded in what he planned to do. He'd be dead soon, anyway. What mattered now was the game, the freedom that came from knowing his death was certain.

What was Carter doing there? How had the Project found him? Why? They couldn't know what he was planning. A road sign flashed by. He was a half hour out of Srinagar.

He analyzed the situation. *They wanted to kidnap me.* If they were willing to go to extreme lengths like that, it meant time was running out. He reached down to touch the stone, wrapped in cloth in his jacket pocket. It felt warm under his fingers.

His secure phone chirped. Rao looked at the screen. It was Prakash Khanna. Khanna was in New Delhi, at RAW headquarters.

"Yes."

"Ashok, what's happened?"

"What do you mean?"

"Security has been in your office, tearing everything apart. You're to be arrested and held for investigation. The Secretary himself was in here, looking pissed. He asked me if I knew anything about the riot at the mosque."

Rao tensed, the fine, high sense of freedom gone in an instant. His body buzzed, as though filled with electricity.

"What did you tell him?"

"What could I tell him? Nothing. They're waiting for you to show up, here or at your apartment."

"Where are you now?"

"Outside headquarters. I didn't want to call you from inside the building. "

"Don't do anything," Rao said. "Deny everything. In a short time it won't matter." Rao paused. "You've been a good friend, Prakash."

"Ashok..."

Rao clicked off.

They must have learned I set up the riot, he thought. *Or they could have found out the truth about Manila. That would explain why Carter was waiting.*

The more he thought about it, the more Rao was convinced that was what had happened. It changed everything. He had to act now, before the security forces closed in on him. Returning the Eye to the temple would have to wait. There was no more time.

He felt the hard shape of the card with the missile launch codes in his jacket pocket. There was one missile site in Kashmir, not far from Srinagar. It was armed with Agni III intermediate range missiles, exactly what Rao needed. Agni III carried a 20 kiloton warhead. It had a range of 4000 kilometers, overkill for nearby Islamabad.

It will be on them before they can respond, Rao thought. *I'll have Ijay meet me in Srinagar and fly me to the site.*

Rao knew that General Chatterjee, the commander of India's missile forces, had scheduled a surprise inspection at the site today. He'd call Chatterjee. Tell him he was coming to talk with him about something of vital importance to India's security.

Like Rao, Chatterjee was a nationalist who hated Pakistan. Rao thought it was even possible he'd cooperate in the launch, but it didn't matter. If Chatterjee and the security detachment on site resisted, Ijay and his men would take care of it. With the card and codes he didn't need Chatterjee. Once the missile was in the air, the end of Pakistan was a forgone conclusion.

He reached for the pill bottle and decided to take two more. He swallowed them down and called Ijay.

"We have a problem."

"Sir."

"Is the helicopter ready yet?"

"We're just finishing up. We'll be in the air in a few minutes."

"I ran into some trouble. Consider yourself on high alert. Meet me at the field in Srinagar," Rao said.

"Yes, sir. When will you be there?"

"Half an hour. General Chatterjee is on an inspection trip at one of the launch sites. We're going to pay him a visit. Get moving." Rao broke off the call.

He thought about Lakshmi and Arjuna, his wife and son. Karma that he'd met her, karma that Arjuna had been born, karma that they'd died. Karma was unavoidable. Whatever karmic debt he incurred because of what he was going to do, it meant nothing compared to avenging their deaths.

It wasn't far now to the airfield where Ijay would be waiting.

Lakshmi, my love, Rao thought, *soon I'll make them pay.*

CHAPTER 57

Rao's call to Khanna was captured by Stephanie's program. When Rao was done talking, Elizabeth called Nick.

"Cobra's been on his phone," she said. "Put Selena on."

Selena listened to the conversations. "In the first call, Cobra's talking to a man at RAW headquarters named Prakash," she said. "Prakash told him security is waiting to arrest him if he shows up. The second call was to Ijay. Cobra is meeting him back in Srinagar and he wants to fly to a missile site. He said General Chatterjee would be there on an inspection tour."

"Chatterjee is in charge of India's nuclear missile forces," Elizabeth said. "Why would Rao go to a missile site? I don't like the sound of that."

"He can't do much without the launch codes," Nick said.

"Chatterjee has those," Elizabeth said, "but only the prime minister can authorize a launch."

Nick laughed. It sounded harsh over the comm link. "In a perfect world, sure. It's bullshit. What happens if the prime minister is dead?"

"Then Chatterjee could launch."

Elizabeth shivered and her skin got little bumps. Her father used to say it happened when a goose walked over your grave.

"You see where this is going," Nick said. "Cobra has set up a war. We know he hates Pakistan. He knows he's blown. He's going to amp things up and launch a missile before they shut him down."

"He'd need Chatterjee to do it."

"He'll have Ijay there with his men. He can force Chatterjee to cooperate. Why else would he suddenly want to go to a missile site?"

Elizabeth's left eye twitched. She could feel a headache lurking. Her intuition began sounding alarms.

"You may be right. You have to intercept him," she said.

In India, Nick slowed for a bored looking white cow with long ears standing in the road. No one seemed to pay attention to a cow in the middle of traffic. They just detoured around it. Nick did the same. The cow looked at them as they went by.

"We don't know where he's going," Nick said.

"I can track Cobra's phone," Elizabeth said. "You've got to get a helicopter and go after them."

Nick thought of Akron, Langley's aging agent with the cowboy hat. "Langley's guy here has a chopper. Get Hood to light a fire under him and have him fueled up and ready to go."

"I'm going to warn the president," Elizabeth said, "but I don't think there's much he can do. If you're right and Cobra is going to try and launch, there isn't a lot of time. You're all we've got. You have to stop him."

"Yeah, sure. Out." Nick broke off the connection. "You all heard that," he said.

"Just another day at the office," Lamont said. "Where's our cowboy friend got his bird?"

"I don't know," Nick said. "Selena, call him. Find out where he's got the chopper stashed. If he hasn't heard from Hood, he will. He's number 3 on speed dial."

He handed her his phone. She called. Akron picked up.

"Yeah."

"This is Selena. We met the other day. Remember me?"

"Darlin', how could I forget? What can I do for you, Sweet Pea?"

Selena had the phone on speaker.

"Sweet Pea?" Lamont said. "Is this guy for real?"

"I heard that," Akron said. "What do you want?"

"Sounds like you haven't talked to the DCI yet," Selena said. Her voice was flat.

"Why would I? He doesn't talk to peons like me."

"You're about to get a call from him," Selena said. "Get your ass in gear and get your helicopter ready for us, now. We need to know where it is. We'll meet you there."

Nick smiled. Selena didn't get called Sweet Pea every day. He suspected it was a first. "Darlin'" would have been enough to piss her off.

"Whoa, don't get riled up," Akron said. Lamont shook his head. "Hold on, I got another call. Call me back in five." He disconnected.

"That will be Hood," Nick said, "Sweet Pea."

"Don't start," she said.

Nick pulled over. "No point in going farther into the city until we know where he's got his chopper."

His phone signaled a call.

"Carter."

"Guess you got some clout," Akron said. "Sorry I pissed off the lady."

"Lady?" Selena said.

"Don't make it worse," Nick said. "Where's the field?"

Akron gave directions. "Where are we going?" he said.

"I don't know yet. Just get the engine warmed up."

"We going in hot?"

"You could say that," Nick said.

CHAPTER 58

Akron's directions took them to a grassy field outside the city surrounded by a rusted chain link fence. A metal hangar with a white roof was the only building. A weathered wooden tower with an orange windsock stood at the far end of the field. A large sign next to the gate advertised sightseeing tours and special excursions. It listed a phone number. The helicopter was parked on a concrete pad in front of the hangar.

"Where the hell did he get that?" Nick asked. "An Army-Navy surplus store?"

"That bird's gotta be fifty years old," Lamont said.

"What are you talking about?" Selena asked.

"That's a Huey," Nick said. "An old one. You can see where the U.S. markings are painted out."

"I'll bet it's left over from Vietnam," Lamont said. "Be about right for this guy. It's what he flew over there."

The Huey was painted olive drab and had seen better days. The big side cargo doors were open. A row of seats had been fitted inside for sightseers but they didn't appear comfortable or like they belonged there. The bird still had the military look. The only things missing were M60s mounted at the doors.

Akron came out of the hangar. His cowboy hat was gone. In its place was an olive green radio helmet. He wore faded green fatigues with his name stenciled in black on the breast pocket, combat boots and aviator style sunglasses. Nick hadn't seen that style of uniform for years.

"You sure about this?" Lamont said. "He looks like he thinks it's 1968."

"We don't have a choice," Nick said. "We need him."

"Afternoon," Akron said. "Nice day for a tour."

"You really get sightseers?" Nick asked, pointing at the sign.

"Oh, yeah. Not many, but some. Enough to pay for gas."

"How come they let you run a business here?"

"It's a long story. A couple of people owed me favors. A little grease from the Agency didn't hurt either."

"The Indians know you're an agent?" Selena asked.

"Nope. They think I'm a crazy ex-pat with money. Long as I don't make trouble, they leave me alone. It's a pretty tolerant place here, or at least it used to be. That's changing, though. I'm thinking of getting out, going back to the States. Do some hunting and fishing."

While they were talking, they'd drifted over to the helicopter.

"What did you fly in Vietnam?" Nick said.

"Hueys, just like this. Sharks."

"Sharks?" Selena looked confused.

"What we called the gunships," Akron said. "The transports were Dolphins."

He patted the side of the craft. "She's a good bird. Where are we going?"

"I don't know yet," Nick said. "Let me make a call."

Harker answered. "Great minds, Nick. I was about to call you."

"You know where we're going yet?"

"Cobra took off ten minutes ago. We're tracking him now. There's only one site in Kashmir, near a place called Pahalgam."

"Where's Pahalgam?"

Akron heard him. He said, "I know where it is. It's southeast of here. Lots of old temples, health resorts, mountains and rivers."

"They keep a half dozen missiles and their launchers in a tunnel complex there," Elizabeth said. "It's got to be where he's going."

"Send the coordinates."

"On the way," Elizabeth said.

Nick's phone chirped.

"Got it."

"I talked with Rice. He's going to do what he can but I don't think it will be in time to help."

"Any rules of engagement?"

"Just stop him," Elizabeth said. "However you can." She disconnected.

Nick looked at Akron. "You got any weapons?"

Akron smiled. "I figured you might ask. Follow me."

He led them into the hangar. The back was partitioned off for living quarters. Akron went into what passed for a living room and pulled up a faded oriental rug, exposing a trap door in the concrete floor.

"Give me a hand," he said.

They pulled up the heavy door. A narrow ladder led below. Akron picked up a flashlight and started down.

"Wait there," he said. "There isn't a lot of room down here."

They heard him moving crates aside.

"Here you go," he said. He handed up an M-16, then two more, then belts weighted down with loaded 30 round magazines. He handed up a Colt Model 1911 .45 in a leather holster.

"That one's for me," he said.

Akron climbed up and turned off the flash. They closed the trap door and put the rug back in place.

Akron gestured at the M-16 Selena held. "You know how to use that, Sweet Pea?"

Selena started to move toward him. Nick put his hand on her arm.

"Hey Akron?" he said.

"Yeah?"

"Sweet Pea here can shoot rings around you with one hand and kick your ass while she's doing it. So knock off the sexist bullshit, okay?"

"Sorry," he said. He didn't look sorry. "Old habit. I just wanted to know."

They checked out the rifles. Clean and oiled, in good shape. They inserted the magazines. Akron belted on the holster and .45.

Nick said, "Let's get going."

CHAPTER 59

Ijay's helicopter set down on a broad, flat area where the launchers would stage in time of war. A helicopter with army markings was parked to one side. Rao had radioed ahead. General Chatterjee was expecting him.

The entrance to the tunnel was a thirty foot square opening carved into the side of a mountain. The complex was located in a forest of evergreens and surrounded by high, snow-capped peaks. A road to the site continued past the tunnel to an ancient Hindu temple set a mile away on a green hillside. The temple was in ruins, destroyed centuries before by one of the Muslim rulers.

For Rao, the ruins were one more reminder of how Islam desecrated everything he held sacred. He shook out two more of Krivi's pills and swallowed them. He felt full of energy, light, invincible.

The steel doors to the tunnel stood open. Waiting just inside was the first of six mobile transporters. The camouflaged, phallic shape of an Agni III ICBM lay flat along the trailer, waiting to be raised into position. The missile was about forty feet long and six feet around. The nose cone tapered to a rounded point and was painted black. The body of the missile was white. The Indian flag was painted on the side.

Agni III had been designed to provide long range counter-strike capability. It was powered by a two stage, solid fuel rocket that drove it to a speed of over 5km a second. Guidance was provided by a sophisticated inertial navigation system. The twenty kiloton warhead was roughly the size of the bombs that had destroyed Hiroshima and Nagasaki. It was set to detonate five kilometers above ground.

An air burst was more destructive than a conventional impact explosion. Everything within one mile of the hypocenter would be completely destroyed. The blast wave would travel outward at nearly the speed of sound. A mile away from the center it would have enough power to hurl a fifty ton railway car from it's tracks and crush it. Two miles out, the damage would still be severe. Anyone left alive in that two mile radius would receive a lethal dose of radiation.

Islamabad had a crowded population of around two million people. One missile would obliterate the city. Hundreds of thousands of people would die in the initial blast. The radiation would leave the ground poisoned for many years.

The tunnel complex was guarded by a detachment of twenty-four men under the command of a lieutenant. The officer approached and saluted. Four sentries in battle dress and wearing maroon berets stood by the tunnel entrance, armed with assault rifles.

"Secretary Rao? The general is expecting you. May I see some identification, sir?"

Rao showed his RAW credentials.

"Follow me, sir."

Rao glanced at Ijay. They had already determined what they were going to do. They followed their escort into the tunnel.

CHAPTER 60

Nick sat in the co-pilot's seat next to Akron. They were flying a hundred feet above the highway leading to Pahalgam, below Indian radar. Nick hoped it was good enough to fool any antiaircraft defenses at the tunnel. There wasn't anything he could do about them if they spotted the Huey.

He felt himself slipping into pre-combat mode. He was hyper alert, watching the countryside flash by below as they paralleled the road from Srinagar to Pahalgam. Next to him, Akron was in his element. He seemed younger, even happy. It was as if he'd dropped thirty years in a moment. He hummed to himself, one hand on the collective, the other tapping fingers against his leg.

Back in the cargo bay, Selena and Lamont sat in the makeshift tourist seats. Selena cradled her M-16 across her knees. She'd put on a pair of Ray-Bans against the wind rushing through the open cargo doors. Her lips were set in a tight line. Lamont looked relaxed, half asleep, but Nick knew it was an illusion. His rifle was propped against his body under his arm.

Nick heard Stephanie's voice over the comm link. The noise in the chopper made it difficult, even with headphones covering his ears.

"Nick, you hear me?"

"I hear you, Steph."

"Cobra has landed. He's got eight men I can see. The pilot and co-pilot, too."

"Describe what you see."

"There's a wide, flat space where he landed, by the side of a mountain. That would be the staging area. There's another helicopter there. Four sentries visible. Cobra's men are talking with a couple of them or standing around nearby."

Getting ready to take them out, Nick thought.

"What else?"

"That's it. The tunnel entrance is to the left as you come in from the highway. A soldier came out of the mountain and met Cobra. They went inside."

"Any sign of the missiles?" Nick asked.

"Not yet."

"Good. We've still got time."

"At your present rate of speed, you'll reach the target area in about fifteen minutes."

"Is there someplace near the tunnel where we can set down? We come in direct, they'll start shooting."

"There's one road to the site. It follows a valley to the left of the main highway. There's a field where it turns off from the highway. You could set down there. No houses. There's a guard post and gate about three miles in from the road. It's another mile to the tunnel after that. Everything else looks pretty steep."

Four miles was too far on foot when time was short.

"What happens when the road gets to the site?"

"There's a short entry road to the staging area to the left as you come in. I'm sending a real time shot now."

Nick's phone vibrated against his chest. He pulled it out and looked at the screen. Steph had sent a wide aerial view of the tunnel complex and the road. He saw the guard post, the staging area and two helicopters. He could see Cobra's men and the tunnel sentries, tiny figures casting tiny shadows on the ground, unaware they were being watched.

The road continued past the missiles and ended a mile away at a structure on the side of a hill.

"What's that building farther on?" he asked.

"It's a deserted temple. It used to be a tourist spot before they put the missiles in."

Stephanie's voice sounded in his ear. "Nick, the satellite is moving out of range. We're going to lose visual in a minute."

"Thanks, Steph. We're going to be busy for a while. I'll call in later. Out."

He tapped Akron on the shoulder and held up the phone with the satellite photo for him to see.

"Here's the complex," he said, pointing at the flat area. "There's a sentry post here, below. Go up the valley beyond it and touch down here." Nick pointed to a point on the road past the entrance to the complex. It couldn't be seen from the staging area.

"We'll jump off. You keep going, toward this old temple. Make them think you're taking tourists sightseeing."

"You really think they'll go for that?"

"It's worth a shot. Or do you want to try coming in on a hot LZ?"

Akron shrugged. "Wouldn't be the first time."

They were flying along the highway. Nick saw the turnoff and pointed. "There's the road. Follow it up the valley."

The chopper banked left.

Nick hoped they'd be in time.

CHAPTER 61

Inside the tunnel, General Naitik Chatterjee
stood next to one of the massive transporters,
talking with a sergeant. Chatterjee was tall for an
Indian man, almost six feet. His uniform was crisp
and neat. Ribbons from the last three wars with
Pakistan adorned his chest. Chatterjee had been
badly wounded during the Kargil War in 1999. His
left hand was missing two fingers and he was
unable to use his left arm for anything except light
duty.

"That will be all, Lieutenant," Chatterjee said.

"Sir." Chandra saluted and left.

"Hello, Naitik. It's good to see you. May I
introduce Major Gupta?" Rao said.

Ijay saluted Chatterjee. "Sir."

"Major."

"Major, please give us some privacy," Rao said
to Ijay.

"Sir." Ijay saluted again and moved off toward
a group of men working on one of the transporters.

"Ashok," Chatterjee said. "I was surprised to
get your call. Come to check up on us, eh?"

The two men shook hands. "Let's go where we
can talk in private."

"Certainly. Sergeant, tell Lieutenant Chandra
we're not to be disturbed."

"Sir." The sergeant saluted and walked away.

"Over here," Chatterjee said.

They stepped into an office with a window
looking out on the missiles and transporters. Rao
looked through the window. There were six units on
this base. Six missiles, any one of which could

eliminate a major city. Rao saw three men working on one of the trucks toward the back of the tunnel.

"Where are the rest of your men?" Rao asked.

"We're a bit short handed at the moment, I'm afraid. Lieutenant Chandra informed me that three men were sent to hospital yesterday with food poisoning. Another six were rotated out. Their replacements haven't arrived yet."

"But you still have enough to man the missiles."

"Of course. It's a straightforward process. All the men are trained to position the transporters."

For Rao, things had just gotten easier.

"I wanted to talk with you about Pakistan," Rao said. "Lanka seems unwilling to act. Islamabad is bringing up heavy armor, artillery and troop transports. They're getting ready to invade."

"The Prime Minister is a fool," Chatterjee said. "We should have done something years ago about those dogs in Islamabad. Now they're barking at our door again. Yet he still holds back."

"I think we need to take things into our own hands," Rao said, "since Lanka will not."

"Surely you don't mean a coup," Chatterjee said, surprised. "War's a certainty. Now isn't the time for that, even if it were possible. Even if there were enough people to go along with it. Which I doubt."

"Not a coup," Rao said. "More specific than that. Let me show you something."

He took the Eye of Shiva from his pocket, uncovered it and set it on the desk. The jewel glittered with a deep, red glow in the bright glare of the fluorescents overhead.

Chatterjee's eyes widened in recognition. "Is it...it can't be."

"It is," Rao said.

"The Eye. You have found the Eye."

"You remember the prophecy?"

"Of course. Where did you get this? How?"

"It's a long story, Naitik. A Muslim had it, a pawn of Islamabad. I took it back."

Krivi's drugs coursed through Rao's veins. He felt as if his body was almost transparent. His mind was clear, his thoughts sparkles of light. He shifted on his feet and watched the general.

Chatterjee stared at the sacred jewel. "The divine fire," he whispered.

"That is why I'm here," Rao said.

Chatterjee looked at him with sudden realization. "You want me to send a missile against Pakistan, don't you?"

"Think of it, Naitik. One blow, and Islamabad will trouble us no more. No more of their constant provocations, their endless attempts to subvert Jammu and Kashmir. Their contempt for everything we value."

"They would retaliate," Chatterjee said.

"They won't have time," Rao said. "The Agni VI is on line, as you know. You command the missile forces. We can knock out their bases before they have a chance to respond. Even if they get a few missiles into the air, our defense systems will blow them out of the sky before they land. At worst, some casualties. But Pakistan will cease to exist. Mother India will be whole again."

"Lanka will never authorize a first strike."

"You don't need his authorization. You have the codes. You are one of the few who can do this."

There it was. The moment of truth. Rao waited to see how Chatterjee would respond.

Chatterjee was a patriot. He'd given years of his life and shed his blood in the service of Mother India. He had been brought up in a Hindu culture, taught that Pakistan and Islam were India's mortal enemies. He'd seen first hand the results of Pakistan's treachery and ambition.

Now Rao wanted him to act, to unleash the nuclear fires under his command. It was tempting. Sometimes he'd thought about it, in the dark hours of the night. But he'd sworn an oath when he entered the military. In Sanskrit, the name Naitik meant *"one who follows the correct path."* There was only one possible response to Rao's proposal. Chatterjee looked at Rao and knew this was the end of their friendship.

"I cannot," he said. "I'm sorry."

"You disappoint me, Naitik," Rao said, "but I understand. You are a soldier. You have a duty to obey your superiors."

Chatterjee looked relieved. "You do understand," he said. "Good. I would hate to have anything get in the way of our friendship."

"I have always valued our friendship," Rao said. "I always will."

He took a 9 mm pistol from his pocket and shot Chatterjee twice in the chest, right through the rows of brightly colored campaign ribbons. The shots echoed in the hollow interior of the cavern.

Chatterjee stumbled backward. He looked down in disbelief at the blood welling out through his uniform. Then he fell to the ground. His legs kicked in a final spasm and he was still. His bowels let go. Rao stepped back in distaste from the stench.

Inside the tunnel, Lieutenant Chandra and the sergeant came running out of one of the offices.

"What..."

Rao shot them. They spun and fell and died.

Farther down the tunnel, Ijay raised his weapon and opened fire, cutting down the group of men he'd been chatting with.

The shots were the signal to act if Chatterjee proved uncooperative. Ijay's men were positioned by the sentries. Knives came out. The guards never had a chance.

Rao turned his pistol on a man coming at him with a wrench and shot him. Ijay ran forward and let off a burst at the last two men in the detachment. It had taken less than a minute to kill everyone at the complex.

Ijay ejected the spent magazine from his gun and inserted a fresh one. He wiped the metal down with a cloth he pulled from his pocket.

It was important to keep your weapons clean.

CHAPTER 62

Akron kept the Huey low and fast, flying a few hundred feet above the valley floor. They followed a narrow stream toward the tunnel complex. Nick listened to the old, familiar tune of the helicopter blades as the sound echoed from the mountains, *chopchopchopchop...*

...and he was back in Afghanistan, back in the village and the brown dust and the heat, the helicopters lifting away, beating up a blinding storm of dust and grit. He signaled his Marines forward. They trailed out behind him as he moved along the deserted main street, the only street. Somewhere a baby was crying. He could smell the sour scent of his fear.

He held his M4 up close to his face, the selector on three round burst, safety off, his finger laid along the side of the receiver. He came to the market. Strips of stringy meat glistening with gristle hung in the open air of the butcher's stall. Flies buzzed in clouds around the stall, a nasty, irritating sound.

Men with thick beards rose up from a flat rooftop across the street and cut loose with AKs. The bullets shattered the flimsy market stalls, ricocheted off the walls, kicked up dirt at his feet. He ducked into a doorway and began firing at the roof. His men were shouting, firing, the noise deafening. Someone screamed in pain. Dozens of automatic rifles spat out their messages of death. Russian Kalashnikovs, American M4s. All the guns spoke the same language.

From across the way, a young boy ran toward him, screaming about Allah. He had a grenade in his hand. He cocked his arm back to throw.

A boy, no more than ten or eleven. Just a child. Nick's finger paused on the trigger.

The boy threw the grenade. Time slowed. Nick fired, one, two, three, the rifle kicking back against his shoulder. The first shot knocked the boy backward. The second took him in the throat. The third blew open his head like a ripe melon. Nick watched the grenade float toward him. He watched it tumbling in the air, unable to move, Then everything went white...

Akron was shaking him by the shoulder. "You all right, man? You don't look so good."

They were in India, not Afghanistan. He'd been lost in a flashback. It hadn't happened for a while.

Shit, Nick thought. *How long?*

"Yeah, I'm fine."

Ahead of them the guard post on the road was coming up. *So, not too long. A minute or two.* Two men stood looking up at the approaching helicopter.

"Wave," Nick said.

"What?"

"Wave. When we go over. Like we're friendly." He turned around to Lamont and Selena and yelled over the noise. "Wave at the guards down there."

They flew over the barrier, waving and grinning like idiots. Then the post was behind them.

"Keep right on like we planned," Nick said.

In another minute they came up on the staging area, off to the left and up the side of the valley. They flashed past. Nick had time to see bodies lying on the ground. Men in black with assault rifles watched them go by. Then they were around the bend in the stream and out of sight of the tunnel.

Akron dropped down, fast.

"Hot damn," he said. "Just like the old days, 'cept no one's shooting at us."

"Not yet," Nick said.

Akron brought the skids within inches of the ground and hovered. Whatever his faults, he knew how to fly. Selena and Lamont were out in seconds, weapons ready. Nick came right behind. Akron lifted away in a soaring bank and headed upstream. Anyone watching from the staging area would see the chopper reappear from the turn and head straight for the temple ruins.

"Think they bought it?" Lamont said.

"I wouldn't bet on it. You see the bodies?"

Both Selena and Lamont nodded.

"Cobra must have decided to take them all out. He's probably got the general with the codes inside."

"The missiles aren't in position yet," Selena said. "We still have some time."

"Not much," Nick said.

The three of them studied the terrain. The land sloped up from the streambed where they stood, toward the tunnel with the missiles. A shallow ravine ran up the side of the mountain through a forest of evergreens.

"What do you think, Lamont? Up that ravine there? We're probably four or five hundred feet below where we want to be."

"It goes in the right direction."

"I'll take the point. Selena, you in the middle, keep an interval. Lamont, you cover our six."

"What's the plan when we get there?" Selena asked.

"Don't have one yet. As the situation demands. If they're suspicious, they'll send scouts out to look around. Be ready for anything."

"For some reason I thought this time would be different," she said.

"You ought to know better by now," Lamont said.

"Weapons free," Nick said.

Three metallic clicks as the safeties went off.

They set off up the side of the mountain.

*****

Rao came out of the tunnel. "I heard a helicopter," he said.

Ijay pointed at the green Huey flying toward the ruins.

"Looked like a bunch of tourists going to the temple. They were in civilian clothes, except the pilot. I think he was wearing fatigues. "

"Tourists? When war's coming and in a helicopter like that? I don't think so."

"I don't either," Ijay said. "It's too much of a coincidence."

"How many?" Rao asked.

"At least four. I saw two up front and two passengers. If they aren't tourists, we'll know soon enough. It shouldn't be a problem."

Ijay walked over to one of his men. "Sergeant. Take Panav and Darpak." He pointed in the direction of the temple. "Go down the side of the hill and make sure no one gets by you."

"Sir."

The sergeant called out to the two men. In a minute they were gone, out of sight in the trees. Ijay turned to Rao.

"Get one those missiles out here," Rao said.

CHAPTER 63

Selena watched Nick moving through the woods ahead of her. It was hot under the trees. There was no breeze. Tiny insects swarmed and bit her, drawn by her sweat. Her shirt was already soaked through. It felt strange to be doing this in civilian clothes. No boots, no armor. The last time she'd gone into a fight without armor it hadn't worked out well. At least she was wearing jeans and her Nikes. A skirt and regular shoes would have been impossible here.

She'd gotten better over time with the art of moving quietly but she still felt clumsy compared to Nick and Lamont. They made no noise as the team worked their way up the ravine.

She was careful not to dislodge any of the loose rocks in the wash. That's all she needed, kick loose a rock and have Nick give her one of his looks of disapproval.

Damn it, why did she care so much about what he thought? Sometimes she felt like she'd never be able to equal what these men did. They had years of specialized training in warfare she could never match. On the other hand, she could whip both of them in hand to hand, though she wouldn't want to take both on at once. Still, she could kick Nick's butt if she had to.

That thought brought a smile.

They came to the end of the ravine. The land sloped up for another twenty feet and leveled out. Nick held up his hand to stop.

He signaled Lamont. *Go left, then up*. He pointed at himself and up. *I'll take the center*. To

Selena, he signaled right and up. He pointed at them and at his eyes and then himself. *Watch me. Follow my lead.* He gestured ahead. *Go slow.*

She began working her way to the right, the rifle cradled under her chest. The hard metal pressed against her breasts. The ground scraped her elbows. She reached a point where she could look over the edge. Nick was behind her to the left and beyond him, Lamont. She risked a glance toward the tunnel.

The staging area was fifty or sixty yards away from where they lay. She saw a dark shape move under the trees, a man walking down the slope toward the valley floor. She ducked back and looked at Nick, pointed toward the base, held up one finger and pointed toward the stream below. *One hostile, moving down.*

He nodded, held up two fingers, pointed.

Two more, she thought.

She got ready to fire. There was little cover. If they were seen, they'd try to get off the first shots. Those were the ones that counted.

Better if they weren't seen. Selena wished she was wearing clothes that blended in with the landscape. Not blue running shoes and a pale blouse. She tried to scrunch down behind a dead limb lying on the ground. It wouldn't stop a bullet but at least it gave her some psychological comfort.

Nick signaled. *Back to the ravine.* He looked at her, touched his lips. *Quiet.* Then he smiled.

Smartass, she thought. *He's like a big kid sometimes. Playing war. Except the bullets are real.*

They crawled backwards down to the ravine. She had a dry, metallic taste in her mouth, the taste of fear. Off to her right she heard someone step on a dry branch and curse.

They waited. The air was still and hot. The only sound was the whine of insects and her heart pounding in her ears.

Noise shattered the silence. Diesel engines starting up, big ones. There was only one possible explanation for that. Cobra was moving the missiles out of the tunnel.

CHAPTER 64

The first of the transporters emerged from the tunnel entrance. The truck was painted in camouflage tan and brown, as if the natural colors somehow made the white body of the missile invisible. It was a big vehicle, low to the ground. The Agni III missile lay waiting and silent, clamped to the ramp that would raise it skyward for launch.

A box-like station behind the cab housed a control board and the electronics to initiate the firing sequence. The Agni III had an inertial guidance system augmented by GPS, a recent upgrade that improved accuracy. Targeting was controlled on site. The target data and launch codes were entered by the operator on a computer keyboard or by way of a pre-programmed card. It only took one man to initiate a launch if everything else was ready, unlike the two man systems common in the older ICBM silos.

Rao watched the first transporter move into place. A second crawled from the cavern into the sunlight. Ijay came over.

"It will take us another fifteen minutes to bring out the others," he said.

"We don't need them," Rao said. "These will be enough. Get them ready for launch."

"We only have one man familiar with these," Ijay said. "He has to tell the others what to do. It will slow things down some."

"Just get them ready," Rao said. "There are satellites up there. We don't have a lot of time."

Ijay's headset crackled. It was the sergeant he'd sent down the hill.

"Yes."

"We're down to the valley floor. No sign of anyone."

"Good. Come back up. Stay alert." He turned toward Rao. "No sign of intruders."

"Very good," Rao said. "I need to make a call."

He walked to the edge of the area and called Krivi.

"My friend," Krivi said. He was speaking English. "How are you?"

"Your pills are wonderful, Krivi," Rao said. "I feel good. I wanted to let you know that we're about to proceed as planned."

"Excellent," Krivi said, "excellent. India will always be grateful, Ashok. You will be remembered for generations. What you do today is only the beginning. Others will follow you."

In Virginia, Elizabeth had just finished arguing with the Pentagon about re-tasking a satellite to give them visual coverage of the missile site in Kashmir, with no success. Stephanie's program picked up Rao's call and put it on the office speakers.

Elizabeth said, "Who's Krivi?"

"I don't know," Stephanie said, "but at least Cobra is speaking English for a change."

"We're almost ready to launch," Rao said. "Perhaps fifteen minutes. Islamabad will cease to exist."

Krivi was still talking but Elizabeth wasn't listening.

"Shit," Elizabeth said. "What are the GPS coordinates for that base?"

Stephanie wrote them down.

"I'm calling the White House."

Elizabeth got up and went to her office and called Rice on his private number. The president picked up after two rings.

"Director."

"Sir, we have an emergency situation in India."

"Go on."

"There is about to be an unauthorized nuclear missile launch from Kashmir, aimed at Pakistan. My team is on site but may not be able to stop it in time. I am requesting a strike. We have a window of less than fifteen minutes, no more."

"You're certain."

"Yes, sir, absolutely."

"Director, if you're wrong, we'll be in a shitload of trouble."

"Sir, I'm not wrong. I'm certain."

"Very well." There was a pause while Rice thought it through. Elizabeth realized she was holding her breath.

"I'm connecting us to the Pentagon," Rice said. "Tell them where to go. I'll authorize the mission."

Thank God for a president who's not afraid to make tough decisions, she thought.

A new voice came on line.

"Special Operations Command, General Atkins speaking."

"General, this is the President."

"Yes, sir, I recognize your identity."

"There is going to be a missile launch in India. I am authorizing an immediate strike. Take it out, now. I have Director Harker on the line. She'll give you the target data."

"Yes, sir."

"Go ahead, Director," Rice said.

"General Atkins, this is Director Harker. Here are the GPS coordinates for the missile. It's nuclear."

She read them off.

Atkins said, "Mister President, please hold."

"Who's behind it?" Rice said.

"The same man who set up the attack in Manila," Elizabeth said. "He wants a war."

Atkins came back on line.

"We have a Reaper Q9 running hot out of Bagram over Pakistan," Atkins said. "I'm diverting it to the target."

"Very good, General. Keep me informed."

"Yes, sir, will do."

"Well, Director," Rice said. "We're committed. Better tell your people to keep their heads down."

CHAPTER 65

Nick, Selena and Lamont had worked their way to within twenty yards of the staging area. They watched the second transporter line up behind the first. A man dressed in a black uniform climbed onto the first unit and sat down at the operating console. He set a series of switches on a panel in front of him and then began entering commands on a keyboard.

"What do you want to do?" Lamont said.

"I make it five men, plus Cobra," Nick said. "We take them out, starting with the guy on the truck."

The ramp began to rise on the transporter. In seconds, the missile was aimed at the sky.

"Don't forget the three who went past us," Lamont said.

Nick's ear began itching. Harker's voice sounded in Nick's headset.

"Nick, there's a Reaper on the way. Don't get hurt."

"How soon?"

"Soon. What's your status?"

"There are two missiles out in the open. One's ready. It looks like there's only one guy who knows what he's doing. He finished with the first and now he's gone to the second to set that one up. That one is still down on the bed of the transporter."

"Nick, whatever happens, that missile can't launch."

"Yeah, I know."

"Wait. If the drone doesn't get there in time, stop it any way you can."

"Copy that."

"Good luck."

"Yeah."

Nick looked at the others. "You heard Harker. We'll wait. If it looks like they're going to push the button, concentrate your fire on the guy at the console."

"We'd better move back some," Lamont said. "They're likely going to drop a 500 pounder or two. We're too close."

"All right. As long as we keep line of sight on that console."

They moved back into the trees.

"That's far enough," Nick said. He looked at his watch. "Can't be more than a few minutes, now."

Sudden shots splintered chips of bark from trees nearby. The three sentries had found them. Selena moved behind a tree just as bullets kicked up dirt where she'd been standing. She reached around the trunk and fired blind at the shooters. Nick and Lamont opened up. The afternoon quiet vanished in the sharp explosions of automatic weapons.

Up on the staging area, Rao and Ijay heard the shooting. Rao ran over to where Ijay's man was working on the second missile.

"Is it ready?"

"Not yet. The other one is."

"Leave this. Get over to the other. Here."

Rao took the card Krivi had given him with the codes and programming for the missile out of his pocket. It went into a slot on the console. Once loaded into the computer, the flick of a switch would send the missile on its way.

"You know what this is?"

"Yes, sir."

"Use it. Fire as soon as you can." He gave the card to the soldier. "Hurry up."

The man ran over to the transporter and climbed up onto the back, the card in his hand.

Ijay signaled his men away from the launch. Rao moved to the safety of the tunnel. It wasn't a good idea to be near the tail of the missile when it ignited.

Nick fired at one of the soldiers shooting at them and brought him down. He looked around and saw Ijay's man climbing onto the truck. He swiveled and fired and an empty casing caught in the ejection port. The gun jammed.

On the truck, the operator inserted the card and activated the firing sequence. He got up to leave the unit for cover. Nick cleared the jam, aimed and fired and the man fell off the truck.

Seconds later the Agni III came to life. Flame and smoke erupted from the base of the missile.

"Fire at the missile and the control panel," Nick yelled.

Selena and Lamont turned. The three of them stood and emptied their magazines at the console and the missile. Nick saw holes appear in the white body. It began to rise. Nick dropped a magazine, jammed in another, and emptied it at the console with it's switches and gauges. He could see fragments fly off where the bullets hit.

Ijay's men were still shooting at them. A bullet plucked at Selena's sleeve. She turned and shot another man. One man still came on. She shot him too. He fell to the ground, clutching his gut and screaming. She couldn't hear him over the roar of the rocket engine. She turned back to watch.

The missile climbed toward the sky on a
column of orange fire and billowing white smoke. It
began to pick up speed. The noise was deafening.

"Too late," Nick said. "We were too late."

Then the missile slowed. It tilted to the side and
fell back toward the launching site, the rocket
engine belching flame.

"Jesus," Nick said.

They dropped down flat. Selena covered her
head with her arms.

The missile hit the ground and exploded.
Flaming bits and burning fuel fell back to earth in a
hellish rain.

Then the Reaper struck with a 500 pound
bomb.

The explosion ripped branches from the trees
and sent them flying through the air in a lethal
storm of splinters. Selena covered her ears. The
shock lifted her body from the ground. A huge,
burning tire from one of the transporters crashed
into the dirt a foot from her head and rolled away
down the hillside.

She lay there, waiting. There were no more
explosions. Slowly, she stood and looked around.
Everything was muffled, as though her ears were
stuffed with cotton.

Fires burned in a dozen places. It wouldn't be
long before the forest of pines where they stood
would be in flames. The staging area had been
destroyed. The transporters and helicopters were
twisted hulks of charred metal. A breeze brought an
unpleasant odor of burning rubber.

"We'd better get up there before these woods go
up," Nick said.

They climbed the rest of the way to the top.
The fire spread through the trees below. Small fires

dotted what was left of the staging area. The bomb
had left a gaping crater in the smooth surface.

A body lay near the tunnel entrance on its back,
eyes staring toward the sky. The dead man's face
was marked by birthmarks that looked like spots.
Debris smoldered in front of the tunnel. It looked as
though the interior of the complex was intact.

Lamont brought his rifle up. "I saw movement
in the tunnel."

"We have to go in," Nick said. "I'll take point."

They entered the cavern. Scraps of metal and
smoking bits littered the first ten yards. The
remaining missiles lay silent at the back of the
cavernous space. There were bodies on the floor,
one in the uniform of a ranking officer. It was dark
inside except for light from the entrance and the
window of one office. They heard someone singing
to himself.

They kept up against the wall and reached the
office. Nick took a quick glance through the
window and ducked back.

"It's Cobra," he said. "He's sitting at a desk. He
has a pistol in his hand."

"How you want to do it?" Lamont said.

"He's the only one left," Nick said. "I want to
try and take him alive. Ready?"

Without waiting, Nick stepped into the door of
the office and pointed his M-16 at Rao.

"Game's up, Rao. Put the gun on the desk and
your hands behind your head."

Rao swiveled in the chair, the pistol coming up
as he turned, but it wasn't pointed at them. He held
it in his right hand, the barrel pressed against the
side of his head. In his left, he held a great, red
stone.

For a second, Rao's face was a mask of anger. Then he smiled.

"Carter," he said. "How did you know?"

"We've been listening to your phone calls," Nick said. "Put down the gun. Slowly."

Rao held up the stone. It blazed with color under the lights.

"Do you know what this is?" he said.

"It's pretty," Nick said. "Put down the gun."

Rao laughed. It trailed off to a giggle. Selena and Lamont looked at each other. Lamont twirled his finger by his head.

"Pretty," Rao said. "You are looking at the soul of Mother India and all you can say is it's pretty."

"Why don't you tell me about it," Nick said. "I'm willing to learn. But put down the gun."

Rao ignored him. "I think the lady knows what I'm holding. Don't you, Doctor Connor?"

"You know who I am?" Selena said.

"Of course. And Mister Cameron, AKA Shadow. Unfortunate about Sergeant Peete, wasn't it? Did you know he died this morning?"

"You son of a bitch," Nick said.

Selena knew he was going to shoot. "Wait, Nick," she said. "He's lying. Elizabeth would have told us."

"Maybe." But he relaxed, just enough.

"So, Doctor Connor?" Rao held up the jewel.

"If I'm right, it's a jewel called the Eye of Shiva," Selena said. "No one has seen it for centuries."

"Very good," Rao said. "Doctor Connor, are you an honorable person?"

"What do you mean?"

He's nuts, Nick thought. *I should shoot him.* He watched Rao's gun.

"Are you honorable? Do you keep your word?"

"I believe in keeping my word. I guess that makes me honorable."

"If you give me your word about something, I will put down the gun."

"What is it?"

"I want you to take the Eye back to where it belongs. To the temple of Shiva, off the Peshwa Road in New Delhi. Anyone can tell you where it is. Give me your word that you will give it to the priests there. They'll know what to do."

"If I give you my word, you'll put down the gun?"

"I will."

"All right," Selena said. "You have my word. I'll take the Eye back to the temple."

Rao sighed. "I would have liked so much to bring it myself. Not much chance of that, now."

He leaned forward. The gun never wavered from his head. Rao slid the jewel across the desk.

"Pick it up," he said to Selena.

"Careful, Rao." Nick said. His M-16 was aimed at Rao's head, his finger on the trigger. "I'll shoot if you blink wrong."

Rao smiled again. Selena moved forward, keeping out of Nick's line of fire, and took the stone. It felt cool. The jewel was heavy in her hand. She stepped away from the desk.

"Islamabad would have been destroyed," Rao said.

"Put down the gun," Nick said. "I won't tell you again."

"I miss Lakshmi," Rao said. His eyes looked sad. Then he smiled. "It's not over."

He pulled the trigger. The side of his head blew out in a geyser of blood and tissue. The body slammed back and fell from the chair.

"Shit," Nick said. He lowered his rifle.

"What did he mean, it's not over? Who's Lakshmi?" Selena asked.

"I don't know," Nick said. "Let's get out of here before the whole Indian Army shows up."

"I hear a helicopter," Lamont said. "Might be too late."

They ran outside. The forest was burning all along the side of the mountain. Thick clouds of brown and black smoke billowed upward. Tongues of red and orange flame leapt high into the air. The heat was intense. Pieces of metal wreckage lay scattered in every direction. The crumpled black nose cone from the missile lay in the path of the advancing fire.

"How come it didn't go off?" Selena said. She gestured at the warhead.

"It was probably set for an altitude burst," Nick said. "There's a firing sequence that has to happen or it won't detonate. It's the way they're designed. A way to keep them safe."

"Safe. Who are they kidding? Lucky for us," she said.

Akron's Huey circled in and set down near the edge of the crater. They ran to it and climbed in. Seconds later they were airborne. Nick settled into the co-pilot's seat.

"Figured you might want to get out of Dodge," Akron said.

"You got that right."

"You don't mess around, do you? You should have seen that from over there by those ruins.

Biggest Roman candle I've ever seen. If I had that on film, I could sell tickets."

"Yeah. Take us back to Srinagar."

"I got a feeling it might be better if we took the long way around," Akron said. "Might get a little bumpy."

"Just get us back without getting shot down," Nick said.

"Roger dodger, Captain."

They lifted off in a steep bank. Nick grabbed for whatever he could find. Lamont uttered a string of obscenities in the bay behind him. Akron headed away from Srinagar.

"Where are you going?" Nick said. "The city's that way."

"So is the Indian Air Force. Trust me."

Akron flew at fifty feet above the highway for a few minutes. Then he banked to the right and flew into a narrow canyon that disappeared into the mountains. The walls of the canyon seemed inches away from the spinning blades. Akron was whistling as he flew, twisting and turning along the torturous route of a river below. It would be almost impossible for the Indians to find them here, unless they knew where to look.

Akron looked over at Nick. "Yesssir, you folks put on quite a show," he said. The chopper came close to the canyon wall.

"You mind watching where you're going?" Nick said.

Akron looked hurt. Nick called Harker.

"Director, we're on our way back."

"What happened?"

"Rao shot himself. We brought down the missile, but it was a close thing. The launch site is unusable and there's a hell of a fire burning. Rao

had this big ruby. He made Selena promise to take it
back where it came from."

"The Eye of Shiva," Elizabeth said.

"Right."

"Where are you?"

"On the way back to Srinagar."

"The Indians are kicking all foreign journalists
out of Kashmir," Elizabeth said. "You qualify, as a
documentary crew making films. The plane has
been released, along with your passports. Get back
and get out of there."

Nick remembered what Rao had said. He had to
know. "How's Ronnie doing?"

"No change."

Nick took a deep breath.

"Nick, that jewel is important. It has to go to
the government. You can't take it back."

Nick looked back at Selena. She was watching
him, listening to the conversation. They all had ears
on the link.

"Why not?" Nick asked.

"It's a national treasure. Bring it home and we'll
return it with the proper diplomatic protocols."

"What?" Nick said. "You're breaking up." He
made rasping noises.

"I said..."

Nick made crackling and hissing sounds. "...up.
Can't...what...say..."

He ended the connection and turned back
toward Selena.

She smiled at him and his heart missed a beat.
Her violet eyes were bloodshot. Her face was
scratched and streaked sweat and dirt. Nick thought
she'd never looked more beautiful.

"Thanks," she said.

"You're welcome."

The adrenaline surge was long gone. Nick was exhausted. The journey back to Srinagar passed in a blur. Once they saw a flight of six military helicopters go past in the distance, headed for the missile complex.

At the hangar, they gave Akron back his guns.

"Thanks," Nick said. "You did a good job with that bird."

Akron said, "Wouldn't have missed that for anything. I haven't had that much fun in a long time, but I admit it could have turned out different. Tells me it's time to pack it in. I'm going back to the states."

"What about this?" Nick gestured at the Huey, the hangar.

"Doesn't matter," Akron said. "It's mostly junk. My guess is the Indians are going to figure out that was my bird out there. I don't want to be around when they do. I'm out of here." He turned to Selena. "Sorry I got you mad at me, Sweet Pea."

He grinned at her and walked away.

"What an ass," she said.

"Yeah, but at least he's a consistent ass," Nick said.

CHAPTER 66

They drove to the airport and were cleared to leave Kashmir. The Eye was concealed with the guns in the camera equipment. Nick waited until they were in the air and Srinagar was receding below before he asked Selena what she was going to do.

"What would you do?" she said.

"You heard what Harker said. Turn it in. There must be a national museum for antiquities. That's where it belongs."

"I gave my word."

"To a dead man who tried to get us all killed. And then there's Ronnie."

"That's a cheap shot," Selena said. "You know damn well I haven't forgotten Cobra was responsible for what happened in Manila."

"You're right. Sorry, I didn't mean it to come across like that."

"I gave my word," Selena said again.

"It's a historic treasure," Nick said. "It's priceless. How long do you think it will last if those priests put it back on display?"

"That's not my problem," Selena said. "Besides, if you didn't think it was the right thing, why did you tell Elizabeth you couldn't understand what she was saying?"

"Because I wanted to give you the choice. Like you said, you gave your word."

"Did you tell the pilot we're going to New Delhi?"

Nick sighed. "Yes. I thought you might be stubborn about it. But I think it's a mistake."

Nick looked out the window. They were already in the approach pattern for New Delhi.

They got a cab at the airport and went to the temple. A Hindu man gave them a disapproving look as they stood by the entrance. Three foreigners.

"We have to take our shoes off," Selena said.

She pointed at a stone shelf by the temple entrance. They placed their shoes on the shelf and entered the temple.

Inside, it was cool and dim, the air heavy with powerful incense. Lamont looked up at the high ceiling and then at the fierce statue of Shiva.

"I wouldn't want to mess with that guy," he said. His voice was quiet.

The head priest stood motionless in front of the statue, watching them. He was old. It was hard to say how many years he was carrying. His face was like the weathered side of a mountain. He wore an orange robe and had a red dot painted on the center of his forehead.

"I think he's waiting for us," Selena said.

"How could he be? He couldn't know we were coming."

Selena said. "Wait here."

Selena stopped in front of the priest, steepled her hands together and made a slight bow.

"Namaste," she said.

He returned the gesture. "Namaste." His voice was soft, deep. Selena sensed hidden depth in it.

"I have something for you," she said in Hindi.

The priest showed no surprise. "I know," he said. "You are an honorable woman."

How did he know about that? she thought. She withdrew the jewel from her pocket. It felt hot in her hands. She held it out to him.

"Ah," the priest said. "Thank you."

There was a sudden smell of jasmine in the air. The priest took the stone and looked at her.

"Perhaps you don't believe in karma," he said. "No matter."

He bowed and turned away. He went through a beaded doorway.

That was weird, she thought.

CHAPTER 67

The next day they were back in Virginia, meeting in Harker's office. Nick was jet lagged and bone tired.

"Ronnie is going to be okay," Elizabeth said. "He's already complaining about the food. I talked with his doctor this morning."

"The good looking one? Fairchild?" Nick said.

"Good looking? Selena raised an eyebrow.

"For a doctor," Nick said. "Competent looking. You know."

"No, I don't know."

Elizabeth cleared her throat. "I thought we'd go over there later. Before that there are a couple of things we need to talk about. One good thing that came out of this is that it was a wakeup call for India and Pakistan. Rao's near miss scared the hell out of them. They were within minutes of annihilating each other and they realize it. China is brokering a peace conference. They're meeting tomorrow in Beijing and the armies have pulled back from the border. So that genie is back in the bottle, at least for now."

"Cobra was crazy," Lamont said. "You should have seen him. But he's out of the picture now."

Stephanie said, "There were more people involved in this plot than Rao. One of them is another agent at RAW named Khanna. He's under arrest. The problem is that we don't know who else. I may have identified one of them but even if I'm right, there's no proof. Nothing we can act on."

"Who is it?" Nick said.

"Rao made a call to someone named Krivi, right before he attempted to launch. I back traced it to Geneva."

"Switzerland? Who's Krivi?"

"I think it's a man named Krivi Dass. He owns a pharmaceutical company based in Zurich with manufacturing facilities in Switzerland and Mumbai. It's a big company, with sales worldwide. Dass is one of the world's richest men, worth billions. Rao thanked him for his pills. I'm pretty certain he's the one Rao was talking with."

"There's more," Elizabeth said. "The nose cone and guidance computer on that missile were recovered, mostly intact."

"We saw it lying on the side of the hill," Nick said.

"The Indians were able to recover the data on the computer. The missile wasn't headed for Pakistan."

"It wasn't? Where was it going?"

"China. It was targeted on Chengdu."

"Holy shit," Lamont said.

"Exactly," Elizabeth said. "A missile hitting China would have provoked retaliation against India. It would have meant nuclear war on the sub continent and the Chinese mainland."

"That doesn't make sense," Selena said. "Rao wanting to nuke Pakistan makes sense. He thought Islamabad was responsible for the death of his family. But why China?"

"We don't know why," Elizabeth said. "Then there's the question of how the missile was launched. The computer shows that the targeting coordinates and go codes came from a pre-programmed card. The commanders on site didn't have anything like that. Someone had to give it to Rao."

"Rao said Islamabad would have been destroyed," Nick said, "right before he pulled the trigger. He thought that missile was going to Pakistan. Then he said, 'it's not over.'"

"It's not over? You're sure?"

"That's what he said."

Elizabeth picked up her pen and began tapping it on the desk.

"Rao planned this operation with Krivi," she said. "At least that's how it sounded during that phone conversation. Krivi was pleased when he learned that Rao was going to launch. He has to be one cold son of a bitch if he can be pleased at the prospect of nuclear war and all the death and destruction that would bring."

"Not on Switzerland, though," Nick said.

"No. Not on Switzerland."

Nick said, "People in Krivi's league don't do things like this on their own. There are too many links. Anything that affects big profits world wide would be planned in consultation with others as rich as he is."

"That's a small club," Stephanie said.

"We've seen something like this before," Elizabeth said. They all looked at her.

"AEON," she said.

"I thought we'd finished with them," Nick said.

"So did I, but now I'm beginning to wonder."

"We'll watch Krivi," Stephanie said. "There isn't anything else we can do without more information."

Elizabeth said, "We all need a break. You three need sleep. Let's go see Ronnie and we'll think about this tomorrow."

CHAPTER 68

The restaurant was new and good and still undiscovered. Nick and Selena sat where they could watch the entrance. Selena had picked up Nick's habit of never having your back to the door. They'd rearranged chairs so they could face out, to the waiter's disapproval.

Nick ordered a bottle of Silver Oak.

"Remember when you brought out a bottle of this in California?" he said.

"Right before we ended up in that mine."

"With the spiders and rats."

"This is a lot nicer," she said.

She gestured at the dimly lit room. The tables were set with crisp, white linen. The silverware was heavy, the plates of good china. The glassware was leaded crystal. Soft music played in the background. Once the word got out, it would be filled with self-important people wheeling and dealing. For now it was just a pleasant place to have a good meal and a glass of wine.

"Ronnie looked a lot better," she said.

"He'll be fine. It will be a while before he's ready to get back in the field, though. He was circling the drain. It doesn't get any closer than that."

"He could decide not to go back."

"That would be bad for the team," Nick said. "Might be good for him, though."

The waiter brought the wine and poured. He took their order. When he was gone, Nick said, "I was thinking."

"About what?"

"Us."

"What about us?"

"I think we should go back to that jewelry store. And as many others as you want, if you don't see what you like there."

She hadn't been expecting that.

"What if it doesn't work out? Us?"

"Then it doesn't. But we won't know unless we give it a shot."

"It will be different if we get married," Selena said.

"It could be better."

"Or not. We get on each other's nerves."

"Yeah, but then it's okay again. Isn't that how it works?"

She sipped from her glass. "I suppose so."

Nick studied his glass, looked up. "You don't want to do it."

"Honestly? I do, but I'm afraid it will change things in a way we don't like."

"We spend almost all of our time together anyway,"

"Yes, but it's not the same."

He picked up the bottle of wine and topped off their glasses.

"I wasn't thinking about anything except how much I wanted you when I asked you. Then later it seemed like you were having your own doubts. It's why I put off getting a ring."

"I was having doubts," she said.

"Do you still have them?"

"I'll probably always have them."

The food came. They stopped talking until the waiter had left.

She looked at him. *I love him*, she thought. *He's not going to keep asking forever. You'll never know if you don't try for it.*
"All right," she said.
"All right what?"
"Let's look for a ring."

New Releases...

Be the first to know when I have a new book coming out by subscribing to my newsletter. No spam or busy emails, only a brief announcement now and then. Just click on the link below. You can unsubscribe at any time...

http://alexlukeman.com/contact.html#newsletter

The Project Series

White Jade
The Lance
The Seventh Pillar
Black Harvest
The Tesla Secret
The Nostradamus File
The Ajax Protocol
The Eye of Shiva

Book 9 will be out early in 2015.

Reviews by readers are welcome!

Acknowledgements

My wife Gayle. Being the wife of a writer is not an easy task. She patiently listens to me struggle with the plot line and deals with the mood swings that accompany good writing days and bad ones.

Neil Jackson, who designs the covers for the Project series.

Special thanks to Michelle Briere. Also to Nancy Witt, Paul Madsen, Seth Ballard, Eric Vollebregt and Gloria Lakritz.

Notes

I like to mix fact and fiction together in the PROJECT stories.

In *The Eye of Shiva*, some things are true and some are not. The story of the treasure looted by Naher Shah during the sack of Delhi in 1739 is true. The treasure eventually reached Persia and was so large that all taxes were suspended for three years in the kingdom. Among the treasures taken was the Peacock Throne, a fabled construction of solid gold built for the Mughal Emperor Akbar Khan. The throne was decorated with precious jewels and golden peacocks. But nothing more is known about the throne after it left Delhi. It disappeared from history. What happened to it?

The jewel in the story, the Eye of Shiva, is fiction, as is the prophecy attributed to it. The Koh-i-Noor diamond and the Timur ruby are real. Abdul Afridi's terrorist group ISOK is a fictional equivalent of a real group called Le T, short for Laikshar-e-Taiba. Le T is responsible for many murders and deadly attacks in India and Kashmir and is closely tied to Pakistan's Inter Services Intelligence Agency. Abu Sayaaf in the Philippines is real. These are bad people. Like ISIL in the Mid-East, they are fond of beheadings, robbing banks and murdering civilians.

The mosque at Hazratbal in Srinagar is a real location and does indeed house a relic of the Prophet Mohammed.

The Agni III missile described is far too real. So is it's bigger, more destructive brother the Agni VI. Pakistan and India are both armed with enough nuclear weapons to obliterate a significant part of the planet. Hindu and Islamic fundamentalism make a bad mix and tensions are always high in the region.

The Research and Analysis Wing is real. India's CIA has its headquarters on Lodhi Road in New Delhi. Ashok Rao bears no resemblance to the real Secretary of Special Operations, whoever that person is.

I've been to India, an amazing, dynamic country. The incident with the truck that almost wipes out the team is based on personal experience. Driving in India is not recommended.

As to AEON, it remains to be seen if it is real or not...